SEA & SKY

MOONFIRE TRILOGY BOOK 2

PATTY JANSEN

GET FREE EBOOKS

Visit pattyjansen.com
to sign up for Patty's mailing list. You get four series starter ebooks
for free!

CHAPTER 1

THE CAMEL PLODDED over the crest of the hill late in the afternoon, when the low sunlight cast long shadows over the dry fields that surrounded the town of Ysherra. At this time of day, the barren soil turned orange and the light, soft and hazy.

After having been away for what felt like a long time, Javes was surprised how familiar this terrain looked to him. Compared to the untamed country of the windwalkers, this piece of miserable land with its stubble fields and sparse olive trees was oddly civilised.

He had, he realised, enjoyed himself in the desert, and the objects he had taken from Karlen's cave would help him in his research. His experience would help him return to the windwalkers later on.

He rode past the olive groves and the white-painted house of the grumpy old fellow who lived in the valley with the goat farm. He knew the fellow would be watching from behind the curtains, but he didn't show himself. Javes rode past the sprawling house on the top of the hill that belonged to the town administrator. This man was the only person in town who had any money at all, and he liked to flaunt it, with the house's paved driveway and opulent gate. There were no goats to be seen here, only hideous statues of winged horses and other mythical animals. The proper name of the hill was Sooty Hill because of the dark basalt stone that broke the surface, but townspeople called it Snooty Hill.

When he had passed that opulent house, he rode down the hill into the town of Ysherra, a loose collection of blocky houses interspersed by the odd olive tree. He passed the carpentry business on the edge of town, and the pens where donkeys and goats for sale stood quietly awaiting the early start of tomorrow's livestock auctions. Next came a metal junkyard and then a seller of agricultural equipment. All these businesses had evidently closed for the night, because there was not a person in sight. A couple of geese crossed the road ahead.

It was odd, because Javes had not known the townsfolk to stick to such city notions as opening times. If there was business to be done, the shops were open, regardless of the time of day.

By the time Javes came to the grocery corner shop, which was also closed, the back of his neck was pricking with suspicion.

The streets were never this quiet. There were never any crows fighting over scraps of food in the middle of the main street at this time. Early evening was when the people came out of their houses after the heat of the day. This was when they would go to the eating houses.

There were no neighbours standing at front fences, watching everyone coming down the road. No children playing, no people going to the bathhouse. No one at the outdoor tables of the tea house either. The only person at the teahouse was the owner, and he was stacking the tables, giving Javes a nervous glance before ducking into the kitchen.

Javes didn't think that this was about him. He got on well with the teahouse's owner. He looked over his shoulder.

Behind him, the street was deserted. A crow cawed.

His neck pricked. There was something very, very odd going on.

He stopped the camel and looked around. Everything in town appeared *normal*, except for there being no people.

He could get off the camel and go into the teahouse to ask the owner what was going on, but he was afraid of becoming involved in yet another problem that wasn't his, because he already had more problems than he could deal with.

He was tired. He'd just go to Pashtan's house, which had been his home in Ysherra, and decide what to do tomorrow, after he'd slept. So he kicked the camel's flanks and it continued walking, even if he sensed he was being followed or observed, and he had no idea who could be watching.

Yet on his way through town, he saw no signs of violence, just closed shops, deserted streets and puzzling emptiness.

Then he turned the corner to the street that led out of town and he could see Pashtan's house with the familiar olive tree in the front yard.

But what had happened to the neighbour Arukat's house? The sloping roof was stained with streaks of soot. The front veranda sagged, because the posts that supported the roof had been burned. The side of the house was entirely black, and the shed that formed one boundary of Arukat's property, and where he stored his metal wares, had fallen in.

Pashtan's house looked fine, but the side gate was smashed.

Heart thudding, Javes led the camel into the back yard. The goats were all gone. Half the hay bales were missing from the barn and the roof of the shed sagged ominously. Some words were scrawled on the back fence in white paint, but he couldn't read them. That blocky script was Aranian, wasn't it?

His heart was thudding.

He tied the camel to the post, righted the water trough, went to the tank—it was empty, because someone had made a large hole in the side.

Well . . . damn it.

There was still a good amount of water in the water bags, but the trough was too big to waste it, so Javes ventured into the shed to find a bucket—and someone had trashed the inside of the shed and left a big, stinking turd in the middle of the floor.

Ugh. What sort of barbarians had been here?

Aranians. Whatever *they* were doing here. Even in Tiverius, people knew there were no border patrols in this area.

What was the point of this destruction? Where were all the people?

A dark feeling came over him.

What to do? Was this place still safe?

First, he needed to rest and feed the camel. Reorganise himself and decide the best path to take. He needed a bucket to let the camel drink.

Pashtan's tools had been ripped from their hooks on the walls and lay on the ground. The broom handle was broken. Spare lampshades and glass jars for preservatives lay in shards on the floor. The buckets, though, were metal and unscathed except for a few dents.

Javes picked one up and went back outside. From the step to the door of the shed, he could see over the fence into Arukat's yard. All his sheds along the back and side fence had been burned. Any scrap metal that had not burned and twisted into useless heaps had been flung everywhere. The sand cart was gone, and so were the donkeys. The veranda at the back of the house sagged, and the chairs where Arukat and his wife would sit at night had been slashed so that the stuffing came out of the cushions. The door stood open and the windows were broken.

Arukat's water tank lay on its side. It normally stood in the corner of the yard.

There was no sign of life. No donkeys, no chickens, no goats, no geese.

With a sick feeling in his stomach, Javes wondered what had happened to the family.

He brought water to the camel, took all the packs off the saddle and carried them to the back door—and when he put down the water bags, he could hear the bleating of a kid. *Inside* the house?

He carefully opened the door. Something leaned against it that made a scraping sound over the floor as he pushed it aside. It sounded like the table. Before the door was far enough open for him to go in, a goat squeezed itself out. It ran into the yard, bucking, leaping and kicking its back legs. Two more hairy heads stuck out of the door.

He recognised the brown- and black-spotted goat and the grey one as Pashtan's. The third was white and had to be someone else's. How had they ended up locked inside? Unless . . . someone had deliberately locked them in.

He called at the door. "Hello? Hello, anyone there?"

There was no reply, so he pushed the door further. The rest of Pashtan's goats, or at least most of them as far as he could see, also ran out, accompanied by two more white goats.

And then, nothing.

The door gaped like a dark maw. In the waning light, Javes could only see a small portion of the floor, strewn with goat droppings.

He grabbed the bottom half of the broken broom: a short stick with the broom head on one end, and on the other a jagged, splintered piece of wood. He wasn't sure what end to hold in front. The broom head would be most effective against an irate goat, but if there was something else, he might want the sharp end of the stick.

Carefully, he advanced into the house.

He could see next to nothing in the darkness. The air smelled of goat and fire. The thing that had been behind the door was indeed the table, and he almost tripped over the chair that went with it.

He stopped, waiting for his eyes to get used to the dark.

A small sound came from the left side of the room.

"Who's there?"

No reply.

His heart was thudding. That noise sounded too big to be made by a goat.

He took a step to the right, and another one, hoping to give whoever or whatever hid in the room a way to escape. He waited.

Nothing moved or made a sound for a long time. Javes was tired and hungry. He wanted this intruder out of the house. He took a few steps further into the room, stepped in something soft, which was probably goat poo—

And someone shot out of the darkness, brushing past him on the way to the open door. In a reflex, he grabbed a hand full of the person's clothing. The intruder screamed. Judging by the voice, it was a woman, and she was quite small.

"Stop, stop, shut up. I live here. If you're honest with me, I won't harm you."

She turned towards him, and by the feeble light from outside, he could see the glittering of her eyes. She was not a woman, but she was only a young girl. Arukat's daughter. Her lips trembled. "You're a ghost."

"It's me, Javes."

"Can't! You're a ghost. You're tricking me! You're dead! They said so."

"I'm certainly not dead. Who told you that?"

"The men in the bath house. Yoshi at the telegraph office. The neighbours. They all said it."

"What do they know about me? I never told anyone where I was going."

"They said you disappeared and you got what you deserved because you didn't want to work here anyway."

Trust a child to be painfully honest. Not only that, it was true, and it was a sign of how much loyalty the town had towards him. Just as much as it had shown towards Pashtan. He hadn't been a local either, and many years of trudging down local weather stations did not change that.

Ouch.

Javes blew out a breath through his nostrils. "Well, let's make a light and get my things inside. Then we'll see what we can do."

Then again, he dreaded looking at the state of the house. He'd already stepped in a few goat droppings, so he could only figure out what the room must look like.

In fact, once he'd lit a light, that estimate proved optimistic. Not only were there goat droppings everywhere—including on the bed—but someone had made a fire in the middle of the room, and had used pages of Pashtan's books to light it. The books were all over the desk, ripped apart. One of the table legs had broken. The cushions on the couch had been slashed. Stuffing was coming out and there were dark brown stains all over the fabric.

Great.

Just great.

He looked around, a feeling of despair creeping over him. Up there, on the shelf, the slate with his list of aims still stood. In neat writing, it said,

1. *Retrieve cart and bodies. Funeral.*
2. *Appoint someone to take care of goats*
3. *Train someone to take measurements*

Compared to the situation he faced here, those aims were almost laughable.

"Is there any food in the house?" he asked.

"There is milk," the girl said.

Javes went to the cold box. The cover cloth that kept the inside cool was dry as the desert. The box itself was made out of earthenware in a rattan basket. Normally, the terracotta felt moist and cool because you had to keep it wet, but it was completely dry. The goats had eaten part of the basket. They had also nosed aside the cloth and eaten some of the cheese, which, without any cooling, didn't smell very good anyway. In the corner stood a jug with milk. He lifted it out.

Ugh. The smell of the rank cheese spread through the stuffy space.

"Maybe we should go outside."

"No! The men will come back!"

"Which men?"

"The big ones with the red faces." Her eyes were wide. "They burned everything. I ran away from them. Please, please don't make me go outside." She shrank away from him.

"All right, all right, calm down."

"Have they been back since they . . ." He gestured helplessly in the direction of Arukat's house. He should probably have asked a whole raft of other questions first, but he'd been too preoccupied with his own needs. But what had happened to her parents?

"They come into town and steal people's things. If people try to defend themselves, they're killed."

"They come every day?" It unsettled him to hear a young girl like that talk about death.

"Most days. Usually in the morning or at night. I hide in here."

My, she was dirty. Had she lived in here with the goats since he left?

Javes found a mug that was relatively clean, and poured milk. "Any bread left?"

She shook her head. "The goats ate it."

Not the only thing the goats had eaten, by the look of things.

Javes drank. The milk was on the verge of going off and he had to hold his breath in order to get it down. Ugh, ugh, ugh. He had some leftover salt meat in his packs, but he'd get it later. Tomorrow, when he could see enough to find it without having to carry a light into the yard.

He pulled the blankets off the bed, sending goat poo bouncing over the floor. The mattress was reasonably clean, he thought. He sat down.

"What's your name again?" Pashtan had introduced her when he first came, but he'd forgotten.

"Tali." She sat with her arms clamped around her pulled-up knees.

"Well then, Tali. Tell me exactly what happened, when it started and where everyone went."

She told him that one morning when she was milking the goats, there was a lot of noise in the town, and when she went to have a look, a lot of men in black leather were running through the streets. They had horses and carts. They stopped in front of her house and went into her father's junkyard. "I couldn't see them, but I heard them yelling at my father and smashing everything up. They asked him where something was, and he said he didn't know what they were talking about, and each time he said he didn't know, they smashed more things to bits. They said my father wasn't allowed to sell to anyone else."

"Do you know what they were talking about?"

She shrugged, and gave him a shifty look.

"Did your father tell you not to talk about it? He was selling wind-walker artefacts, wasn't he?"

"I don't know. I don't care. I don't know what those weird things are. They scare me. My father should never have started buying from the windwalkers."

"Do you know who he was selling to?"

"People from out of town. I don't know. He always tells me to go inside when they come to the yard."

"So, these men, what did they do?"

"They smashed the house, and then they set fire to it. They put my parents in a cart and rode out of town. No one knows where they are."

"Did you see the men?"

She nodded, her eyes wide. "They were very big. They wore black and a couple of them had shaved heads and had red paint in their faces."

"Did they write the letters on the fence?"

"They did. I don't know why they did that. No one can read it."

Knowing Aranians, and especially the high-class ones who bore the red tattoos on their faces, Javes figured that the words were probably some obscene insult, like the turd in the shed. What he couldn't figure was what they were doing here and why they had singled out Arukat's shed. He shouldn't have sold to someone else? Did Arukat sell to Aranians? He'd never seen Aranians in town. The border—if one could speak of borders in this desert—was a least a full day's ride away.

"Did they go to other people's houses?"

"Oh, yes. They smashed the telegraph office, pulled down the wires. They wrote all over the town hall and inside the bathhouse. They stole all the grocery shop's food."

"Are there any guards in town?"

She gave him a blank look.

In Tiverius, the town guards were employed by the doga's local arm. He had definitely never seen any guards since coming to town, and Ysherra had no doga office, so he guessed that answered the question. "What were the men doing in the rest of town?"

She didn't know. In fact, the detached way in which she told her story disturbed him. He would have expected a girl whose parents were taken away to cry or be upset, but she seemed numb more than anything.

"So while this was happening, you hid here all the time?"

She nodded. "Yes, with the goats. You should have seen what they did to my father's donkeys. The goats saw that, too, and they wanted to come inside."

Javes shuddered, seeing ribs and chunks of meat in the desert. "Where did the men go?"

"I don't know. I couldn't understand what they were saying to each other."

"How many of them were there?"

She shrugged. "Many. Maybe a hundred, maybe more."

"And they have been back since?"

"A few times."

It worried him. Aranians in town. What for?

Well, the goats would have to stay outside for the time being, but Javes did worry about his camel. It was a silly and sometimes stroppy beast, but he liked it and would hate for something to happen to it. Unfortunately, camels didn't fit inside the house.

Javes attempted to clean the smell of goat from the bed. He turned over the mattress, only to find that the fabric on other side was badly worn. He put a blanket over the top, but the straw still stuck through the rips in the cover. The fact that he used the blanket meant he had no blanket to sleep underneath. There were additional blankets for winter, but he needed light to find them in the cupboard, and the goats had probably eaten them. He also had a blanket in his packs, but again he couldn't be bothered to rummage around in the dark.

Tali insisted on sleeping on the floor. There was the couch which had served him as a bed, but no matter what he said, she wouldn't go anywhere near it. On closer inspection, there were wet patches on the cushions, and they smelled funny—probably goat's piss.

Javes was too tired to worry about it. He slept.

JAVES WOKE up when it was still mostly dark. He stared into the darkness until he remembered where he was: Pashtan's house, the devastation of Arukat's house, and Tali, who lay sleeping on the floor.

His stomach rumbled and gurgled. He'd hardly eaten anything last night. The sky through the little window next to the door showed a faint blue tinge. The back of the house looked out to the west and so if the sky was blue there, the sun must be about to come up.

He rose, walked around Tali and stumbled through the dark to where he had left his packs near the door. He was rummaging through his bags for some raisins or anything to eat when there was a sound from outside. Footsteps?

Heart thudding, he froze and listened.

Some shuffling and thumping sounded very much like a camel. He fumbled around for some sort of weapon, found the broken broom and went outside. No one was getting his hands on his camel or his goats.

He opened the door, looking into the yard in the pale predawn light.

The camel stood in the pen, curiously looking past the side of the house in the direction of the street. The goats were all asleep in the shade of the broken shed.

Javes patted the camel's neck and walked along the side of the house as quietly as he could.

An unfamiliar cart with two horses stood in front of Arukat's house. People in town didn't use horses. The cart was a flatbed vehicle with a simple wooden bench for the driver. The back was filled with various metal junk.

The sound of soft voices came from the back yard, and the clinking of metal.

Javes went back into the back yard of Pashtan's house and peeped through a hole in the fence into Arukat's yard. He could see two men, but there might be others, who were collecting bits of metal in a heap. A third man came into view.

These were not Aranians, but peddlers who came to scavenge. He dragged a bucket to the fence, turned it upside down and climbed on top of it so that he could see over the fence.

"Oy!"

The men looked up. One had a face with deep canyons, dry and engrained with dust like the desert , hidden under a cloak with a cowl. The other two were larger, younger, possibly his sons.

"What are you doing here?"

"Getting the stuff," the old man said. "It's not that he'd be needing it."

His mouth was missing several teeth.

"His daughter lives with me. You're stealing from her."

"Well I've never seen no one here."

"That's because she's afraid and hiding."

The two younger men gave their father uncertain looks. One had been carrying an armful of metal junk that he put down.

The old man nodded. They collected their empty baskets and made their way back to the cart. Javes followed them on his side of the fence and met them in the street.

"Nice horses."

"Don't worry about us. We're going already." He jerked his head at his sons.

"I was just wondering if you knew any more about the Aranians who did this." He glanced at the burned house.

The old man shrugged. "They're Aranians. What other explanation do you need?"

"What're they doing here? Is it common for Aranians to come here?"

"You're not from here, are you?"

"Neither are you."

The man gave him a blank look.

"People here don't use horses. Too hot for them."

"Aw, all right. We're from out Watya-way."

"All the way out there? What are you doing here?"

"You know, looking for stuff."

"What sort of stuff?"

"Mostly metal. Things that people find."

"People. Like, windwalkers?"

He cast a shifty glance to the side. "What do you know about those?"

In other words: yes. "Not much, not much, but saw one, once. At the Field of Bones."

The old man snorted. "Robbers of the dead, that's what they are."

"You're selling this 'stuff' to the Aranians, right?"

"Why are you asking if you know it already?"

"What do they do with it? Why do they pay so much money for it?"

"There's smart people who can make it rain, more than can be said about the loafers in Tiverius, who are still talking about whether or not they'll build the railway they promised ten years ago. Tell you what, the railway will never happen because we haven't the people to use it, because it doesn't rain so no one wants to live out here. Make it rain, and it solves all the problems. The people can grow their crops, they can eat, the towns will fill up and the railway will be built. That's my view on things anyway."

"And these Aranians can make it rain?"

"Sure can. They got all kinds of magic."

A chill crept over Javes' spine. *Magic* was what the meteorology department measured as sonorics. It was related to low pressure cells and rain. The dust devils caused sonorics spikes. Were these artificial phenomena?

The man continued, "Anyway, we best be out of here." He flicked the reins and the horses started moving.

Javes watched them leave, his hand over the pocket where he still kept the globe that Karlen had given him in the graveyard. He couldn't shake the feeling that everyone was looking for artefacts like this, maybe even this particular one, and that the Aranians were looking for Karlen. Not that Javes knew where Karlen was, or even *who* he was. Karlen had been wrapped up in cloth like all windwalkers, and Javes had not even seen his eyes.

CHAPTER 2

*L*ANA HAD ALWAYS BEEN adamant that she would never become one of those vain girls who agonised for hours about what to wear in front of the mirror before going out, but she spent all day going through her wardrobe deciding what to pack for her trip to Ysherra with Viki.

Because, though she might not be concerned with what she *looked* like, she didn't want to be dressed inadequately on the trip. Ysherra was hot, so she packed cool chemises, and wide skirts. Also some trousers, despite Dad's belief that she shouldn't be wearing any. She packed sandals, but didn't want to wear them for the first part of the journey—the train ride to Watya—because sandals weren't appropriate wear for a lady; so she put the sandals in her bag and would wear closed shoes on the train.

What books should she take? Her notebook, for one, but books were heavy. Would there be any libraries where she could use the books she needed? Should she take any instruments? What about her spyglass? It came off the stand, and the tube and stand separately fitted snugly in a neat little box. There was a place called Red Hill to the north of Ysherra where people came to observe the stars, where it was said that the night sky was lit up with them even if there was no moon. The moon had vanished to a pinprick and would not foul up any night viewing.

It would be a pity not to go up there if she had the opportunity.

But when she put everything she thought essential in her bag, she could barely lift it. That wasn't going to be practical. So the books came out. The spyglass case was nice, but in hindsight quite heavy, and if she wrapped the tube in clothes and stuffed a sock in the lens opening it would be nicely protected.

There. That was a bit more manageable. She picked up the bag and carried it down the stairs. It was still very heavy, and she wondered if she would be required to carry it large distances. She hoped not.

Myra came out of the kitchen. "Oh, you're ready? When are you leaving?"

"Viki will bring the truck here after midday." The train would leave in the late afternoon and would arrive at Watya tomorrow morning. From there, it would be a two-day bus ride to Ysherra.

"I'll pack you some nice goodies for the journey. Just leave your bags here, and I'll put a nice parcel on top."

Lana dreaded how much Myra would give her to bring. She had so much to carry already.

She went into the kitchen. It was warm in there, the cook was ladling steaming soup into plates, and her mother sat in her chair at the table.

She smiled at Lana when she sat down. "Your father will be here soon."

"I thought he had to go to meetings?"

"He does, but he still made some time to be with us before you leave."

Words were on Lana's tongue about it being only a trip of a few weeks, and that she wasn't even leaving the country. But she understood some of the worries about Aranians and a potential war, even if her father didn't want to share those with her.

"Do we wait for him?" The soup smelled wonderful and she was hungry. She reached out for the bread that lay, still warm, on a cutting board on the table.

"That would be nice, don't you think?"

Lana withdrew her hand from the bread. She tucked her hands between her knees, and then didn't know what to say.

"You will have a nice trip," her mother said after an awkward silence.

"Are you going to be all right while I'm gone?"

"Of course. Myra will just have to keep me company."

A small stack of books and papers lay on the corner of the table. Lana knew that her mother was working on collecting names of people from the City of Glass who had died, for a monument to be put up in their name, but her mother rarely spoke about it. Now she nodded at the stack. "How are you getting on with the monument?"

Her mother gave a wan smile. "I have most of the names that I will ever be able to get. I only need to write to a couple of people now."

"To get the monument built?"

"No, the Knight Council has already voted to do that." She looked at the table. "I'm going to write to all your half-brothers and half-sisters who are still alive. I want them to know that I have never forgotten them and that I would have looked after them had that been possible."

Lana raised a hand to her mouth. All of a sudden, she understood what her mother had been doing. She didn't often speak about the concept of being a breeder in the City of Glass, but Dad had told her about it. Lana wasn't even sure how much Dad understood. It sounded like an incredibly horrible life.

"You must invite them so that they can see you." And that would need to be done before the disease ended her life. Dad never spoke of it, but Lana wasn't stupid.

Her mother looked at her hands. "Not all are still alive."

"The ones who are should come."

"They might not want to see me."

"They should be allowed to make that decision. Give Dad the names. He will tell them to come. I'm sure he will."

"Someone here talking about me?"

Her father had come into the kitchen. He looked flustered, red-cheeked, and very tired. He sat down at the table and thanked the cook for giving him soup.

Lana repeated what she'd said to her mother.

He thought for a while. "It would be nice for you just to see them once, but inviting them here might be a little bit trickier than you think. Some of the men who hire breeders in the City of Glass are very high up in their aristocracy. The children themselves may not like to be reminded that they come from breeder background, or their families might be embarrassed to have the name of their breeder so publicly revealed."

"You can try," Lana said.

"Yes, we could."

They ate for a bit.

Then her mother said, "How was this morning's session?"

Dad sighed. "We have a lot to deal with."

"Did they find out more about this poor man who died delivering the message from Arania?"

"The Aranians aren't bluffing. They have a lot of troops stationed on the other side of the border. Several people have confirmed that. For now, they don't appear to be doing anything."

"I guess that's good?"

He shrugged. "I don't know. The fact that they're there at all worries me. And that they appear to have weapons based on sonorics. And that they are still not willing to engage in any kind of meaningful discussion with us."

Lana thought of the turd in its little ornate box in the cabinet next to Dad's office. Every child in Chevakia visited the doga and was told the story of Arania's smelly reply to Chevakia's efforts to reach out and forget about the past; and was taught that it was evidence that it was all right to ignore Arania, because they were rude and stubborn and refused to talk the doga and hey, we beat them badly in the last war, so why should we?

Probably Arania had been pretty angry during all that time. There hadn't been an ambassador for a great many years.

"But let's not worry ourselves too much about it today. Let's talk about your trip."

His face carried that expression that told Lana that he had to force himself to be cheerful and forget about the bad news.

But she told him about the itinerary Viki had sent her, and Dad told her about any of those places he had visited. In Watya, apparently, she should look out for the water towers and aqueducts that were a marvel of engineering. He had never been to Ysherra, but said that others had reported it as a small and tight-knit place, where the capital Tiverius was so far away as to be irrelevant and where it paid not to be too cocky.

He said, "A lot of the people in the north believe that meteorologists control the weather."

And then they discussed customs and superstition, one of their favourite subjects. It felt just like the old days, when her mother was healthy and Lana had been at school.

They'd long since finished eating when there was a commotion in the hallway. A moment later, Viki came in. He wore sturdy trousers and a travel cloak, probably a little bit frumpier than he would appear in class.

His gaze sought out Lana. "Ready to go?"

"Yes, sure." Lana rose nervously.

"Well, there you go, then," her father said. "Into the big world."

"Thank you for letting me go." Lana hugged him and then her mother. She felt so thin and fragile.

"Take care out there," her mother said. Her eyes glittered.

Lana went into the hall, where the luggage waited. Myra had put a sizeable parcel on top of Lana's suitcase. Lana half-despaired at seeing it, but she knew it was full of nice edible goodies and would probably not make it to Watya.

Orsan took her big suitcase, and Lana her smaller overnight bag and the parcel, which was heavy enough.

She followed Viki down the path through the yard to the truck that waited in the street. Big clouds of steam drifted past the side, and Lana had to bat them away to climb into the cabin. The driver shut the door.

Her parents stood on the doorstep of the house, her mother in the chair, her father behind her with his hands on her shoulders. Lana waved and they waved back. The driver dropped the truck into gear and the house and her family slowly slid from view.

Lana had to blink a few times. She stared out the window, embarrassed that she would get emotional over something she had wanted for so long. But her parents looked so . . . lonely, and she was all they had. What if her mother *died* while she was away?

She swallowed hard a few times.

Slowly, the truck made its way through the stately tree-lined avenues of the city. It was autumn, and the golden sunlight cast the city in a warm glow.

The main station in Tiverius was a big sandstone building adjacent to the marketplace, not far from the doga. Lana had taken short train trips plenty of times, but she had always looked wistfully at those big engines with lots of carriages that went to other parts of the country, hoping that one day she could go on those trains. Sometimes the engines were dusty, sometimes their fronts were covered in bugs. There were always a lot of people around these trains, including station staff helping passengers board and loading mail bags.

And today, she *was* going on one of those trains and didn't at all feel as glamorous as she had thought it would. In fact, it felt rather scary.

The activity on the platform appeared rather chaotic. There were lots of people with bags. The stationmaster was arguing with a man about the booking of a cabin, while the man's family sat around on their suitcases, blocking the way for everyone else.

Viki used his status as chief meteorologist to interrupt that conversation and get the tickets checked. Lana waited for him.

Further down the platform was a lot of freight, including crates of fruit, potatoes and other produce, wrapped-up parts of an engine and many pallets of dusty white bags that looked like cushions. Big clouds of steam drifted from the engine over the platform.

"Come, we're at the front," Viki said.

Lana followed him, weaving between yet more families with lots of bags and children.

"What's in all those white bags they were loading onto the train?"

"Where?"

"Behind us."

Viki looked over his shoulder. His expression turned serious. "Those are old sonorics suits."

"Why are they being taken to the north?" Way back before she was born, they used to stockpile these suits in all towns close to the borders with Peria, in case the sonorics barrier failed. Since the destruction of the machine in the City of Glass, the suits had been stored in army sheds, where they had gathered dust for twenty years.

"They are stored in the region as a safety precaution—ah, this is our carriage."

It was painted green on the outside. A man was helping a woman with a long, frilly, utterly impractical dress up the narrow steps. When she had made it in, Viki jumped up and held his hand out to Lana.

She felt kind of strange, going with him instead of attending class where he lectured at a big group of students.

The inside of the carriage consisted of little cabins with cloth-covered seats and little tables in between them. Further down the carriage was a narrow corridor with sleeping cabins on either side. Viki checked the numbers on the doors.

"This is yours."

Lana looked in. The cabin was tiny and mostly taken up by a bunk bed. She put her overnight bag on a shelf to the side, underneath the tiny window. The only thing she could see from the window was the red side of another train, with dark streaks where raindrops had run across the paint.

"Is everything all right?" Viki asked from the door.

"It's cute. Will anyone use the top bunk?"

"No. This is just for you. My cabin is next-door."

He stepped into the cabin and put a cloth parcel on the bottom bunk. "Put that in your overnight bag."

Lana picked up the parcel. "What is it?"

"Sonorics suit."

She frowned at him. "Why would *we* need it?"

"You read that comment about dust devils, didn't you?"

"Yes, I did, but . . ." She looked from the suit to him. She remembered her father talking about the machines that the Aranians might have made.

"Several of our barygraphs have been recording sonorics spikes near Ysherra. I'd rather lug these suits around and not need them than need them and not have them."

That was true, but still . . . sonorics? "Where would it be coming from? I thought sonorics was made by that machine under the City of Glass."

"That's what we all thought. And it *was* made by that machine, but there may be other machines."

"Near Ysherra?"

"We don't know." He was silent for a while and an expression of worry came over his face. "Maybe. Maybe not."

Lana put the parcel on top of her bag since it wouldn't fit inside. She was pretty sure she didn't need to be as careful with sonorics as other people. Her mother was from the City of Glass and all Perians had a very high resistance to sonorics. Lana would have inherited at least some resistance from her mother.

"Let's find our seats," Viki said.

They went back to the section of the carriage with the little cabins. Viki was checking his ticket to find the number that corresponded with the number on the little round label affixed to the cabin door.

Their seats were in the third cabin from the back.

Lana sat next to the window, and Viki settled opposite her, with the table in between them. Through the cabin's glass door, she could see a lot of activity still on the platform, if not in this particular carriage.

Most of the passengers went into the carriages at the end, which had only seats. Lana asked where those people slept, and Viki said they slept mostly in their seats, or didn't sleep at all.

"We get free first class travel for the doga, because otherwise a lot of representatives would never go home and never talk to their people about the things that the doga is proposing."

That made sense.

Lana eyed the empty seats. "Anyone else coming in here?"

"Only when it's busy."

And the trains to the north were never busy, Lana had heard. It was the main reason that the railway had never been extended, even though her father had promised it years ago.

They sat down and waited.

"I hope your family won't miss you too much," Lana asked after a slightly awkward silence.

He smiled. "There is so much noise in my house that they may not notice I'm gone."

Viki had no less than ten children.

Eventually, people stopped coming onto the train. Some station guards walked past, one with a flag. The clouds of steam became thicker.

Men's voices rang out on the platform. Someone yelled, "Make it quick. Train's about to leave."

A door opened in the carriage and a number of talking and laughing men climbed in. Their heavy boots clonked on the floor and the carriage moved with their weight. There were a lot of them, and they came through the corridor past the cabin where Lana and Viki sat, a line of big, sturdy men silhouetted against the light.

A horn tooted on the platform, the engine hissed and clanked and chugged.

Very slowly, the train moved away from the station. A couple of men stood outside the cabin door. Someone called out further down the corridor.

Viki flicked his eyebrows. "Soldiers."

The train was going through the commercial part of the city, where the windows gave a view into the back yards stacked with crates and other rubbish. Then they went through a part of town where people lived in apartments four or five floors high. There was a fence along the tracks, and weeds grew along it. They crossed the iron bridge over the river with the sound of metal on metal that Lana could sometimes hear at night when the window in her bedroom was open. On the other side of the river the track crossed an area of small farms with little fields where farmers grew vegetables and flowers. The tracks turned, giving Lana a splendid view of Tiverius. The golden light of dusk reflected off the dome of the doga assembly building, where her father would be standing at his dais. To the right was the gently sloping part of town where the well-off families lived, where her mother would sit in the kitchen with Myra and maybe Myra's husband Farius. The Scriptorium's tower stuck out above the tiled roofs of the merchant quarter.

"Excuse me, sir?"

The door to the cabin had opened and a military officer looked in —quite a high-ranking one, judging by the stars on the band around his upper arm.

He nodded at the empty seats. "Is anyone using those seats, sir?"

"No, we're not," Viki said. He had brought a book to read, and he moved it from the seat next to him to the table.

The door opened further and four men came in. All were in military uniform: sandy brown trousers and shirt; a broad leather belt with a dagger, all-purpose tool, water bottle and pouch; heavy high boots of brown leather; and a blue beret.

Clean-shaven and well-groomed, they looked quite similar, although one wore a row of gold stars on his chest. He was ranked much higher than the others. They sat in the remaining seats in the cabin.

The high-ranking man sat next to Viki. The man next to Lana was much younger, maybe only a few years older than she. In addition to the dagger, he also carried a gun, which he took off and placed in the luggage rack above his head.

He sat down again, nodding to Lana. "M'lady. It's not appropriate to carry weapons in the presence of a woman and a senator."

His face was so serious that Lana almost burst out laughing. *M'lady?* Was this guy for real?

"I wasn't aware that the military used civilian trains," Viki said.

The high-ranking officer said, "We don't normally, but we were told to go to Watya, and there were no trucks available."

"I'm guessing with the balloon division, you don't normally use trucks anyway."

"That's correct, sir. I believe you're Senator han Marossi?"

"I am indeed. This is my student, Lana han Chevonian."

He bowed to Lana. "We're pleased to meet someone as distinguished as our proctor's daughter. I'm Patrol Commander Ramatius and these are my junior officers Jarendran, Daferius and Yaishan."

The officer next to Lana nodded again. She thought he was Yaishan. What sort of name was that? Regional, for sure. His skin appeared darker than that of the others, and he was taller and broader.

His eyes had an unnervingly honest look that made her turn away.

The train was going through the forest now. It was getting dark and there was little to see except a wall of increasingly dark trees whizzing past the window.

A railway attendant came to each cabin to light the lamps with a flame on a long stick and a bottle with a narrow spout to refill the oil basins.

Viki and the commander had moved to talking about balloons. All four men wore a little medallion on their uniforms that, when the light fell on it a certain way, showed a group of flying swans, which Lana guessed to be the balloon division's emblem.

Yaishan, next to her, leaned back in his seat, glancing at the couple of soldiers in the corridor, who didn't appear to have found seats.

"How many of you are on this train?" Lana asked in a low voice.

"Our unit is forty-eight strong."

"Do you fly balloons?"

"Yes. Each vessel has twelve crew."

"I would love to fly on a balloon one day." Another thing that her father would never allow her to do. "Why don't you fly to Watya?"

"Too slow. A balloon is a tactical combat vehicle, not a transport vehicle."

"But balloons do fly long distances?"

"They can. But very slowly. And they're highly sensitive to the wind directions. I guess you know all about the wind as meteorology student." He was very serious.

He sounded a bit like that arrogant boor Pavin from her astronomy group, but Lana wasn't sure that was such a good comparison. She didn't think he *was* like Pavin.

"Have you ever been to Watya before?"

Now a ghost of a smile played over his face. "I was born in Watya and grew up there."

The train rumbled on into the darkness. Yaishan told Lana about Watya, and then Viki suggested they get something to eat. The six of them moved to the dining car, past the other cabins in front of theirs, out a little door across a walkway between two carriages, where the cool night air made Lana shiver, and into the warmth of the dining car. Dinner was a piece of steamed duck with sour cabbage and raisins and cooked barley. It was a very traditional Chevakian meal such as she only got when she went home with her friends. Myra came from the City of Glass and cooked more modern meals.

Lana sat opposite Viki on the long table. It was noisy in the car with the talk and laughter of all the soldiers and, on the far end, all the second-class passengers waiting for their turn to eat.

"Did you ever hear anything back from Javes?" Lana asked Viki.

"Apart from the reports he sent, no."

"It's very strange. He wrote me a letter asking for some information about Dust Devils. I wrote back to him, but he never replied. I'm not even sure that he got my letter."

"He might not have received it. Communication isn't the best."

"Wouldn't it be just the mail, like we get in Tiverius, or that we send to Twin Bridges or Solmeni?"

"Yes, except a lot of people travel to those places, and there is quite a lot of mail. Only a few people live in Ysherra, and those that do are not interested in sending anything to Tiverius. So it takes a long time for the mail office to collect enough mail to be worth sending."

Oh. "What about the telegraph line?" There was one, because Javes had used it. She had learned that meteorological field stations were in all places where there was a telegraph line so that weather data could be sent to Tiverius.

"It's only a single line, and it's very sensitive to bad weather. It goes out for days on end."

So maybe he hadn't even received her information. That was annoying. Maybe he thought she was thumbing her nose at him. "Does he know that we're coming?"

"No. I've heard nothing from him for a while. I presume he's busy making the rounds of the weather stations. He also had a lot of trouble after his tutor died. The town wants him to stay there, but I wouldn't send an inexperienced meteorologist to Ysherra. That's why I sent him to Pashtan, because he's very experienced."

"Pashtan?"

"His tutor. The one who died."

"Oh. Did you know him?"

"I did. He was one of the students in the Scriptorium when I was there. He's from Watya and at that time, the railway didn't even extend that far. It was a long way away. We all thought he was a bit strange and probably treated him worse than he deserved. He probably hated all of us, but after I finished, I came to know him as capable and reliable, more than can be said for any of the previous meteorologists in Ysherra."

"Why did he choose to go there? I mean, it's a long way from his home if he's from Watya."

"Yes, and so is Tiverius. There are many reasons why people do this. The family can both be a reason to stay and a reason to leave. Not all people are blessed with a loving family like you."

He gave her a bittersweet smile.

Viki, of course, had a very large family. It occurred to her that his wife might not like him to go away for so long, or that maybe he wanted to go away for a bit to escape a house with ten children. What a noisy place that must be, especially because some of them were very small. Lana remembered when the youngest was born, only a year or so ago. A fellow student had mentioned the word "jackrabbit" and she had thought that was a very nasty thing to say.

The dining car was busy and there were still people waiting at the far end of the carriage. Everyone got up as soon as they had finished to make way for others to eat.

The soldiers had shovelled all the food off their plates in mere moments and all the ones who had been in their cabin had gone already. Lana had overheard some talk of a briefing.

Sure enough, they found all the soldiers jammed up in the little passage along the first cabin. Some of the men were in the cabin and the rest were in the corridor, making it quite impassable to other people.

Viki and Lana waited while Commander Ramatius explained about what was to happen the next morning. Military talk was full of funny words, she concluded. Disembark, "exit" when they meant "leave"—who ever said things like that?

One of the men yelled, "Get out of the way! Senator coming through!"

The soldiers shuffled aside and pressed themselves against the walls to let Viki and Lana through to their cabin. Viki said he wanted to do some reading. Lana had also brought a book, but spent most of the time looking at the reflection in the window against the ink-dark sky.

She was thinking of her mother, alone in the kitchen, waiting for her father to come back. She thought of her mother wanting to see all her children one last time, and of her father worrying about Arania. And she thought about Javes who didn't know that she was coming, and who hadn't written back since her letter about dust devils.

The dining room staff brought tea, and then it was time for bed. The soldiers appeared to have gone to bed already.

In her cabin, Lana opened her suitcase and took out her familiar nightgown.

She let down her hair and combed it out while sitting on the bed, put her slippers under the bunk, turned down the wick in the lamp until the flame died and lay down. The bed was quite comfortable but she found it hard to sleep because the mattress creaked and the train rocked. But most of all because it wasn't *her* comfortable bed at home. But then she thought about adventure and new places and the fact that she had always wanted to travel and that she would have exciting stories to tell when she returned for lectures.

Eventually she dozed off.

She woke up while it was still dark. The train had stopped. Why? Where were they? Men's voices shouted in the night. A door was yanked open. Big booted footsteps sounded in the hallway. The cabin next to hers opened. A man called out.

What was going on?

Lana jumped out of bed. In the dark, she found her slippers under the bed and her knitted vest against the cold. She looked out the window, but it was too dark to see anything. She opened the door to the cabin a little. A man walked past, went to the door and jumped out of the train.

Big clangs and shudders went through the carriage, making her think that some freight was probably being loaded or unloaded.

"I can see it all over," man said outside.

"What the hell is it?" someone else said. His voice sounded disturbed.

Lana tiptoed to the next cabin where Viki slept. The door was open. She found Viki standing outside the carriage with a group of other people.

"Why have we stopped?"

"Just unloading some cargo, I think. But look at the sky."

The entire sky was lit up with shimmering bands of green and pink. Lana had never seen this before. It was as pretty as it was scary. A chill breeze wafted past her skin, making her shiver.

"This can't be a good thing, right?"

"It's what Perians call skylights," Viki said.

"What causes it?"

"It's said to be caused by sonorics."

"But there are no sonorics around here, are there?" As she asked it, she thought of the comments about Dust Devils and the soldiers bringing the suits. But this . . . this was really bad. Her mother described how the sky would glow when the machine that produced sonorics still worked. Even Peria hadn't seen a sky like this for a long time. "Where is it coming from? Not just from Aranians with little machines they've made?"

"We don't know. We truly don't know." The fear in his voice shook her more than the words he spoke.

CHAPTER 3

*J*AVES WENT BACK into the yard, where the goats had woken up and crowded around him, bleating for him to toss them some hay.

Tali came into the doorway, looking scruffy and dusty.

"Sleep well?"

She didn't reply. Her eyes had a hollow expression, fixed at a point over the back fence.

It disturbed him how skinny, dirty and ill she looked. She said she couldn't remember how long ago the men had come, but he guessed it must be some while, because she didn't look like she'd eaten much for a few weeks.

"Did you have any breakfast?"

"There is milk," she said.

Javes eyed the goats around him, their udders full. They hadn't been fed either. "Last night's milk? That's off."

She shrugged and sat down, wrapping her arms around her pulled-up knees.

Well, suit yourself.

Javes crossed to the broken shed and pulled down half a bale of hay. The goats chased the pieces as they scattered around the yard. While they were eating, he could get close with the bucket.

The harvest of milk was poor.

He picked up the bucket, wiped sweat from his brow, and carried

31

the milk into the house. There, he found Pashtan's cooling box cloths and wet both of them from the water bag that was fast emptying. He also poured water into the dish that fed the earthenware cooler, annoyed that Tali had allowed the goats to chew the basket into bits. What was the point of having animals inside anyway?

With the jug of milk installed in the box, he poured himself a glass, and drank it by way of breakfast, supplemented with the last of the raisins.

"Have you bought any food? Do you have any money? Do the townsfolk know that you're alone here?"

Again, she just shrugged.

"Come on, help me. You are allowed to say something, you know. I don't bite."

He was annoyed and hot. This was stupid. Girls were stupid. He'd much rather talk to the camel. At least it *couldn't* respond even if it sometimes looked at him as if it wanted to tell him to shut up.

He fed the camel and then he saddled it up, brought as many empty water bags as he could find and tied them to the saddle.

"I'm going to the well to get water," he told Tali, still seated on the back step.

She barely reacted.

Well, pfff, if she was going to be like that . . . He didn't think he understood girls at the best of times: always giggling in class and talking about clothes and walking in groups whispering together. This girl-child seemed to be positively petrified of him. And he had no idea what to say to her to make her behave normally.

The walk into town did little to improve his mood. The air was extremely dusty; he only spotted a few people, and most of those were scurrying back into their houses. Once a man with a donkey cart came the other way, but he hid his face in the hood of his cape and didn't look up. The tray on the man's cart contained jars filled with water and a crate that contained bread and a sack of onions.

Javes didn't understand the northerners' obsession with onions—they made your breath stink and made you fart—but right now, he'd eat a whole sack of them, and boil them in goat's milk, too, as the locals sometimes did. He was that hungry.

The selection of stalls in the market square was a pale shade of the meagre offering that would normally be there, but at least the markets operated with a semblance of normality: people were buying supplies and lining up at the well for water. No one had brought the animals from the pens to the sale yard, however, and the stalls selling fabric, kitchen implements and other household items were also gone.

The buildings surrounding the square bore the signs of vandalism by the bandits—Javes refused to call them invaders, because they were simply destroying things and looting for their own wealth, not conquering land on behalf of anyone else.

As Tali had said, the telegraph office was burned out and the wires were down. The building lay abandoned, and there would be no messages from Tiverius, or any way of sending those messages, not to Viki and not to his parents.

Well.

He guessed this absolved him from having to collect weather data.

That meant he could try to get out of this place. He searched his pockets for loose coins, of which he had far too few to be of any use. Several times, his fingertips touched the metal globe that he'd received from Karlen. If it was really worth that much, he could use the money, but he also had a bag of camel hair. He got two eggs for that, and then he bought some bread, and breakfast was starting to look up. He'd seen the firebricks in the shed, and if worse came to worst, he'd make a fire in the yard from the fence palings and cook the eggs over a campfire.

Now water.

He lined up for the well and found himself behind the owner of the teahouse, who told him that Aranians had come into town on a couple of occasions.

"They were looking for someone or something," another man said. "Takin' all the people who might know prisoner. Askin' questions. Beatin' people up if they don' like the answers. Woe betide if you happen to be a girl. Swearin', filthy, rapin' gits. I'll cut off their dicks if they give me a chance. Cut 'em off and roast 'em as sausages and feed 'em to the pigs."

Javes tried not to stand cross-legged after hearing that threat.

While the men relayed stories about having saved their wives and mothers, the line moved forward. Javes got to the front and filled his water bags with milky, muddy-looking water. How long before it ran out and life in Ysherra became impossible? Many people were already leaving, he was told. A bus left daily for the two-day trip to Watya. With the camel, however, he'd have to walk.

He loaded the bags onto the back of the camel's saddle, but something had spooked it and the stupid animal kept tossing its head. Javes had become quite handy with the camel and managed to keep hold of the rope while he walked back to the house, but the camel was *not* happy. It kept snorting and blowing and pulling sideways.

Javes patted the furry neck. "What is wrong with you?"

The camel gave him a disdainful look, which was the normal state of affairs for a camel. Javes trusted the camel, because it couldn't listen to reasoning. If it was unhappy, there was a reason.

Yet there were no dogs in the street, and no other camels to spook it.

But boy, the air had gone dusty all of a sudden.

That was not a good sign.

He reached Pashtan's house.

When he first came into the back yard, he thought it was empty. The gate to the animal pen was closed, but the goats were all gone. The back door of the house was shut.

"Tali?" Javes called.

The sound of a voice came from inside the house, and the bleating of a kid. What? He'd just cleaned out the room. Had she let the goats back in?

The camel went up the back steps of the house, pushing the closed door with its head.

Javes pushed it aside. "Get out of the way, you silly animal. You don't even fit in there."

But as soon as he opened the door, the camel stuck its head in and then tried to worm itself into the house.

Javes pulled at the rope that dangled from the camel's headgear. "Whoa, whoa! Come back. What's going on here?" He managed to push the camel out of the house, quickly shut the door behind him— and was nosed in the crotch by a goat.

"What the hell possesses all these animals?"

Tali sat cross-legged on the desk. "They come in when they're afraid."

Javes retorted in an annoyed tone, "That doesn't mean they *should* come in. You've spoiled them." He pushed the goats aside so that he could walk into the room.

"Then you try to keep them outside. The little ones climb in through the window and the big ones headbutt the door and bleat until you let them in, or until they break the door. You can't sleep, and the neighbours complain about the noise."

"Then what are they afraid of?"

"I don't know? Things we can't hear?"

That reply filled Javes with a horrible foreboding feeling. "Things we can't hear," like sonorics spikes prior to dust devils?

Like unusually dusty air?

Pashtan's shelves contained two barygraphs, but neither contained paper. There was also a pocket barymeter, but it didn't show anything out of the ordinary. The spikes had always been really short and it could be that the spike had passed already. The goats wanted to go back outside, right?

He opened the door. The goats rushed past him into the yard. He opened the gate for them—and noticed that the camel had broken the latch, so he went to find a length of rope in the shed—where he still hadn't cleaned away the turd, that, by now had gone very dry.

He took a shovel and carried the offending object to the outhouse.

Then, with the camel and goats back in the pen, he stood at the back step, looking at the sky. The air was still dusty, but there were no signs of clouds and there was not much wind.

Javes went inside and instructed Tali to help him clean up the house. He moved the furniture to one side, swept up the dust and soot and goat poo and then did the same on the other side. The blankets were filthy and he wanted them washed, but he'd already made a trip to the well, he didn't have that much water and, besides, Pashtan's washtub had been dented badly and he would have to bang it straight first.

There was just so much to do, and he needed to decide if it was worth doing.

He had to decide whether he'd bother staying here, or whether he'd take the risk of saddling up the camel and walking it all the way to the train station in Watya.

But damn it, he had no money for a ticket to Tiverius.

Well then, he could turn south and walk the camel all the way to Tiverius.

With Tali?

She had no relatives in town. He'd already asked and surmised as much from the fact that no one had helped her after she had been left behind.

Damn it, that was annoying. Not only didn't he have any money, he was saddled with this girl, too. He thought of his mother, a refined rich Tiverian lady, and what she would think if he suddenly turned up with a camel and a little girl. He liked to think that she would be happy enough to see him again that she wouldn't mind Tali, but he feared that his parents weren't as nice as that. They would see a thin, dirty child from a poverty-stricken area and they'd go, "We don't hire people like that. They steal." Even if he said she was a friend—which she wasn't—they would look funny at him. And that was before they saw the camel. He could just about see it ripping out all the neatly cultured bushes in the front yard of his house.

At times Javes wondered if his parents cared all that much about him. Enough to find somewhere to house the camel? His father would complain about the money it would cost.

And he wanted to go home, badly.

But he couldn't leave Tali, because she was too young to look after herself.

And what if Arukat came back and found his daughter missing?

People captured by Aranians don't come back.

Where were her other relatives? Uncles, aunties, grandparents. They should look after her.

But no matter how many times he asked, she said she'd been a little girl when she last saw her other relatives. They lived in another town, and she couldn't even remember the name of the town.

Javes named all the towns in the area he knew, but she didn't remember, or didn't *want* to remember. He was probably wasting his time pursuing that avenue. Javes had found that when families didn't live close to one another, there was usually a reason.

She would have to come with him.

But his parents . . .

And so his thoughts went around and around. Meanwhile, they cleaned the house and carted more water, because Javes did want to wash both himself and the blankets. He beat the washtub back into a useable shape and found a piece of soap that the goats hadn't eaten. He put the tub in the back yard, filled up water in a bucket, undressed, stood in the tub and poured the water over himself.

Ah, that was good.

He scrubbed himself with the small piece of grainy soap and poured water over himself again.

Tali sat watching on the back steps. He had asked her to make tea, but she seemed more preoccupied with staring into the distance. Seriously, he had always thought she was pretty capable, but she'd been useless since he'd discovered her in Pashtan's house. If only she would just talk, and say what she wanted, or have an opinion on anything.

"Want me to wash you, too, before I make the water dirty with washing the blankets?"

She shook her head.

"Oh, come on, I don't bite. I'll go inside and won't watch if you want."

She shook her head again. Her gaze was fixed at a spot over his head. Javes turned around and looked—

Big orange clouds billowed in the sky, blocking out the view to the west.

Dust Devil!

Oh shit oh shit oh shit. He scrambled out of the tub, stark naked and wet, and ran across the yard into the house—shit, the animals. He ran for his pack in the shed, yanked out big handfuls of the cloth that used to cover the donkey cart, and dragged it outside.

The camel stood in the corner of the pen, underneath the shelter, looking out over the fence at the approaching menace. The goats huddled next to the fence.

He pulled the rope on its headgear. "Sit."

The camel sat.

Javes strung the cloth onto the fence, and then onto the posts that held up the shelter's roof, so that it covered the camel.

He shooed the goats underneath.

The wind picked up, whipping up sand. A gust picked up the empty washtub and sent it rolling through the yard. He managed to catch it, and dragged it behind him into the house. Sand bit into his naked skin. He wrestled the tub inside and shut the door, panting.

Tali sat on top of the desk, her favourite spot, with her knees drawn up to her chest and her arms looped around her legs.

"I could have used some help!"

She stared wide-eyed at him, and his male appendage in particular. Oh. His clothes. Where the hell were his clothes? He'd left them on the back step, but hadn't seen them on his way into the house.

Great. His clothes had blown away.

The wind howled around the house. Sand blew into the little high window next to the door. Javes pulled a cushion off the couch and stuffed it into the hole.

There.

But now it was really dark inside.

The noise of the wind drowned out all other sounds. It got cold in the house. Javes rummaged around on the shelf for the oil light. He struck a match and lit the wick, hands trembling.

"Are you cold?" he asked Tali.

The expression on her face was empty. Her eyes were wide and staring, her face pale and sweaty. She moved her lips, but no sound came out.

"Uh, Tali?"

No reaction. Something banged against the roof.

"Tali?"

He rummaged on the shelf. He needed a hammer to nail down whatever was flapping. He closed his hand over the pocket barymeter and held it up to the light. What the . . . eighty motes per cube.

Damn it, where *were* his clothes? It was really starting to get cold.

The cushion blew out of the window and a whoosh of air entered the house. Clouds of sand blew in, the door crashed open, the horde of goats bolted in.

Tali screamed and pointed. A dark silhouette moved within the dust-red clouds. Its eyes were hollow and its mouth open in a howling sound. *The mud monster.* Javes tried to push the door shut but either the wind was too strong or the door was damaged.

He had to make an effort not to look outside. He crouched behind the door against the wall.

Tali screamed, "No, no, the men are coming back!"

She was absorbed in her own fears. The Dust Devil was playing with their minds.

The goats all crammed under the desk, the whites in their eyes showing.

The storm was over as quickly as it had come. The wind died down, the dust stopped whirling and bleak, blue-tinged sunlight returned.

Javes rose, cursing. All the work they had done this morning had been for nothing. Sand lay ankle-deep on the floor. The door had fallen off its hinges. The couch and bed were covered in sand, and he still couldn't see his clothes anywhere.

But his pack stood against the wall.

He took the *temuz* he'd worn on his trip out of his pack and pulled it, and the matching trousers, on. Both were also seriously in need of washing and the smell of old sweat made him gag.

"I don't know about you, but I've had enough of this place. I'm leaving."

He didn't wait for Tali's non-response, but jumped down the back step into the yard.

What a mess. The fence had blown over, the shed leaned sideways, the roof of the animal pen's shelter was missing. The camel still sat under the cloth; it raised its head off the sand when he came. A thick layer of sand had collected on the lower parts of the cloth.

"At least you survived." He rubbed the camel's furry neck. Dust coated the animal's long eyelashes. He freed the camel of the sand-burdened cloth so that it could get up. The goats were already nosing around the yard, digging up—

"Hey, that's my shirt!"

He shooed the goats aside and pulled out his shirt. The wash tub was there, too, but his pants were nowhere to be seen.

He walked past the side of the house to the street. He barely recognised the scene there. A thick layer of dust covered the road. Fences had blown over, roofs blown off, and walls had fallen. The olive tree had lost several branches. The neighbours on the town side of Pashtan's house were walking around, collecting bits of wood and metal sheeting that had blown off the roof.

The house across the road had fallen down in a heap. Javes hadn't noticed the grumpy old fellow who lived there since he'd come back from the windwalkers, and hoped he wasn't inside.

Tali had come to the front of Pashtan's house. She met Javes' eyes with a horrified look.

"What is wrong?" he asked.

"You're leaving, now?"

He looked at the sky. "Not before I've packed. You can come or you can stay here. That's up to you, but there is nothing here for me, and no reason to stay."

She stared at him, her throat working. "Where are you going?"

"Eventually, Tiverius."

"But I don't want to stay here alone."

"Then you can come. It's up to you. This place is just going to be overrun with Dust Devils, and if I have to die, I'd rather do it while trying to get home."

"I don't want to die." Her voice was small.

"Me neither, so that's a start."

"But . . . what if my parents come back?"

"Look, I don't know, and I'm not going to tell you what to do. I barely know myself. Except I want to go home, and I'm not staying here waiting for Dust Devils or Aranians to get me."

The mention of the word Aranians appeared to settle the matter for her.

They went back inside, swept out the house—again—and started packing. Since Arukat's donkeys had been killed and there were no carts left, they were limited in what they could take and the camel could carry.

Javes decided that they would walk as much as possible to spare the camel. There were certain things they absolutely had to take, including a thick cloth against Dust Devils. They were going south, so hopefully they would not need it. But the cloth could also double as a tent in case of rain. And the thought of rain made him feel homesick. He'd not seen rain since leaving home.

He decided to take the pocket barymeter, too.

His clothes had been seriously depleted.

Tali had nothing to take.

"Nothing at all?" he asked her. "Why don't you go into your house and see if you can bring anything that you can still use."

She shook her head.

"I know it's not easy, but an extra jacket or a blanket or a water bag might mean the difference between life and death. It's cold in Tiverius."

She shook her head again, so fervently that her plaits swung around her head.

Javes had been told that it was improper to say rude things to women or children, but he was tempted to say something rude to her. From the moment he had discovered her, she had done *nothing* useful and he was really sick of it. She was just *sitting* there.

And because he was tempted to say something rude, he stomped off into the yard to Arukat's burned-out house. He could even understand why she didn't want to go back, but he was also struggling to cope. He could use some *help* or just someone who responded normally to things he said.

He climbed over the fallen-down section of the fence separating the two back yards. A rake stood in the shed, one of the few items that had not been strewn about by various groups of scavengers. He pulled it out of the dust before climbing the burned veranda steps to the back door.

Once he stepped between the blackened walls of the house, he became aware of a foul smell that wafted from within the house.

He knew what it was before he came to the kitchen, where he found two burned bodies on the ground. The fire and decay had made them unrecognisable, but who else could they be except Arukat and his wife?

And Tali had said that they'd been loaded onto a cart and taken away by Aranians? What else had this girl told him that was a lie?

He stood there for a moment, gathering his frayed thoughts.

Part of him didn't want to travel with this silent, one-syllable-response girl with serious personality issues.

The other part of him knew that he could not just abandon her, because he would never be able to look at himself in the mirror ever again.

A third part of him wanted to run out of this house, this place of death, because whatever had happened here, Tali could not speak of it.

But the sensible part of him knew that the reason he had come here—to see if he could find anything useful—was still very valid.

He gave the bodies a wide berth when crossing the kitchen into the living room.

The fire had not touched this room quite as much, but the scent of burnt wood, combined with the stench of decay, was a powerful mixture. Javes held his nose while looking around, because if the smell made him vomit, it'd be a waste of good food as well as a waste of time. In a cupboard, he found some money. He felt dreadful taking it, but, as he had said to Tali, it could make the difference between life and death, so he took it. In the other drawers, he found various business implements, including an abacus and a few slates. Javes had little use for slates. He wanted some loose sheets of paper so he could write to his parents when he reached a place where letters could be sent. There was no paper in the drawer, but underneath the slates, he found a metal shape cut from a flat sheet. It looked a bit like a key to him—it had a narrow end with notches. It was made from the same type of metal as the globe he'd been given that was tucked away in his pack.

He had no idea what this thing was, but it appeared that people paid good money for this stuff and that Arukat had thought it important enough not to keep it with the rest of his stock. Javes could sell it later.

In the other drawers, he found a few old coins and a pendant on a silver chain. In the bedroom, he found a blanket, a heavy men's coat and two shirts and trousers that looked like they might fit Tali. There was also a pair of sturdy boots, but they were much too big for him, so he left them and made his way back to Pashtan's house.

He rearranged the packs to include his new things. Then he gathered all of Pashtan's maps. The road map interested him most. He'd taken the road south a few times, but all the larger towns were further south than he had gone.

Tali sat on the desk, her knees drawn up to her chest.

He suggested that she might like to do something, but she didn't move, so he packed the bags, filled the waterbags, hauled the saddle, fashioned a rope harness for all the goats. He didn't intend to take them all the way to Tiverius, but he'd set them free somewhere they could survive in the wild.

This was going to be one long trip to Tiverius.

CHAPTER 4

*T*HE TRUCK PULLED AWAY from the house, leaving Sady with a deep dark hole at the bottom of his heart. Next to him, Loriane wiped a tear from her cheek.

"She'll have fun," Sady said, to cheer himself more than anything, to fool himself that he wasn't terribly worried about the signs he was getting from his spies. At least when she was out of the capital, Lana was safe.

He wheeled Loriane back into the house, to the kitchen, where Myra stood at the stove, her face red. She wiped her cheeks.

"We'll all miss her," she said.

It was true. Sady remembered the day Lana was born, his first and only child. He remembered holding her for the first time when the midwife put her in his arms, all red-skinned and wrinkled. She was the baby in the household and had always remained so. Myra's son Beido, who had come from the City of Glass with her as infant, was a couple of years older, and he had gone back to the City of Glass to serve as Eagle Knight. Myra and Farius had never had children.

Orsan came in, ready to take Sady back to the doga assembly building. Myra gave him a cup of tea while Sady got ready. He went up to the bedroom to collect his gown which he had left on the bed.

Loriane's book of names also lay there.

He should ask her for the names of her children so that he could write to them. That would keep her happy until Lana came back.

43

Wouldn't it be nice if they could travel to the City of Glass together one last time to meet the children?

On the way back to the doga, Sady sat next to Orsan in silence. Although Orsan had been a faithful guard for more than twenty years, Sady knew that he adhered to a code of confidentiality, and Sady had learned not to trust or rely on him too much. Unlike his house staff, Orsan was employed by the doga and he protected the institute, not the person.

So he did not in general discuss personal things with Orsan. He'd only recently learned that Orsan was married and had three children and two grandchildren. Yes, they were all starting to get old.

Sady had left the assembly at the beginning of lunchtime. Normally, the doga's kitchens would serve a meal for the senators when the assembly was in session. Not having taken part in the lunchtime gossip, Sady felt oddly detached. In a way, he wondered if this was still his fight. A younger generation should take over.

When he went into his office, his advisor came after him. "Proctor, did you hear the news?"

"I went to say goodbye to my daughter who's off to Ysherra with Viki. I didn't hear any news."

"The news reached us just now that the Aranian crown prince Nayek has been killed."

Sady stopped, turned around and stared at his advisor. Prince Nayek was *not* the crown prince, but people often called him that. He probably would have become crown prince once the king chose his successor from his hundreds of sons. Nayek—whom Sady had never met—was said to be in the best position to take over from his father. As Sady understood, that was determined by his usefulness to the king, and how many sons he could sire.

The race for the position of crown prince was typically Aranian, and, Aranian-style, often went over dead bodies. He shouldn't have let this news surprise him, especially now that King Orik was getting old.

This fight for the throne was going to affect the whole world.

Although still a boor, Nayek was considered a moderate influence in Arania.

"Well," he said, and sat down at his desk. And again, "Well . . . what does that mean for us? Who are the likely contenders to take over? I don't think we'll be invited to the state funeral."

The man laughed wryly. "We'll be talking about the Aranian succession at the assembly this afternoon. If you approve, that is. General Selidas has been invited, as well as some of our Aranian advisors. I drafted up this agenda." He passed Sady a piece of paper.

Sady read.

Positioning of spies

Positioning of army units, including balloon divisions.

Security of border towns.

Emergency fallback line.

Potential sonorics protection.

Sady nodded. "That looks fine. I have no doubt people will come up with other points as the meeting goes on."

"Will we allow the agenda to be modified during the meeting?"

"Yes, but close the doors. I don't want any public panic over this."

Yet. His head was reeling. This reminded him of the war councils he'd attended twenty years ago, when the sonorics cloud was coming from the south. Those meetings had been with General Finnisius. Poor Finnisius, who was very old and very frail and, on the occasions that Sady visited him, very confused.

Sady collected his papers and a pen and made his way to the assembly hall. A couple of guards stood outside, blocking the usual path where the public could enter the gallery to observe the meeting. Several people were arguing with the guards.

"I always come here, every time the assembly sits," a man was saying, his voice laced with outrage.

Sady recognised him from having seen him in the gallery many times.

The guard said, "Today's meeting is closed for the first half. There will be a statement from the doga later."

A young teacher with a class of children waited by the side of the entrance, looking unsure what to do now. Sady usually encouraged those visits, because the more youngsters became interested in the processes of government, the better the doga's accountability. He quietly instructed one of his assistants to take the class through a guided tour of the building. He would make an effort to see them later, if there was time.

The atmosphere in the assembly hall was tense. Senators stood in their benches talking and the very noisy clangs made by the guards shutting the big doors did not quieten them.

Sady put his papers on the central table.

His assistants were already there, most importantly Senator Shara from the Watya district—which made him think of Lana, and a stab went through him.

His secretary came up from behind. "Proctor, I managed to invite, at short notice, a few people who know more about Arania. They're waiting on the bench."

Sady could see the people in question. The only one he recognised was a tutor in warfare from the Scriptorium. Well, that was a good sign.

He pushed away unease while he walked to the dais.

When he asked for quiet, people actually stopped talking. It never ceased to amaze him that, after all those years, people still listened.

"The news has reached us that the Aranian contender for the crown, Prince Nayek, has been killed."

Senators wanted to know more details, but no one knew any.

Some suggested that it might be some form of false propaganda, to which senators with knowledge of Arania made counter-arguments that prince Nayek was no friend of Chevakia and that all princes made threats to Tiverius.

"Prince Nayek is friendly with Peria," a senator said.

They debated that angle for a bit, although no one could say what Peria's role in the matter was, or even if Prince Nayek's death gave Peria any advantage.

"The City of Glass has become a major hub for commerce. It would be crazy if they did not deal with Arania."

Another senator agreed. "Other than power, there is one thing these Aranian princes need: money to maintain their harems and armies. They'll go anywhere there is business to be had, especially if business is easy and relatively unencumbered by rules." That brought some outraged calls, because it was seen as a stab at the business administrator, who had made real efforts to stamp out the rampant black trade that avoided tariffs, costing the doga handfuls of money. Yeah, some people didn't like those new rules.

Sady cut in before the meeting degenerated into a discussion about tariffs and brought the discussion back to the likely effect of the prince's death on Chevakia.

No one really knew, so it was hard to keep the debate on topic.

There was some discussion about the power of the Aranian king in general. Sady called the doga's Aranian expert forward. This man was Aranian, and had fled from there about ten years ago. Like many Aranians, he was a tall man, but the lack of exercise had made him lanky and thin. His grey eyes were deep set, with a heavy brow and glossy dark hair that he wore loose without any adornments.

"The direction Arania will take depends on who wins Prince Nayek's place as the favourite for the throne," he said. "We have two likely options. First, Prince Denori, who was a long-time favourite before Nayek came onto the scene. He is older than Nayek, and his mother is Yala, who is highly respected, although now too old to bear the king any more children. Nayek's mother is Selwa, who is still fertile, but he is her second son. Her first son is Sferuk, who is the other rival."

Sady tried to remember when and in what context he had last heard those names. Prince Nayek was often talked about, but the others, not so much.

The expert went on, "Denori is a brute who gives the impression of being dumb, but he has more intelligence than people give him credit for. He has military interests. He has amassed a vast army and continues to send men to fight his rival's forces. He is also said to be developing new methods of warfare. Sferuk is an administrator. He excels at trading favours, and tricking his associates into agreeing to unfavourable contracts. He is also said to use force to get people to agree or part with information. He has a vast network of informants, including people who inform on his brothers. Unlike his rival, he does not use solely men, but employs the disgruntled women in his rival's harems to give him information."

Sady did not like the sound of either of those two men. He had never met Prince Nayek, but he appeared to be at least moderately outward-looking. Aranian culture could be so terribly insular and unrelentingly harsh on their own citizens. He remembered Milleus' observations on winning the war and pushing into Kadrish with the army.

"They were slaughtering their own men," Milleus had said. "Those who were perceived to be at fault for their own defeat died by the hand of the king's guards, not by ours. The fall of Kadrish would not have been such a blood bath if that hadn't happened."

Sady remembered thinking that was a strange way to run a country, but he'd been a lad at school during that time, basking in the glory of his brother's great victory. How much of that victory was part of the implosion of Aranian infighting and rivalry?

Similarly, how much of that rivalry would now be fought out over the heads of Chevakians?

"What should our course be?" he asked. "How should we react to the prospect of either man becoming the crown prince?"

The warfare tutor from the Scriptorium said, "Neither of them are good news. Prince Nayek was valuable to us in a way, because he was interested in trade. If there was money to be made, he would not fight. He understood that fighting is expensive and has the potential to turn public opinion on him very quickly, if losses are heavy and beloved people die or cherished towns are lost. These two men . . . are much less refined. They will start a war."

Coming from an academic, it sounded detached and unemotional. *They will start a war*. Just an observation. Did all these young people who had never lived through hardship even know what a war meant?

Sady stepped up to the dais. "Well, we won't have a war if I have anything to do with it. We won't engage and we won't jump to their tactics of trying to provoke us."

"They will provoke us, because they have nothing to lose," General Selidas said. "Those are the hardest enemies to defeat. Those men in the Aranian military see it as an honour to die for their country so that their blessed mothers can rise in status. They get their names inscribed on a wall after their death. The conditions in the Aranian military are bad enough that some men *want* to be killed. The Aranian generals consider them their spearhead elite troops."

A chill went over Sady's back. "Are these the type of troops that are amassing just over the border?"

"We've had no indication that those are elite troops. I don't think those camps are there for any other purpose other than to make us feel uneasy. The Aranians are likely posturing to see if they can get a reaction out of us so that they can gauge how strong we are. If there is going to be an operation across the border, then it won't be at those places."

"Would they really go to war, seeing the history?"

"With those princes trying to curry the favour of the king, anything can happen. If either of them can put a significant victory over us to his name, it will lift his status immeasurably. It is a favourite pastime amongst the Aranian populace to blame any hardship on Chevakia. Common people of the current generation have forgotten the suffering brought about by the war. They are happy to donate their sons to the cause. If they're poor, they can sell their daughters, but they can't sell their sons, and their sons can't buy women. Sending them into the military and hoping for a glorious death is the family's only hope to win favours."

Sady shook his head. "It's a crazy country."

The general shook his head. "It makes for dangerous opponents."

That was true.

The military experts then went on a discussion about potential tactics. There was some doubt about whether the action came only from the camp of prince Denori, the military man, but the Aranian experts had analysed the note that the dying soldier had brought to Sady's doorstep.

The Aranian adviser reported, "The handwriting resembles that of prince Sferuk, which means that he is also involved, although likely not in command of large armies, but of smaller elite groups of soldiers. They're potentially more dangerous than armies, because they can remain concealed and penetrate deep into the country. It could be that prince Nayek had a networks of spies in place, and those will be called to join either prince."

"And all this while their father is still alive."

"They're trying to impress him and the Aranian people."

It was a crazy situation, but not one the doga could do much about; and so, after giving the general the mandate to do whatever was necessary to gain more information and to prepare for a conflict that would hopefully never happen, Sady ordered the doors to the public gallery reopened. The meeting proceeded with the day-to-day points of running the country.

After the meeting, Sady went to his office, where his assistant notified him that Rodi wanted to see him. That was Rodius han

Deverus, the academic acting as the doga's Chief Meteorologist in Viki's absence.

Sady told his assistant to let him in.

The appointment of this man as Viki's second had surprised Sady. He knew that, despite having worked for the doga for many years, Viki still had an academic streak, but Rodi was a full time lecturer at the Scriptorium and poorly versed in the processes and mysteries of the doga assembly. He was also a bit old for a replacement and had, in the past, displayed a disdain for politics and how it influenced his discipline that was . . . just call it unhelpful.

He understood that Viki got on well with the man, but unfortunately he couldn't say the same for himself. The man was so *old school*, despite being thirty years younger than Sady. It was infuriating. One would think the younger generation would jump on the new sciences.

Rodi came into the office carrying the telltale weather maps.

"Good afternoon, Proctor." His voice was dry and without a shred of friendliness.

"You asked to see me?"

"I did, and I've waited for you to come back."

"I was at the assembly meeting, which you are welcome to attend." Which he probably *should* attend, since Viki was going to be away for a couple of weeks.

Rodi cleared his throat. "The reason I've come is that we're detecting a system that will break the drought in the northern districts."

Well, at least something looked to be going the right way.

Rodi unrolled his maps on the desk. As soon as Sady saw the dense concentration of lines across the north of the continent, he knew that this was not just a storm.

Rodi explained the extent of the system that spanned most of the northern half of the continent. He admitted that large sections of land were uncovered by measurements because there were no stations.

"What are the readings for Watya like? And Tamyra and Ysherra?" Viki and Lana were there. He hoped they wouldn't get stuck in an inconvenient place. If the Aramys River rose, it could be weeks before the crossing at Watya was passable.

Rodi pulled out a table with the rain, temperature, air pressure and sonorics data from the weather stations in the region. "This is from today."

The first thing Sady noticed was the empty lines. "Why are there no reports from Ysherra?"

"There weren't any. The line must be down."

Well . . . damn it. That made Sady's heart jump. "Any idea why?"

"A problem with the wires? They're all above-ground up there and vulnerable to weather."

Yes, that was true.

He looked at the rest of the data. Some rain had already fallen at stations south of Tamyra. Then he noticed something else. "The sonorics readings are rather high."

"Yes." Said with conviction, as if he was glad that Sady noticed.

"But that is . . . it's the *north* of the country. There is no acceptable level of sonorics for Tamyra. There has never been *any* elevated sonorics measurement taken in Tamyra. And it's not just Tamyra, it's the whole region, all these stations, except the ones where we have no data—"

And the cold chill turned into a blizzard. Was it that they had no data because of the elevated levels of sonorics, which were known to upset telegraph lines?

And he had just sent his daughter into that region, thinking she'd be safer than in the capital.

CHAPTER 5

*I*SANDOR SEETHED with anger.

He sat at his desk, staring at his hands, ripping pieces of paper to shreds with trembling hands. Waiting.

He'd written to Ledor of House Mara, asking for explanation, asking, no, demanding, that he give up control of his twenty-nine year old daughter so that she could marry the man she loved.

What gall did the man have anyway, forcing her to refuse an offer from the king. *The king!*

Trouble was, Isandor didn't feel like a king.

King Caldor, Isandor and Jevaithi's great-grandfather, had been a dark magician, using icefire to do wonderful things for his family and other nobles and terrible things to most of the common people, especially those who raised questions.

After he had been deposed, Perian laws had severely curtailed the power of kings. Isandor could never hold a position higher than that of Jevaithi's consort, and he couldn't be that because he was her brother, and the position of "brother of the queen" held no legal standing.

No matter that he usually led the Knight Council, no matter that he organised the rebuilding of the city, that he ran the palace and that he made the decisions.

It was always all about Jevaithi. She took the limelight with her pretty dresses and her cultured speech for which she had been trained.

Isandor had not minded being in her shadow. He didn't have a showy personality that required everyone to pay attention to him. He *liked* being able to get on with the job without being hassled by people.

But just now, the fact that he did all the *work* hit him hard. He did the work, and got no reward, and when he found someone he liked, Jevaithi had the gall to *complain* and some other stuck-up prick dared deny him the only thing he had ever asked for himself for the last twenty years.

That got in his craw.

And there was another Knight Council meeting this afternoon where he could just turn up and pretend nothing had happened, that he wasn't terribly upset at Jevaithi's manipulation of Rider Barton—which would be all for nothing anyway—that he wasn't ready to slap her in the face for being so stupidly stubborn, that he hadn't been taking his gun out of the drawer in his desk and pointing it at the door as if Ledor would walk in any moment, that he hadn't lain awake in bed the last two nights with the tears streaming down his face, reliving that moment Tamerane turned away from him and ran out of the teahouse.

Where was she now?

Did she lay awake at night crying as well?

How could he reach her and snatch her away without risking the anger of all the old noble families in the City of Glass, who still had a lot of money and influence, and without violating the rules about power that he and the council had worked so hard to establish? He could not just snatch her and elope. He could not use violence against the family. He could not have a nasty public argument.

But oh, how he felt like doing all of these things.

And his mind blanked out on reasonable thoughts, things he could actually do and that might work.

All he could see was seething red anger.

So he ripped sheets of paper, his hands sweaty. He let the pieces fall to the floor.

The stack of papers on his desk for the Knight Council meeting stayed untouched. The meeting would start soon, but he had not yet done anything.

He was *through* with being grateful, being patient. He was through with putting aside his own wishes for the good of the country.

Clearly Ledor of House Mara thought someone or something else more important than the leader of his own country. And Isandor was going to tell the man exactly what he thought. And since he wasn't replying to his correspondence, he was going to his door, in person. Two days was a reasonable time to wait, wasn't it?

Isandor rose.

His legs were cramped from sitting at the desk in the same position since the early hours of this morning.

He went to the bedroom and dressed in his official clothes. He put on his shorthair cloak, including his belt and dagger. He pulled the medallion and chain with the crest of the Thillei clan on top of his shirt where it glittered in the light. He put on his pretty boots with the gold buckles. He combed his hair and put it in a ponytail. He had not shaved for several days and debated doing that, but he didn't want to appear too desperate to please.

He left the room.

Striding through the corridor, he met several of the Eagle Knights going the other way into the council room. He said nothing. They said nothing. They assumed that he would come back to attend the meeting.

He rejected the guard's offer of a coach at the door, and walked through the garden. The sky had gone misty again, rendering the city in muted greys—a miserable and wet day that reflected his mood.

No one questioned him at the gate. He could do exactly as he wanted . . . and no one cared enough to ask him if anything was wrong. The only person who really cared about him was the one he'd been told he couldn't have.

He strode into the street. People moved out of his way. Some made greetings. He wished for his former life as butcher's assistant, or even as Eagle Knight, where he could just take off his uniform and become a normal person again and walk through the streets without people noticing, without people gossiping about where you were going and who you were seeing.

He hated the onlookers, the rubberneckers, the gossips.

Those people still had their happy lives. He'd given so much to this city since coming back, and what had it given him in return? He'd been too patient, too gentle, too accommodating.

No more.

He entered the gate to House Mara. The front yard was tidy. A dusting of snow had fallen last night and it softened the stark contrast between the white fence and dark walls.

He climbed the steps to the front door and dropped the heavy knocker on the wood.

He waited, his heart thudding.

And waited.

The curtains over the windows on both sides of the door were closed. They didn't stir from curious people watching behind.

There were no sounds, no voices, no footsteps within the house.

He knocked for the second time and waited again, but that didn't change the lack of response.

That was strange.

He went down the steps, off the path and across the snow-dusted gravel that covered most of the yard. A small door led into the area between the side of the house and the wall that went around the yard. The gate was bolted from the inside, but a crate of the type that was used for firebricks stood against the wall. He dragged it to the gate, put it on its side and heaved himself on top of the gate. Whoa, that was wobbly. His breaking and entering skills had definitely suffered a lack of development while he was in the palace.

He swung both his legs over the gate and jumped onto the gravel with a crunch.

The windows at the back of the house belonged to the formal room, where he had come during his first visit here. Through the window, he could see the table and the couches. The hearth was empty. Another window looked into the dining room where twelve chairs stood around the ornate dining table. The family's pretty tableware was displayed in a cabinet with glass doors against the back wall. Again, the room was tidy, with no sign of inhabitants.

Isandor knocked on the window, but predictably no one came.

He could believe Ledor or Tamerane or the entire family being away. But to take all the staff as well or instruct them not to open doors? That was very, very odd.

Then he remembered the notes he had seen written on an account belonging to Ledor's business in Zaina's office, where Zaina had made a note to do no more work for them unless there was upfront payment. He'd assumed that Ledor was just one of those arrogant men who thought that payment deadlines were for idiots. On the other hand, he'd been happy enough to take Isandor's money for Tamerane. Ledor would not have agreed to the contract if he had no need for money.

So the family was in financial difficulty and Ledor had sacked the staff?

That made no sense either, because if that was true, Ledor would happily negotiate about marriage. They'd signed for more than five thousand Golden Eagles for a child. Taking Tamerane as wife would have to be renegotiated, and would require a higher fee. If Ledor really needed the money, he would not refuse that. He would also not lightly do something—like vanish—that tarnished the family's reputation and gave rise to gossip that something was going on.

In other words: something *was* going on, something that transcended the noble family's wish to keep up their appearance. Maybe Ledor was secretly pleased that the king—powerless as he was—wanted to marry his daughter. Which father would *not* be pleased? He had certainly seemed pleased with the breeding contract.

That brought everything back to that one thing Tamerane had said at the teahouse: something had happened. Nothing trivial, but something that scared Ledor so much that he *had* to leave town, damn gossip and reputation. Something that was a matter of life and death. Tamerane couldn't mention it to him because she didn't want to endanger her family.

Where would they have gone?

What clues did he have?

He could try the staff, maybe, if they had been sacked, and if he could find them. Unfortunately, Isandor remembered none of the servants well enough to know where to start looking.

Or he could investigate Ledor's business, except that he didn't know where it was housed. But he did know someone who used to have some dealings with them.

He went back around the side of the house and left the yard, carefully shutting the gate behind him. He made sure he closed the front gates as well. The housing shortage was such that groups of youths would sometimes force their way into buildings and houses that were clearly empty. They'd steal all the contents and make fires inside. He didn't wish that to happen to anybody's house.

In the street, he debated running to the palace for a coach to the Harbour District, but once he went back, he'd be dragged into the Knight Council meeting. Let Jevaithi deal with it.

So he walked down the hill to the tram stop. He had a few coins in his pocket which he used to buy a ticket. People gave him strange looks. Many bowed, and many others didn't quite know how to behave. Some even seemed hesitant about whether he really was the king or merely someone who looked like the king and dressed up to fool people.

It made him angry with himself. Having grown up sheltered, Jevaithi could be excused for not wanting to go out on the street, but he had no such excuse. He had neglected the people while he'd thought he was helping them.

WHEN ISANDOR REACHED THE WORKSHOP, Jadan and one of the boys were working on a brand new truck, and the were parts spread all over the floor, laid out on oil-stained rags.

Jadan got to her feet as soon as Isandor came into the workshop, surprised to see him there. "I'm sorry about the mess. I would have cleaned up if I knew you were coming."

"I won't be long. I only need to look up one thing. No word from you boss?"

She shook her head. "To be honest, I wouldn't know how she could contact us from out there, wherever she is."

No, but the palace hadn't heard from the expedition either, and that was more worrying. "I'd like to look at your accounts once more."

"I've already shown you everything we have."

"I know, but there is something I need to check."

She showed him back into Zaina's cramped office, where he pulled the account books off the shelves. The account with Zaina's warnings all over it was the only one she had for the company.

Clearly, Ledor had taken his business elsewhere. Isandor took the sheet out and showed it to Jadan.

She frowned at it. "Did Zaina ever do business with *them?*"

"That's what it says. It's a long time ago, though."

"True. It also has lots of warnings. That was a while before I came to work here."

"What does that company do?"

"They have some engines and ships. That's all I can say with certainty. However, I'm pretty sure they don't use that office anymore, because one of our other customers rents the place next to it, and the shop is a bakery now."

"Where did they move?" He could barely comprehend how often people moved in this area.

Jadan spread her hands. "They're not our customers. They've probably moved into the main city."

Isandor remembered there being another mechanic workshop in town. If Zaina didn't service their ships anymore, the other shop probably did.

Isandor found the workshop one block away, behind the large warehouses on the waterfront. This was a much quieter area, where most of the buildings housed businesses rather than shops. The streets had less pedestrian activity, and so more coach and horse traffic. Businesspeople, not merchants and shoppers, walked down the street.

Isandor had to admit that he was thoroughly unfamiliar with this part of his own city. That thought made him uneasy. Once, he had known every street, every alley, back in the time when he had to run from guards, not walk down the street with them.

The other engine workshop was neither as big nor as well run as Zaina's. The owner, a big-bellied Chevakian, was baffled at Isandor's question.

"I'm talking about Ledor of House Mara," Isandor repeated. "He has a business that owns ships."

The man's mouth formed into an "o". He turned around and went to the small, very messy desk in the corner. He rummaged around between paper and engine parts and returned holding a grotty book, with edges blackened by oil-stained fingers.

He opened it at a spot marked by a pencil and ran a black finger over the page.

"Here," he said.

Isandor stared at the columns of disjointed, childish writing. There was a substantial amount of money in the column.

"That's what they owe me, as I keep reminding them, not that it seems to do any good. He pays just enough to keep me happy, and then brings in the next order."

"Who is 'he'? Ledor?"

"Oh, no, that guy who's the manager. The Aranian, whatsisname?"

Isandor waited, but the man scratched the back of his head and didn't come up with a name.

So he asked, "What is your judgement of the business? Do you think they don't pay because they're badly organised or that they don't have the money?"

"Funny you say that. I always thought the first, but lately I've been wondering, because there are other businesses providing much better cargo services to both Chevakia and Arania, and I can't imagine that a cargo line just to Curack makes them any money."

"What's in Curack?" It was a southern Aranian port city.

The man shrugged. "I don't know. Maybe they have friends or relatives there."

"How many ships do they have?"

"Three, as far as I know. They're old clunky things that need a lot of maintenance. Aranian-built, of course."

"Where are they?"

"If any of them are in port, you'll find them on finger wharf four on the northern quay."

"Where is the business's office?"

"Above the wharf. One of those that overlooks the water, flashy as anything of course. Don't know how they pay the rent."

Isandor thanked the Chevakian, who kept saying that he didn't know why he should be thanked. The man behaved casually enough that Isandor suspected he didn't realise who Isandor was.

He went to the harbour and found two of the ships in port. The mechanic was right; they were really clunky. He saw no activity on board or on the quay. The gangplanks were out, but a metal gate barred the way onto the deck. Both ships looked clean and tidy, with no sign of what they carried or any of the crew.

Then he found the company's office on the nearby quay—it was closed, with no way to get in, because the window was on the upper floor on the street side.

It was all very suspicious. A business that did well would at least have their office open on a normal working day like this. They would have accountants and office clerks.

He now wished he'd investigated earlier.

He might send some of his hunter Knights back here, maybe tonight, to see what they could find out. He'd even like to come, even though he wouldn't—his breaking-in skills were rusty, and it wouldn't look good for the queen's brother to be caught breaking in.

But even if he wouldn't be doing this himself, it felt good to be doing *something* again, other than waiting for Jevaithi and attending long and boring Knight Council meetings.

And then, because he came past the *Silver Gull*, he went to have a look at the room that had supposedly been occupied by the man who was said to be the Aranian prince Nayek, who had been killed.

The inn owner definitely had no trouble recognising him. He bowed and kept making suggestions for Isandor to come into the main room and sample the seafood.

A glance into the room in question revealed dark wood tables and chairs on a worn tiled floor. A waft of stale air drifted out.

"No, thanks; just show me the man's room."

The inn owner bowed. "As you wish, Your Majesty. But the guards have done a pretty thorough job of combing the room already."

"I understand. I'm not here to investigate. I leave that to the knowledgeable people."

He accompanied Isandor around the side of the building through an alley where a couple of hookers were coming out for the night, into a little foyer where pairs of shoes were lined up all around the walls and up the stairs.

The room was at the very end of the hallway, in the corner of the building, and looked out over the street and harbour.

Guards had strung a rope across the doorway. As the owner had said, they had combed thoroughly through the room, and had taken all the man's personal items. Isandor had already seen those, but not the room they had come from. Not that there was much to see: just a regular inn room with a bed, a small table, a stand for a washbasin and a jug of water, a desk and a chair. Through the window, Isandor could see the clunky ships belonging to Tamerane's family on the other side of the harbour.

The owner of the establishment still hovered at his back. "I was wondering when we could use the room again, Your Majesty. Are the guards finished with it? I would like to get tenants again. I'm down on customers because this man is dead, and I'm down because this room is empty and I can't hire it out. You'll understand that this is my best room."

"I'll raise the issue with the guards." He was sure the guards had a reason to keep the room like this. "Do you happen to know where this man died? Where is the body?"

"Oh, it's gone to Arania, I imagine."

"He didn't die here, did he?"

"Nah, somewhere out of the city. The mountains, they say. No idea what he was doing there."

"Then how did you know he died?"

"There was a lot of to-do amongst the Aranians downstairs in the main room. I overheard that it was about the prince. I asked them what was going on and whether he was going to come back here and pay his rent, because he was behind. Then the Aranians said he was dead."

That was how the guards had first heard the news, too. But Isandor was unsure how that news had arrived in the city. He was supposed to have been killed in the mountains. The council had sent two patrols into those mountains and so far neither had reported in.

A chill crept over his back.

No, it was more than a chill. It was a golden glimmer that licked over the corner of the bed like a flame, and then crept over the floor to the desk chair that stood in the middle of the room.

It then detached itself from the chair, forming a glowing mist in the shape of a staff with a pointed object on top. It held the shape briefly before dissipating.

These days, an ever dwindling number of people could see icefire, but he recognised the staff that the two men had used to attack him and Rider Barton, the men they had spotted attacking Jadan.

So those men worked for this prince?

And those men had threatened Jadan—who could also see icefire —and asked where Zaina had gone. By the skylights, he had always thought there was more to Zaina's story. Why hadn't he checked it out earlier? But the Knights *had* checked it out.

Not well enough.

His heart thudding, he turned to the inn owner. "Did you see the prince often?"

"I saw him a bit. He's not the kind of person you enjoy a drink with—wasn't, rather."

"Did you ever see him in the company of a woman?"

He snorted. "There is only one thing that Aranians do with women."

"Well, did he?"

His mouth worked. "There was a woman who stayed up here, one of the longterm residents, who was also Aranian. I did see them downstairs together once, and I also saw them going upstairs together."

By the skylights. "Was there anyone else with them?"

"No. She normally eats with two friends. One is an Aranian who stays at the *Sailor's Rest*, the other a northern Chevakian."

"And her room is in here?"

"Used to be, but she paid up and left."

"She didn't leave anything in the room?"

"No, she travelled light and didn't have a lot of stuff anyway."

Well, it appeared there might have been a reason for that.

CHAPTER 6

*B*Y THE TIME Javes had packed everything, saddled up the camel and caught all the goats and tied them in the harness, it was midafternoon.

He studied his maps. A place he knew, a few valleys down, had a pleasant grove of trees surrounding a well that had once belonged to an abandoned farm. He would sometimes have a break there with Pashtan. The farmhouse had almost fallen to dust, but the well was still there, and last time they visited, it had still contained water.

He gave the rope with the goat harness to Tali and led the camel out of the yard.

The neighbours had swept away a lot of the sand and had already started repairs on their house. The father of the family watched as Javes and Tali and their herd of animals walked out the gate and turned into town.

The Dust Devil had cut a path of destruction through town that included the baths and, apparently, from the rumours that went around, the town administrator's house on Snooty Hill. Javes felt sorry that he wasn't going in that direction to see it, but it was not to be helped.

A group of people were cleaning up the market place, where the flimsy stalls had blown into a heap. They stopped work when Javes and Tali walked past, watched, but didn't say anything. Their faces were hard and sad.

They didn't need Javes to tell them why he was leaving. They saw that their town was dying, that the Dust Devils would come back, that if the rains stayed away for another season, the wells would fall dry and that anyone who had not left by that time would die of thirst. They might be afraid of leaving, might never have travelled far from town and might not have family who lived elsewhere. They might want to fight for their town until it was too late, and might see anyone who left as a traitor, and anyone who tricked loyal townsfolk into leaving as even worse.

And it was not as if Javes didn't understand them or feel for them. This ugly little hamlet on the edge of the vast and unfriendly desert had sent its roots into him. He wasn't proud of leaving, but what else could he do?

They plodded past the last houses on the edge of town, first Javes with the camel, then Tali with the goats. She walked slowly and kept falling behind. Javes had to wait several times for her to catch up.

"Come on," he urged. "We don't have that much time before it gets dark. I want to be there in time to set up the tent."

She made an effort to go faster but soon fell behind again.

What was wrong with this girl? She should be running ahead, but she struggled to keep up with the goats. Sometimes, he thought she was walking with a limp.

So he slowed the camel and allowed her to catch up with him.

"Did you hurt yourself?" he asked. "It's all right to tell me."

"No, it's nothing."

And she straightened her face and quickened her pace, but she did walk stiffly and her face was s mask of concentration. She was not going to walk to Tiverius like this.

"But you can't walk properly," he said a bit later. "Let me look at it. What is it? Your knee? Your ankle?"

She shrugged. "There is nothing to see. I fell."

Javes let it rest. But he really wanted to give that dress of hers a wash, because it smelled rank each time the breeze carried the air from her to him.

They finally reached the grove just before sunset.

A copse of ancient olive trees stood in the valley next to the ruins of the old house. The dwelling had been built with mud bricks,

Pashtan had said, but they had dissolved in particularly heavy rain one year, after the farmer had already moved out.

Why had they left, Javes had wanted to know, and Pashtan said there was a long-running family dispute over this piece of good farming land. Well, the argument had outlasted the land's ability to grow crops.

Although sparse weeds grew on the rocky hillsides, the land had not seen a crop for a number of years, and probably could no longer sustain one.

As Javes remembered, the well contained cool, clean water, though probably not enough to sustain an irrigated crop.

He strung up the cover cloth like a tent while he told Tali to haul up some water for the animals.

He untied the ropes on the goats. They all clustered around him, nosing his trousers. Stupid animals.

"Go!" He waved his arms. "You're free! Go and graze."

The goats drank some water and nibbled from the green bushes that grew under the twisted trunks of the olive trees. They followed the camel around while it tore thin branches off the trees and demolished bushes. In one area, the ground was quite soft. Javes dug a hole there. It filled up with muddy water, which the goats then came to drink. They could survive here, because the winter rains would come soon, right?

He looked up at the cloudless sky where the two bands of the sky path were starting to come out in the east. A group of students at the Scriptorium spent nights looking at the stars. What a frivolous activity. Lana han Chevonian was one of them. Clearly had nothing better to do, not even answer his questions.

In his pack, he had some salt meat and bread which he cut into thick slices. He drizzled some fragrant olive oil over it and the ate it with the last piece of goat's cheese that he had declared good enough to bother with.

Tali had at last made herself useful by spreading out the sleeping mats under the cover. It was barely light enough to see anything, but Javes managed to find his mat.

He was tired, and the ground was not as hard as it could have been, but he still took some time to fall asleep.

Tali, too, was tossing and turning on her mat. Sometimes, he thought he could hear her sniff, and then he thought he should ask if she was all right, but that seemed silly because of course she wasn't, with her parents murdered—and she *had* to know that, despite her story about them being taken away on a cart. She had probably never left town and was scared. Maybe she was scared of him because he was a stranger from big bad Tiverius. He definitely was no good at talking to girls, especially not when they were in this awkward, gangly stage where any word you said would either make them giggle and not stop for days, or make them burst out in tears without giving him the faintest clue about what he'd said or done to justify that.

So he listened to her noises, deciding whether or not she was crying or just had a sniffly nose, and decided that she was crying. But he was unsure about how to help her.

Oh, and the camel snored.

And then his thoughts went to his parents and how they would be sitting at the table, hosting opulent dinner parties while trying to cover up their disappointment about the fact that their son had failed to secure the coveted spot at Solmeni and had been sent to this stupid part of the world instead. That made him angry about how vapid and empty life in Tiverius was, and that the things people cared about were utterly unimportant in the scheme of life.

He must have fallen asleep at some point, because all of a sudden, the sky was turning blue. He raised himself on his elbow, finding the mat next to him empty.

Where was Tali?

Heart thudding, he sat up. The goats and camel were peacefully grazing in the meadow around the well. The air was still fresh, and a faint hint of mist hung over the ground. All but the brightest stars were gone, but although the sky was light in the east, there was no sign of the sun yet.

The grass in the oasis and the rocky hillsides was still grey, and apart from the gentle movement of the animals, he saw no sign of life.

"Tali?" he called, almost afraid to shatter the silence.

There was no reply.

"Tali, where are you?"

He crawled out from under the cover. The dew on the grass was cool on his bare feet. Where was she? He spotted a trail of dewy footsteps on the grass, leading towards a bunch of bushes on the edge of the oasis. One of the water containers was also gone.

Tali was behind the bushes. The moment he realised that she had taken off her clothes, he wanted to withdraw, but for a moment he gaped, staring at her perfect, olive skin, the soft rounded mounds of her budding breasts.

She screamed.

"I'm sorry, I'm sorry!" He scrambled back, but tripped over a branch and fell hard on his backside.

Tali was scrambling around for her clothes, gathering a handful of dirty rags stained with blood.

Javes felt sick. "You're hurt. Let me put a clean bandage on you."

Tali retreated further, shielding herself with the bundle of clothes. "Go away! Go. Away!"

"All right, all right!" He climbed to his feet and ran back to the campsite.

What was going on there?

Why was she acting like that? There was nothing shameful in having an injury.

His heart was racing. In mechanical fashion, he started taking down the cloth and rolling up the mats. Tali's mat bore specks of blood.

Whenever a breath of wind came his way, he could hear her sobbing loudly behind the bushes. What was he going to do about this girl? Why couldn't she just tell him what was wrong? Was he supposed to just know?

He carried all the pack to where the camel sat snoozing. The palest edge of sunlight was just clearing the horizon, edging the fur on the camel's back in soft pink. The dew made little diamond drops that glittered in the light.

Javes couldn't resist rubbing the animal's neck.

"You old grumpy pot," he said. The camel opened its eyes and gave him a baleful look. Javes looped both hands around the camel's neck and hugged it. Even if the camel snored and was grumpy, he understood its needs. Food, sleep, water. He'd rather continue his journey with a thousand grumpy camels than one weird, moody girl.

By the time Javes finished packing up the camp, milked the goats and started on breakfast, Tali had emerged from the bushes, fully dressed but with her face red and blotchy from crying. She carried nothing, and he wondered what she had done with the bandages: left them or rebandaged whatever part of her was injured. They'd been pretty filthy, and he shuddered to think at the disease and filth that they would harbour.

Tali didn't want to look at him. She took the "porridge" made from stale bread soaked in fresh goat's milk without a word and carried the bowl a short distance away. She sat on the grass and shovelled the bread into her mouth with her hands and then drank the rest by the time he had finished less than half of his.

"Wow. Do you want more?"

She held out the bowl, and he gave her a bit more. Not too much, because they wouldn't reach the next town for some days. On one hand, he was glad that she was eating again. That was at least a step in the right direction.

He didn't know what to say, and hid his awkwardness behind activity, by packing everything onto the camel. He was about to make the beast get up, when he noticed Tali looking at him.

"Are you all right? Do you want to ride?"

She shook her head. "No. I'll be fine."

It was with some reluctance that Javes led the camel out of the oasis. Survival there would have been easy. He'd already spotted some wild potato and corn plants that he could have dug up to grow. The well might not be able to support a big farm, but it would support a plot that was just for survival. He didn't know much about the terrain in between here and the next town, which was a small hamlet where he wasn't even sure visitors would be welcome.

He'd filled the water bags as much as he could, and hoped they would not need that much water, but resolved to be careful with it regardless.

The goats, those stupid things, insisted on following them along the road, no matter how much he shooed them away.

Once they were out of sight of the little grove, the landscape turned dusty and bleak. It didn't look like any Dust Devils had come through; but Javes kept his eye on the horizon and on the pocket barymeter, which he had tied to the camel's saddle, just in case.

The day got hot, and then hotter.

Tali made no more complaints, and her limp appeared to have

become much better, but she followed a little behind, talking to the goats more than to him. He was happy that he didn't have to worry about her being unable to walk anymore, even if the mystery of the bloodied bandage remained unsolved. Even when the wind picked up and blew her loose dress up her legs, he didn't see any injuries. All he could think of was seeing her perfect brown skin and her softly rounded breasts, with drops of moisture running off them from where she had poured water to wash herself.

When he thought these things, his ears became hot, and something inside him stirred that he wasn't sure was appropriate, but it was pleasant.

"How old are you?" he asked her when they sat under a very sorry-looking olive tree for a bite of food.

It was midday and the measly tree barely cast enough shadow for them to sit in.

"Thirteen."

And then he didn't know what else to ask. At thirteen, she was a child. At the same age, he had just graduated from playing with building blocks to going to serious school. And she had already seen more death and destruction than most people would see in their lifetimes.

"How old are you?" she asked, returning the question, as if it were a game. A gust of wind blew her black hair into her face and she raked it behind her ear.

"Twenty."

That was the answer right there. Thirteen. Twenty. He should be ashamed of himself staring at the bit of her inner thigh that showed through a gap under her dress.

"What is it like, living in Tiverius?"

"People live in very big houses. There are wide streets with paving and lines of really big trees along them." He stared in the distance, seeing the streets of his home town before his eyes.

"Do you want to go back there?"

He looked her in the eye. Did he want to go back? He did, didn't he? Back to his parents' vapid existence, back to being a nobody at the Scriptorium, back to girls in his class making fun of him.

"Well, do you?"

"I have to go back to finish my studies."

"Why do you need to study to replace barygraph paper? I could do it."

Good question. He bet she could, too. In a town like Ysherra where no one had any formal education, the things that you could learn from study would be impossible to explain.

He rose. "Let's keep going."

They did. He asked her if she wanted to ride for a bit, but she said no, she wasn't tired. He found that hard to believe. *He* was tired. When they got to the next town, he should see about selling some of his treasures in return for a cart and donkey, or better, a second camel. Then they could divide the load and they could both ride.

For most of the rest of the afternoon, they walked through undulating terrain. Javes had come this way once with Pashtan for the weather stations, but the landscape was so monotonous that he had no idea where they had turned around.

Those weather stations still stood there, and the telegraph poles that linked some of them appeared to be intact, but the signal was dead. This was the main line to Tiverius. Javes knew it was out at Ysherra, the telegraph station having been burned down, but this meant that there was trouble further south as well.

He didn't like that one single bit.

At the end of the afternoon, when the hazy light turned orange, they came to a small cluster of houses. Javes remembered this place, too, and was disappointed that they had made so little progress. Pashtan had told him that three brothers and their families lived here, but they disliked strangers, so he never visited them. It was a bit unfortunate that he and Tali now had little option but to stay overnight on the land of this family. Javes made an effort to go past the back of the fields, out of view of the houses, but the little track that he hoped led around the field stopped, and the field of discarded sharp stones looked most unappetising, particularly in view of the camel's soft feet. They had to turn back.

While doing so, he noticed that one of the roofs of the houses had fallen in. The sun was going down frightfully fast, and they needed to find a place to camp. If no one lived at the farm, there might be a shed where they could sleep, and water or other things they could use. Javes wasn't happy with the amount of food they had. Oh, it was enough for a few days; but he liked to have more, because if abandoned places were going to be the norm, what were the chances of getting food in the next town?

"Come," he said to Tali, and led the camel down the drive that led to the courtyard between the houses.

Tali remained where she was. Fine, if she was going to be like that she could mind the goats, which had gone to graze in the stubble fields.

The first farmhouse with the damaged roof was burned out. The other two houses had also sustained fire damage. There was no sign of life but, unlike Arukat's house, the doors were shut and most of the windows intact.

He tied the camel to a conveniently placed tree and went into the farm shed, where he found a cart; but the wheels had been smashed. There were pens for various animals, but the gates were all open. The walls had similar Aranian scrawls as the ones in Ysherra.

He kept looking over his shoulder, hearing little sounds that might be real or imagined.

He called out, "Hello, anyone here?"

There was no reply. He looked around the courtyard, at the dark windows, the broken farm equipment, the scrawls on the walls.

What was the point of all of this if no one could read it?

Should he go inside the house?

But he was afraid of what he might find there. Also, the camel was getting fidgety and he should probably check out why. That animal had a better sense of danger than most humans.

He went to untie that camel and—whoa!

The needle on the pocket barymeter that hung from the saddle was going nuts.

Dust Devil!

On second thought . . . all the times he had encountered Dust Devils, they had come with a lot of wind and dusty air, and the evening was still and clear. He untied the barymeter from the saddle and walked around the yard, checking it everywhere. It jumped from eight motes per cube to thirty and back again when he came close to the buildings. One charred, burned spot even went up as high as fifty. He stepped away and it dropped and came closer and it went up again.

Was it even possible to measure sonorics that accurately?

If so, what was it supposed to mean?

Probably that it was a bad idea to go into any of the houses. The danger about sonorics was that at low-level exposure, damage was not evident, and took years to manifest.

He remembered reading all the reports from twenty years ago of the people who had died in Fairlight, with peeling skin and bleeding from their mouths. He remembered the people who had come into contact with the first refugees from the City of Glass, many of whom had died in years following the disaster of diseases that left them with weeping abscesses on their skin, especially in their faces.

He shuddered.

He kept having the feeling that someone was watching him.

He untied the camel and quickly left the courtyard, past the burned buildings and the sheds.

Tali was sitting on the ground in the middle of the road, her knees drawn up to her chest, rocking backwards and forwards.

He told her, "I didn't see anything that we could use. The stuff is all burned."

She looked up at him with a vacant, distant expression in her eyes.

"Are you all right?"

"Yeah."

"Come."

She didn't react. Was she even hearing what he said?

"Come on, Tali, let's get out of here." He reached for her arm.

She screamed and scrambled away, as if he'd been going to hit her.

"Whoa! Calm down."

"There is evil in those houses! Can't you see, it's written on the walls!"

"Yes, yes, I can see that the Aranians have been here. We're going now. Stop screaming. I'm not going to do anything to you. Calm down."

She looked at him while standing in a crouch, her legs bent, ready to spring. Her face was like that of a wild animal considering whether to bite or run. Her arms and legs were like sticks, her feet dirty in her sandals, her nails rimmed with black. She had not combed her hair since he had come back from the windwalkers and found her in the house, and a huge tangly knot had formed at the back of her head.

Wherever they were going to find people who could offer them help, they would not get it because she looked like a vagrant kid, the type that would typically steal. She would need to be cleaner, with nicer clothes for farmers or villagers to put any kind of trust in the two of them.

Or they would have to turn into scavengers and thieves, and he could never live with that.

He led the way back to the main road and continued toward the south-west. The sun hung low over the horizon. They soon needed to find a place to camp, preferably with some water, but the prospect of finding it did not look good.

CHAPTER 7

THE TRAIN CONTINUED its journey soon after the appearance of the skylights had caused such a distraction. Railway employees walked past the carriages shouting for everyone to get back on board. Lana followed Viki back to their cabins. While the train clanked back into motion, they could still see the shimmering green light in the sky.

"Have you ever seen that before?" she asked him before going back into her cabin.

"I haven't. I've heard people talking about it, but no one said it was this bad."

A couple of soldiers tromped past. It struck Lana that no one had mentioned sonorics suits yet. "What does it mean?"

"That's a very good question. I've had correspondence with Brother Veshi in the City of Glass. They seem to think that the machine that produced sonorics might not have been the only one. It looks like they might have been right. That direction is west. We're not terribly far from the Aranian border. It looks like the machine might be on Aranian soil."

"Does that mean that Aranians are also resistant to sonorics? Shouldn't we be wearing the suits?" A feeling of unrest crept over her.

"The skylights indicate sonorics at high altitude. We don't need to worry yet. But I will take measurements when it's light."

Lana went back into her cabin, but she couldn't sleep. From her bed, she could see the glow in the sky. There were no more trees interrupting her view.

She thought of hearing people talk about the time of the sonorics explosions. When she was little, they occasionally tested the alarms. She could still hear the sound. She remembered the strange little rhyme children used to sing. It went:

Once rings the bell and we stay inside,
Twice rings the bell and school is out,
Thrice rings the bell and we find the shelter,
But when it rings all the time, we run.

Or something like that. It was supposed to train children to know what to do when sonorics danger loomed.

How could anyone sleep while this was going on? They were all going to die.

Dawn revealed endless dreary fields of stubble stretching over rolling hills. Sometimes there would be a dirt road, no more than two cart tracks in between the fields, and sometimes a blocky house made of rough stone. There might be a pen with goats or a donkey. There might be a shed with a cart. But there were no trees and there was nothing else green in the landscape. It was too early for people to have come out, and the only movement she spotted was that of animals, mostly birds.

The sun had just risen when she noticed more evidence of human habitation. Farms and roads grew closer together and the roads were wider. Once she even saw a cart, drawn by two pitiful donkeys.

"Lana." That was Viki, knocking on the door of the cabin.

She opened the door.

He was already dressed in his loosely fitting travel clothes. "We're about to arrive in Watya."

"Do we get breakfast on the train?" She was hungry.

"No time. We'll get something in town. Come on, pack your things."

Lana got changed. The air felt warm, so she put on a thin dress, but she put on an undershirt because she didn't like the look of those clouds on the horizon. But this was the desert and it hardly ever rained, right? They were going to go on a bus. She bet it would be hot. From her experience with buses in Tiverius, it was hot inside even if it was not outside. Even worse, it might be a primitive bus without windows.

Those clouds really did look very black and ominous, desert or no. That looked like a major rain front on the horizon. She didn't remember hearing about rain in this region, and it hung over the western horizon, meaning that it was still coming.

But this was supposed to be a desert. Did they get a lot of rain out of those fronts?

If it rained and she got wet, the thin dress would be too cold.

She truly didn't know what to wear.

She decided to keep the undershirt on. Her nightshirt, slippers and thick dress all went into the overnight bag. But her autumn clothes for Tiverius took up more space than her thin dress and now the bag was too full and the book wouldn't fit. Well, dang it. She'd have to hold it. Maybe she could put her slippers and thick dress into her suitcase when it came out of the train. Slippers were really a very impractical thing when you were travelling anyway. They'd gotten all dusty from last night's small trip outside the carriage, too.

She felt all flustered, disorganised and stupid. She stuffed everything in her bag and dragged it into the corridor, holding her book.

Viki was already waiting. "Got everything?"

His overnight bag was quite small and much more practical. He didn't have to carry a book, either.

The windows on that side of the train showed blocky houses strewn over a gentle hillside. The houses were mostly white, probably made from mud bricks and stuccoed with white clay. Only a few trees poked out from the jumble of houses and yards and walls. The smoke rose into the hazy air. At one place she could see into a yard where a dark-skinned man was throwing rubbish on a fire. A couple of white goats pulled at a stack of hay in the yard.

Wow. She could understand why people from this region acted bewildered when they came to Tiverius. It was so different here, so dry, so . . . colourless.

The train slowed down and rattled across a very long iron bridge. In the middle of the broad sand plain was a riverbed with a tiny trickle of water.

"Did they really need to make a bridge that big for this tiny creek?"

Viki shook his head. "Where were you in geography? This is the Aramys River, the biggest river system in the whole continent. When it flows, this entire basin is a churning brown mass of water."

"This whole area?"

"That, and sometimes more."

Lana stared at the sandy terrain, sculpted with sand dunes and little dips where—she noticed now—there were lines from where water had flowed. She had heard of the Aramys River before, of course. There were songs about it. But . . . that little trickle of water? "That must take a lot of rain."

"All the rain that falls on the northern plateau makes its way to the ocean past this point. This is why Watya is situated here, and not further to the east, since we're actually quite close to Arania here."

Lana remembered her geography. The Aramys River system started with hundreds of little creeks on the plateau, which fed into bigger creeks that eventually formed a large river. It flowed westwards and then did a big loop at Watya, switched back on itself and flowed to the eastern coast. She should have remembered that.

She imagined this whole area covered in water and could not.

The train had slowed considerably. It came off the bridge and entered the town, which looked ancient, dusty. Few buildings were higher than two floors. A tower protruded from the mass of roofs, an ancient-looking thing made from light-coloured stone. The top was an intricate structure of stone carved into latticework. A walkway circled the tower underneath. The centre of the structure consisted of a stone cylinder that stood on a pedestal with four thick, squat supporting legs. A narrow stone bridge led from the cylinder through the town.

"What is that thing?" she asked.

"Watya is famous for its water towers. There are quite a lot of them."

Yes, she could see that now and she remembered her father having said something about it. Where was her brain?

The train slowed further and came into the station in a big cloud of steam.

A station attendant walked past the carriages and opened all the doors, shouting, "Watya!" into each carriage, as if anyone would have missed it.

The group of soldiers were all lined up in the corridor. The commander Ramatius was yelling at his troops to keep out of the way of civilians and not disembark—there was that word again—until everyone else was off the train.

Lana followed Viki to the door. The last soldier in the line was Yaishan. He looked very dapper in his uniform with his pack at his feet.

"Welcome home," she said to him.

He touched his beret. "Thank you, m'lady."

Oh, soldiers were funny.

Viki helped her off the train onto the crowded platform. There were people unloading luggage, people meeting travellers and a lot of people with packs, sitting around. Maybe they were waiting for the train to leave again? Many of these people were families with dirty children wearing dirty clothes.

"Come, the luggage collection is this way." Viki set off towards the end of the platform, where people waited for others to slowly carry their bags, children and sometimes animals, down a set of stairs.

"It's so *busy* here," Lana said. She hadn't expected that.

"Yes, it surprises me a bit, too. It wasn't this busy last time I came here. Admittedly, that was some time ago."

They made their way down the stairs one slow step at a time. All around, people spoke in the dialect that Lana had only heard from one or two people in Tiverius, when they, as it turned out, did their best to make themselves understandable.

Here, they might as well be speaking another language.

They came out in a hall where—surprise—there were more queues at the counter for collecting luggage. It was stuffy here, and before long Lana thoroughly regretted having put on that undershirt. By the time Viki had managed to retrieve their suitcases, said shirt was soaked with sweat.

Viki led her to yet another counter, where he gave a man some money and received a couple of chips in return. Lana had no idea what they were for. Viki gave the man his suitcase and told Lana to put hers next to his on the trolley. So much for trying to offload some of the surplus things from her overnight bag.

She had the feeling that everyone was looking at her, from the other passengers to the children to the man with the little table next to the hall's exit to the street. He was selling something in halves of orange skin.

Viki stopped at his stall on the way out and bought two of the half oranges. He gave one to her. The fruit had been hollowed out, the flesh cut into pieces which were put back inside mixed with a white substance and sprinkled with a dusting of red powder. A tiny wooden pick stuck out of one of the orange pieces.

"Breakfast," Viki said.

They walked out of the station hall. Walking was awkward while carrying the orange and the book and her overnight bag which bumped into her side and threatened to slide off her shoulder.

Viki stopped. "Oh, drat. I'd hoped to sit down on that bench."

The bench in question, in the middle of a patch of dirt surrounded by date palms, was surrounded people. Not just people, tents. There were people sitting in front of the tents, cooking even, and hanging out washing.

A couple of little children came forward. "Please, you have any to spare?"

Any what? Lana wondered.

"Beggars in Watya?" Viki sounded appalled. "What are all these people doing here?"

Lana had no idea.

The bench was out of the question, and they eventually found a wall surrounding a yard. Lana was grateful to be able to put down her overnight bag. He shoulder was aching from carrying both the bag and the book. She was hot, too.

The orange was sweet. She was less certain about the white substance, which was probably goat's cheese. The red powder was chilli. The ensemble tasted . . . odd.

"Is this what people normally have for breakfast?"

"No. They have porridge or bread. I just wanted to make sure we made the bus."

"That's what the chips are for?"

"They are. The bus leaves on this side of the station. Usually, it's a return service, and usually, the bus arrives before the train does. But it has been a long time since I was last here, so it might have changed."

"There were a lot of people on the platform."

"I have no idea what all those people are doing here, or the ones in the tents."

"My father said something about people fleeing the drought and that they couldn't afford the train south."

Viki nodded, staring at the ensemble of tents. "Ah. There is the bus."

A dusty, ochre-yellow vehicle entered the square. It didn't slow down much, and pedestrians and animals alike scurried out of its way. It turned in a circle around the tent camp, and stopped in front of the station entrance. Many people in the camp had gotten up and were making their way to where the bus had stopped.

Were they all passengers, too? Lana felt ill. It was so hot and muggy here, and with all those people in the bus, it would be terrible. They would be *smelly*, too.

The bus was full of arriving passengers. Many had already stepped out, but she could see the silhouettes of more people waiting to get off. A station attendant had climbed up the little ladder on the side of the bus and started handing—or throwing—down packs. Anything that was soft, and the mailbags, he threw off the back, where the item landed in a cloud of dust, and the personal suitcases he handed to a helper. One parcel was a cane cage with two puppies, yelping and carrying on while they were being handled.

There were so many *people* on that bus.

But eventually, the stream dried up. Some people went into the station, some met with acquaintances camped on the patch of dirt in front of the station. Some even started setting up tents themselves. The crowd dissipated, and the bus was just left by itself. The driver retrieved a broom and started sweeping the inside of his vehicle.

"All right, our turn," Viki said. He shouldered his bag.

Lana was still holding her orange skin. "What do I do with this?" Viki no longer had his.

"Give it." Viki held out his hand.

She gave it to him and he tossed it over the wall. A couple of brown pigs ran out from the shelter in the corner and jostled each other over the morsel.

All r-i-i-ight. Was that what people did here? Throw their rubbish out for the pigs? They were funny pigs, too, with reddish brown hair and sagging bellies.

The driver was still sweeping.

"That's strange. I thought the man said that the bus would be leaving soon. Where is everyone else?"

Lana couldn't see any people waiting.

Viki called into the bus, "Oy!"

"Oh, sorry sir . . . *Senator*. It's an honour to have you in this dusty town." He wiped his forehead and sweat and dust made mud, which he smeared over his face. "What can I do for you?"

"Are you the service to Ysherra?"

The man gave Viki a startled look. Then he looked at Lana and back to Viki. "You got a ticket *to* Ysherra?"

"I believe we did. I have a student there and I want to do some study."

"Senator, please, there must be some mistake. No one travels *to* Ysherra. See all those people there? They've just come *from* Ysherra. They're leaving, fleeing drought and dust devils—"

"I've got equipment to study dust devils."

Again, that incredulous look, as if in his wildest dreams he couldn't imagine that anyone studied dust devils. "There are pirates, too. The place is unsafe, especially for a pretty young lady."

Dusty and sweaty as she was, Lana felt anything but pretty.

"So, you're not going to Ysherra, then?"

"I am, picking up more people."

"Then we're coming."

The driver gave a *suit yourself* kind of shrug and took Viki and Lana's suitcases. "We're leaving soon. We stop overnight at Tamyra, which is a bit rough because rogues came through recently, but I have a friend there with a barn where we can sleep safely. Ysherra will be the next day."

Lana didn't like the sound of a barn, and she was starting to wonder if this trip was such a good idea after all. She had assumed that Viki would be staying in stately guesthouses. But of course weather stations and such were often in out-of-the-way places. Her father had known that.

She sat on the bench behind the driver while Viki spread out across the aisle from her. He had taken his book and was reading, absolutely calm. Things must be all right, then.

The driver was dusting the inside of his steering panel with all his pressure gauges for the boiler and water levels. Another truck had come from a side street, bringing water. Fuel was loaded onto the roof and consisted of bricks of pressed stubble and dung.

"You haven't by any chance taken a young man from Tiverius called Javes, have you?" Lana asked the driver.

He chuckled. "I take so many people. Do you expect me to know them all?"

"He would look different."

"When people are dusty and tired, they all look the same."

She guessed that was true.

Viki glanced at her. "Javes would not have left his post. It is the meteorologist's task to stay and continue to send data. The doga pays a stipend, anyway."

Yes, but what if there was nothing left to buy?

They waited.

The driver cleaned. Some of the people in the camp gave the two of them funny looks. Viki ignored them and continued to read. Lana didn't understand how he could. She had an unsettled feeling about this trip. Part of her wanted to join the queue to go back home. It was only an overnight trip. Soon, they would be much further away from civilisation.

But if she came back, everyone would laugh and consider her a coward.

So she said nothing.

No one else came, and after the driver had loaded a couple of boxes with carrots, bundles of long beans and other food and a cage with, of all things, three pigeons, he looked around. "Ready to go?"

He clunked the vehicle into gear and, slowly, they moved away from the station.

Lana looked out the window as the buildings of Watya slid by. There were indeed a lot of water towers and those narrow bridges were aqueducts that delivered water to the houses. How clever. The water was carried up to the reservoirs—the round towers—by windmills. The water came from the river, but at this time of year, when the river was low and the water foul, the town would run it through beds of sand to clean it.

"What happens if the water runs out?" she asked.

"The Aramys River never runs completely dry. If you know your geology, you can stand on a hill in the desert and you can tell by the land where you need to dig to find water."

"At any rate, it doesn't look like the river will be low for much longer."

"Yeah," Viki said, looking through the side window. "Out of all the potential problems we've run across today, I have to admit I like that one the least."

"Wouldn't it be good if it rained? Everyone is complaining about drought. People can go back to Ysherra."

"It's not quite that simple. Desert rains bring floods before they bring prosperity."

"We'll be in Tamyra before it hits," the driver said.

Except he was wrong.

It was about midafternoon, and Lana was getting numb from being jolted around on the rough road, when the first fat drops hit the front window. A gust of wind whipped up dust which stuck to the drops, making a mess of the front window. It was so hard to see that the driver had to get out and clean the window, and while he was using a wiper on a stick, the heavens opened.

The rain *hammered* on the roof of the bus.

It leaked, of course, and soon the water ran down the inside of the windows. Lana sought out a dry spot, but water formed puddles at her feet that ran across the floor each time the bus turned.

Viki seemed tense. Once, he went up to the driver and spoke to him, but Lana couldn't hear any of what was said, because the rain was making too much noise.

The driver argued, waving his hands and gesturing at the road. He looked frustrated.

They came down a hill and—whoa! The deepest point of the road through the valley was under water. It was not very deep, and the bus crept through the creek. But on the next valley, they had the same problem. The bus had to slow down. The water was deeper here, and there was more of it.

Up the next hill and down into the next valley. This one was still dry, but the valley after that had another creek running through it.

The bus plunged into the water and continued across, then started climbing up the other side, and stopped. The engine was going and the wheels were spinning, but the bus wasn't going forward.

The driver swore, opened the door and jumped out. Rain lashed against the side of the bus.

Viki's expression was dark. "I told him to go back. He said we'd be all right."

There was a sound of the luggage compartment opening and something being taken out.

"I better go and help him." Viki also went outside.

Lana stared at the drops running down the outside of the window. The sky was leaden grey without any visible clouds. In Tiverius, that would mean lots of rain.

There was a sound of a shovel squelching in mud, and then someone hammered. The driver came back in, put the engine into gear and—crunch! The bus listed. The back wheels span. Viki, still outside, yelled and ran through the water, waving for the driver to stop.

He swore and went back outside.

Lana got up from her seat and stuck her head out the door. "Anything I can do to help?"

"Help us get this under the wheels." Viki tossed her a piece of netting, wiping rain out of his face.

Going out there in the pouring rain with a dress was going to be impractical, but her trousers were in her suitcase. She took her shoes off and stepped gingerly into the mud.

Her feet sank in past her ankle. Eeeew. It was so soft, and when she pulled her foot out, it made a sucking sound. Then she put down her other foot and almost slipped.

"Here, grab this." Viki tossed her a rope. He tossed the other end underneath the bus to the other side.

He struggled around the side of the truck. At the back he had to walk through the water, which flowed quite fast. Lana felt silly standing there, not knowing what to do with this rope.

"Pull it up!" Viki yelled from the other side of the bus. Lana pulled. She almost slipped but managed to keep herself upright. The rope went taut. A course knotted net rose out of the mud, attached to the rope. She and Viki dragged it as close under the back wheels as possible.

Viki got to his knees, crawled under the bus and jammed pieces of wood under the net.

Rain was coming down in sheets. Lana noticed that she'd dragged the hem of her dress in the muddy water.

The driver had crawled underneath the bus with Viki, and was jamming planks under the wheels with the hammer.

That done, he went back inside and started the engine. The wheels slowly rolled up the planks, very slowly, a bit further and a little bit further.

Viki raised his thumbs. Water was dripping out of his hair into his eyes.

The engine hissed and steamed. The driver gave it a bit more, and little bit more. Soon, they would be free of the mud—

And then—CRACK! One of the pieces of wood broke. The right back wheel slipped. The bus listed. The wheels spun, throwing up a spray of mud. Viki managed to jump out of the way, but not before he got sprayed.

The truck sank into the mud almost to the axle.

The driver came out, swearing.

They tried to dig the wheels out but that only made the bus sink even further. There was no point. Everything was wet. It was cold.

They gathered for a measly meal inside the damp cabin.

"There is nothing we can do except wait," the driver said.

Viki asked, "How long before the road is passable?"

"Could be days. Maybe we can dig ourselves out when it stops raining."

"At least we won't die of thirst."

"Nope."

"Well I guess we won't see many dust devils, either," Viki remarked.

"Nope."

They sat in silence. Lana poured a bit of water over her hands and washed her face. Ugh, there was mud everywhere. Her dress was covered on it. She could taste it on her lips. No doubt she was a real sight.

The driver sat up. "What's that?"

He looked out the window where the view was blurred through condensation and raindrops running down the outside of the window. The muddy fields vanished in the mist.

Beyond the quickly rising creek and the hills, Lana couldn't see much.

But wait—a group of people plodded over the hill. They led horses by the reins and wore long coats against the rain. There were about fifteen of them, all men, and they were broad and tall.

The driver cursed. "Where did they come from? The road is cut south of here. If they want ill, we're stuck."

There was nowhere to go, no bushes, no old farmhouse to hide in.

Viki said, "Surely they're just fellow travellers. They may give us a hand getting the bus out of the mud."

"Don't know about that. Anyone with a horse is likely to be a foreigner."

"Do you mean Aranian?"

The driver didn't reply, but continued to look at the group.

Viki said, "Get between the seats, Lana."

The urgency in his voice made Lana's heart jump. She did as he said, although the floor was wet and there was nowhere to sit.

Viki and the driver stayed outside.

Slowly, the sound of footsteps came closer. An accented man's voice said something.

Viki replied, "We are going that way."

A rough voice replied. Lana didn't catch what he said.

The Viki said again, "No, there isn't."

And the driver said, "This is my bus."

Someone laughed and this was followed by a shout and a big splash in the mud. Viki yelled something, but she couldn't make out the words. There were some further thuds and slaps. Another splash. The bus rocked. A man came in. He was huge. In the hood of his coat, he had a dark face and pale grey eyes. He grinned with a mouth full of crooked teeth.

An Aranian soldier.

CHAPTER 8

*T*HE MOTHERS' HOUSE was in one of the most pleasant corners of the citadel, the jumble of palaces and temples in the centre of Kadrish. Perched on the edge of the original hill that housed the citadel, it rose significantly over the roofs of the surrounding part of the city. As a result, many of the cool, high-ceilinged rooms in the three-storey building looked out over the sea, catching cooling sea breezes that came in from the west.

As a man, Kotori could enter the Mother's House because he lived in the citadel, and also because of his profession: to tell the fortunes of the king and the princes and of the women carrying the royal children, especially those about to give birth. Today, he had been called to attend Selwa, one of the most revered mothers, from the harem of the king himself.

Already, there was a lot of activity inside the audience room through a door on his left on the ground floor of the building. The flower vases had been put on the stage, a couple of men were setting out rows of chairs, and the musicians were putting the last touches on their drum routine. The light was dim in the room, the curtains drawn and two pedestals contained fire bowls, to give a dim light. To see too much would be distasteful, but this way they could be there and encourage Selwa's birth in spirit.

The woman in question, Kotori had been assured by the doorman, was still upstairs. Kotori continued down the hallway. The smell of cooking for the after-birth gathering wafted through this part of the building. The gathering would be held in the garden room. A wheelchair stood to the side so that Selwa would not need to miss any of that party.

Kotori walked past all that, clutching his astrologer's case and holding his back straight. It was an extremely significant honour to be asked to tell the fortunes of a birthing mother, especially one as highly ranked as Selwa. Kotori had provided the service for years and had lost track of the number of birth ceremonies he had attended, in private for first-time mothers or when an earlier casting had predicted trouble, or, like this one, in public.

The first guests were already arriving, bringing cake and presents, or some ill-disguised bottles of homemade fruit wine recognisable by their shape. It was not considered virtuous for mothers to drink wine, but many did so anyway.

A group of mothers came down the stairs, greeting Kotori as he was ready to go up. One of them was Rissa, whose birth fortunes he had predicted not half a year ago, and who was already showing signs of being with child again. Prince Denori did not let his women lie idle for long.

They bowed and continued to the audience room. By their dresses, all soft pink, Kotori guessed that the women were part of the choir, which sang gentle sweeping songs and provided the birthing mother's voice when she needed to scream but was better off concentrating on the monumental task of bringing a child into the world.

Kotori came out into the upstairs corridor.

The building had many luxuriously appointed lounge rooms with couches and cushions and gauze-like curtains, cute little trees and flowers, soft carpets, gently spoken attendants and incense. The whole building reeked of it.

Kotori suppressed a shiver over his dislike of incense. It reminded him of his youth, spent in the children's house next door, where high-born princes terrorised minor princes; where to complain about bruises—or worse—was akin to treachery; where minor transgressions resulted in whippings meted out by the most senior princes; and where he'd go to sleep in fear of his life every night with the smell of incense wafting in from next-door.

From the sophistication of the top floor of the Mother's House, that cruelty was hard to imagine. The children's voices sounded so *nice* when they drifted on the wind. Children were always playing, weren't they?

Kotori found Selwa in one of the quiet rooms. She reclined on a couch in the company of two younger women who sat on either side of her, fanning cool air over her with intricate paper fans.

Like most older Mothers, Selwa carried a lot of extra weight. Her hips were broad, her thighs soft and fleshy.

She wore only a singlet, and a loincloth that covered a small strip immediately between her legs. The skin to either side bore signs of having hair removed: little nicks from a shaving blade or regrown hairs from a past waxing treatment. Her tiny singlet was just long enough to cover her breasts. In between loincloth and singlet, her belly was round to bursting, the skin tight and criss-crossed with bright red stretch marks.

Selwa was getting to the age where soon she would no longer be able to conceive. She'd had more children than anyone and was highly experienced. She wore her hair in a bun on top of her head, flecked through with grey. Her skin was no longer perfect but freckled with age spots and, today, shining with sweat.

Her eyes were clear and bright with the glorious pain, that feeling of coming closer to the Mother herself that, as a man, he would forever lack.

"There you are," she said. She attempted to push herself up, and the two other women jumped to assist her.

Kotori bowed. "I'm sorry my lady. I came as soon as you called."

"I don't know why I bothered."

"Lady?" Kotori did a double take, but at the same time, he knew what this was about.

"Don't feign ignorance. Maybe I still let you come because the king put in a good word for you. But you did not even predict the death of my favourite son. I very much doubt that you could predict what you'll have for dinner tonight."

Kotori winced. The scolding was deserved. Prince Nayek's body had been brought in yesterday and it now lay, awaiting burial, in the cellar. And no, he had indeed not predicted anything of the sort, because he had not seen the signs in the stars. He didn't need to be reminded of his misstep. In the last few days, he'd thought of little else.

"I can only apologise profusely. Rest assured that I will study the reason for my failure and I will remedy it."

She snorted and winced, putting her hand on her swollen belly. "I'll leave that discussion for later. My fortune, please, before this child falls at my feet."

"Certainly, my lady."

He sat down on his knees at the low table at the foot of the couch. He set his case on the floor before him. He took out the embroidered star map and his casting stones. He moved the case aside and spread the map out on the floor.

"Hurry up please. I still need to go downstairs." Selwa leaned back again. She closed her eyes and took deep, calming breaths. One of the women spoke to her in a soft voice. From his position, Kotori could see up her backside where the blue loincloth covered the bit between her soft buttocks. Sometimes, it unnerved him how Mothers had so little shame. Some of the younger ones used no modesty sheet to shield the audience, and they would scream as loudly as they could, just to make everyone squirm.

Kotori's hands were sweaty. He didn't like being told to do things in a hurry. Telling fortunes was serious business. You could not do it in haste, because you might make mistakes. Like missing a vital sign that would predict someone's death.

Prince Nayek was her son, and she derived a lot of status from being his Mother.

He'd forgotten to take the coins out of his case, so needed to open it again and rummage inside for those three fortune coins. He'd forgotten the cup, too, so needed to open the case a third time and retrieve it.

He *had* to get this right.

One of the younger women brought him a lock of Selwa's hair which she had cut with ceremonial gold scissors.

"Hurry up, clumsy fool." Selwa let out a beastly growl, followed by heavy breaths.

Kotori put the coins and casting stones in the cup, held his right hand over the top and shook. He turned the cup over. The stones tumbled over the cloth and came to rest. But one of the coins fell onto its side and rolled off the fabric. Dang it. That was embarrassing.

He put the stones and coins back in the cup again.

"Mother's breath, what are you doing? I told you there is not much time. Do you want me to miss my own birth ceremony? I *am* going to drop this child in your lap, if you keep going like this."

"Just . . . hang on."

He shook the cup again and recast the stones. The three gems and three coins all landed on the star cloth this time. The six elements represented the five Wanderers and the moon. Two of the stones had landed in the Scissors.

Two? One was considered bad luck. Two . . . He couldn't predict bad luck to a Mother on the verge of giving birth. She'd kill him. He'd be the laughing stock of the citadel.

It had to be his nerves. He'd thrown wrong. Too timidly, in fear of making another embarrassing mistake.

Selwa cried out. The two women wiped her face and her belly.

Kotori looked over his shoulder and pushed the stones to the much more favourable Wagon constellation where they would have landed had he thrown properly. There. That was better.

Kotori cleared his throat. "The fortunes speak."

Selwa clamped her mouth, breathing heavily through her nose. Sweat was pearling on her forehead. Her chest heaved.

Kotori didn't need reminding that he had to hurry up. No time for any of the flourishes or poems that would normally go with a reading.

"The sign of the Wagon is an important feature in this reading. The stones of the Small Man and the Great Wanderer are in the sign of the Wagon. This is a great indicator for prosperity. The coin for the moon is in the Lion, indicating swiftness and speed."

"I'll give you speed all right," Selwa panted. "Are you done?"

She was being quite rude, but that was probably a forgivable offence given her level of distress.

"The room is ready my lady," said an attendant at the door.

"I'm coming."

Selwa attempted to get off the couch, but could not. Her helpers pulled her each under one arm, carrying her entire weight on their shoulders. They progressed a couple of steps when Selwa screamed. "Stop, stop, stop. I can't. Oooowwww!"

She stood between the two women, trembling. Her water had broken and fluid was soaking into the loincloth, staining it from sea-blue to dark blue.

The two women looked at each other, unsure what to do.

One said, "Do you want us to—"

"Ow, my back, oh fuck, my back. Ooooowwwww!" She glared at Kotori. "Oh, fuck you. You took too long. I can't go down the stairs like this. I'll miss my last ever ceremony."

Kotori shrank a little with the words. He wasn't used to this. Mothers did not swear. Selwa's face was a mask of pain. She growled. "Call everyone up here."

The two women guided her back to the couch, very slowly, with lots of swearing. By the time she was back at the couch, her loincloth was soaked, so they took it off and draped the diaphanous birth gown over her shoulders. They spread out a white towel over the couch.

There was a commotion in the stairwell of the people gathered downstairs for the ceremony coming up. The girls with the flower vases that had stood on the stage downstairs arrived first. They placed the vases on either side of the couch. The women with the fans moved to stand in front of the couch and continued to fan cool air over Selwa's sweaty skin. Then the drummers, with their big skin-covered drums and their rattles and their jingle boards that tinkled and rattled as they walked, set up and started their routine so as to drown out Selwa's groans of pain. Birth was a beautiful thing.

The audience filed in. The room was quite big, but there was no time to bring the seats up here. Some of the younger men and women sat on the many rugs while the others stood or knelt, letting the more distinguished guests see while they remained standing. Even the king was here, and Prince Denori, who was one of the contenders to take the favourite spot from Nayek. He was a huge man, and had been even at the age of twenty—another of Selwa's sons.

It took a while before everyone had settled and the women of the choir discussed amongst themselves where they were at in their routine. Most birth ceremonies were drawn out events that started with gentle singing and swept into louder and faster songs and ulti-mately into screaming chants that always gave Kotori the chills.

They settled on singing *The Working Man's Wife*, which was a song from somewhere halfway in the procession that described how the man worked during the day and the woman did all her work in turn when she gave birth to his child. The comparison held up only for these mothers of the royal harem, because the mothers of less well-off men definitely worked in the kitchen, the laundry or the fields while they carried the man's children.

Selwa sat on the white towel on the couch through the song. She took off the gown and tied it by the sleeves around the top of her belly. The thin fabric covered her from the waist down, hiding both the red stretch marks and anything that happened underneath, because that would be distasteful.

But she was in a lot of pain. She alternately leaned forward on her knees or turned her face to the ceiling. Her face and arms shone with sweat. Normally, she would sing or move with the music, but this wasn't going to be one of those scripted ceremonies.

She stretched out both arms, a sign that she wanted to stand.

The singers stopped, because this was normally a sign that the birth was imminent.

After another moment of confusion, the drummers rushed forward, carrying their instruments.

A couple of other women brought towels, the bassinette and jugs of water, and held up the cloth that hid the bottom half of Selwa's body from view, allowing her to discard the gown.

The drummers drummed. The women in the choir sang their moaning songs, designed to let the mother get on with the job. But it was not fast. In fact it took a long time. Selwa's hair was wet with sweat.

It was so noisy and the drummers were getting tired and the audience nervous. Selwa stood with her legs apart slightly bent over. Pushing, screaming, panting.

There was something wrong. The birth gown did not show the exact details, but Kotori could see that the child's head was out. And the rest was stuck.

Kata, another of the distinguished Mothers, herself highly pregnant, told the audience that it might be better for them to wait downstairs.

People got up and crowded near the door, while the drums were still trying to drown out Selwa's howls.

Kotori wanted to leave but he was supposed to stay. Despite the noise and panic going on around him, he kept hearing his own words, that the birth would be quick and easy. He saw his own hand moving the coins that had fallen into the Scissors star sign.

He had not thrown incorrectly; those coins had belonged there.

The medic, an older woman, rushed into the room, carrying her bag, with a young student trailing her carrying a second bag.

The cloth that protected Selwa's dignity came down.

Two attendants were trying to get Selwa to the couch, but she wouldn't or couldn't move. Other Mothers ran forward to help her onto her knees.

The medic yelled, "Kneel so I can see what's happening."

A few of the attendants lifted Selwa—cursing and screaming terribly—and put her on the couch bent forward on her knees and elbows.

Kotori both didn't want to look but couldn't look away. A few of the audience about to go out the door also stopped and stared.

Yes, the head was out, bloodied and covered in slime. The medic tugged at the child, and wriggled it up and down. Selwa screamed and howled.

"By the Mother, push . . . yes, like that. Keep going—Mother's breath, what's that?"

A red, balloon-like sac bulged at the child's emerging shoulder.

Selwa pushed.

The balloon bulged. And bulged.

"By the Mother, stop, Selwa. There is something—"

But the red thing grew and grew like an inflating balloon—and popped. The child shot out.

A spray of bloody fluid scattered over the midwives, the drummers, the attendants and the audience and everyone waiting to leave.

People screamed. A guard fainted.

The child lay in a pool of blood on the white towel. It wasn't moving. Selwa had turned around and was staring at it.

Kotori swallowed bile. It came back up and he swallowed it again. A few spectators down, a young woman vomited in the hands that she held clasped over her mouth. Another woman lay passed out on the ground. Blood was everywhere. Kotori felt dizzy.

The room had turned to chaos. Spectators had stopped filing out the door and stood watching. The young woman was crying, vomit down the front of her dress.

Kotori didn't know what to do.

The king was looking straight at him, a hard, furious look.

A chill crept over Kotori's spine.

This was the second time this week that he had been terribly, terribly wrong.

In the past, astrologers were *hanged* for getting predictions this wrong. In school, they'd learned the story of Tomek, who had predicted that if the Aranians invaded Chevakia to quell the eternal rebel unrest that originated from there, even if the Chevakian army tried to retaliate, they would be stopped at the border.

After the crushing defeat of the Aranian army at the hand of the evil Milleus han Chevonian, the butcher of Tiverius, Tomek's head had been displayed on a stake in Kadrish's main square until the birds had pecked all the flesh off the bone and only the skull with the stake driven through it remained.

Feeling sick, Kotori went to the bloodstained, motionless little body lying on the towel that the women had dragged to the side while they attended Selwa, who was crying.

The child's face was like a doll's, the eyes open. It would have looked normal if not for the fleshy appendage on its chest that resembled a deflated sausage.

Kotori poked it—it was soft. He noted the veins going into what was left of the sac. He poked a bit harder, but it seemed attached to the child's body. What was it?

Someone came to stand next to him. It was Mother Kata, putting her hands on both sides of her back as heavily pregnant Mothers often did.

"I heard you predicted a healthy child."

Kotori didn't know what to say. He'd obviously been mistaken about shifting the coins. But he had *not* been mistaken about the time he'd read Prince Nayek's fortune, before he left. The stars really had predicted a safe trip.

"The child's heart grew outside the body. It got stuck when she tried to push it out. It burst when it wouldn't fit."

He felt sick. He tried to look away from the rounding of her belly, knowing that very soon, he'd be called to attend her, too. She probably wouldn't trust him, and she'd probably be right. He wasn't sure he trusted *himself*.

People were filing out of the room, crying or talking in disturbed voices. The king was gone, but Kotori was sure he'd hear more about this.

Women attended Selwa, who sat on the couch, still pale.

Her eyes met Kotori's. "You predicted good luck and an easy birth!" Her voice was hoarse from screaming. "This was the last child I will have for the king. You let me retire in embarrassment."

Kotori bowed. "My lady, I don't know how to make amends. I have failed. Rest assured that your predicament hurts me deeply." He was sweating. This was terrible. He might as well throw himself off the tower before he did anything else wrong.

She snorted. "Rubbish. You have lost touch. Do I even consider getting you to tell the fortunes of my other son? Can I trust you to pick a replacement for me to serve the king?"

"Be quiet, dear," an older woman said. "He will be confronted with the consequences of this, I have no doubt. It is not our place to deal with it."

No, it wasn't. They turned away from him, minding their business.

Kotori slipped from the room. He went down the stairs with the stream of people talking in emotional voices.

He made his way back to the astrology wing, doing his best not to look at anyone.

In his study room, he shut the door and leaned against it, breathing deeply.

All along the walls stood his hundreds of books. He'd read every one of them, learning and always wanting to understand. The giant star map hung on the wall behind his desk. For years he had studied, never having known anything else. Since he'd been a little boy, he'd wanted to become an astrologer.

Was his whole life about to take a turn? Had he lost touch, as Selwa had said?

He went to stand in front of the open window. Warm air drifted in, laced with the scent of flowers and the tang of salt. The view from the astrology tower was amazing. From up here, you could look down into the courtyard, many floors below, and over the roofs of the houses to the ocean.

How easy would it be to jump out of the window and never have to face Selwa's withering glare again, to be free of his embarrassment.

CHAPTER 9

AS IT TURNED OUT, *Sailor's Rest* was an establishment with an even shadier reputation than the seedy *Silver Gull*. Set two blocks back from the waterfront, its patronage obviously consisted of the lesser crewmembers from the ships, and those whose business would not pass muster in the city proper.

Despite being less than ten years old, the building looked tired, with peeling paint, ill-fitting doors and steps worn by the passage of many feet.

It was cold and damp in the foyer. A woman wearing furs drawn up to her ears sat by the light of one measly lamp. Her breath steamed.

Isandor's request to see "the Aranian who stays here" was met with suspicion and hostility, again because the Chevakian woman at the desk didn't recognise him. The owner definitely did, and when he came in, he told the woman to go to the back and then proceeded to speak in a sugary voice.

Isandor was getting very annoyed by this type of response, but he knew it had been the council's fault. They'd more or less left this part of the city to its own devices—as they used to do with the Outer City—and as a result undesirable activity festered alongside burgeoning commerce. What these people thought to gain by crawling on their knees for him he had no idea.

"I've been told an Aranian man by the name of Marek stays here."

"That appears to be right, Your Majesty."

"I would like a word with him, please."

"Certainly. If you could wait here."

He indicated a bench against the wall for the purpose, but the worn velvet cover didn't look appetising, so Isandor remained standing. The man climbed the stairs.

Isandor waited.

A man came in, his hood drawn over his head. He didn't look at Isandor and didn't greet him, but crossed the foyer to the stairs and disappeared up the stairwell, taking the steps two at a time.

The sound of voices drifted down the stairs.

The owner came back in the company of a thin, lanky man hiding in a fur cloak.

Isandor met his grey eyes. The expression in them was sharp and intelligent. He nodded a greeting. Isandor was unsure if the man recognised him.

"I'm Marek," the man said. "You wished to see me, Your Majesty?"

"Let's get something to eat. Do you know a decent place?"

Marek said that he did, and the two of them left the foyer under the stares of both the owner and his receptionist.

"I hope this is not going to cause you trouble," Isandor said.

"No more than the usual suspicion." But he looked uneasy.

"It's about Zaina," Isandor said when they were in the street. "I understand that you're friends with her."

"Is anything wrong with her? She left on some expedition, from what I understand. I'm worried about her."

"I don't know that there's anything wrong. The expedition was sent out by the Knight Council, and they haven't reported. I'm wondering specifically about her connections with Prince Nayek, and what the prince was doing in the City of Glass."

Marek stopped. "Don't."

"What?"

"Don't ask me about it. I can't tell you anything."

"You're not worried about your girlfriend?"

Marek laughed. "She's not my girlfriend. She doesn't go for men."

Did he mean—wait, like Rider Barton had a male lover, were there women who only loved other women?

To be honest, it wasn't the first time he'd heard of it, but it made sense, in Zaina's case. He'd just never met a woman like that.

Marek continued, "Zaina is a friend, and she left town because she's in a lot of trouble. It is, however, *Aranian* trouble, that I don't want to be involved in, and the Knight Council doesn't want to be involved in either."

They had stopped walking, and people were streaming around them. It was starting to get cold, and people had pulled collars up around their necks or hoods over their heads.

"I would still like to talk," Isandor said. "Which is the establishment you were talking about? Is the *Dancing Bear* over there any good? I'm hungry. I care about Zaina. I care even more because she had involvement with the family of *my* lover whom I proposed to, but who has disappeared: Tamerane of House Mara."

Marek's eyes widened briefly before his expression went blank. "I'm sorry, I can't help you."

"What is it that frightens you about what I said?" Isandor gestured to the eating house down the street. "Come on, let's go."

Marek looked over his shoulder. "It's not as simple as that. They're everywhere. Look, I really have to go—"

"We're having dinner." Isandor put his hand on the man's shoulder and gently pushed him forward. "I will pay if you want. I can give you protection of you need it—"

"Protection?"

"Yes. Zaina was scared and she asked for protection. She stayed in the servant's quarters in the palace before leaving on the expedition. She'd been badly beaten up—by Prince Nayek or his men, I presume —but she was safe inside the palace."

Marek looked at him. Isandor could almost see conflicting streams of reasoning warring behind his eyes.

Isandor continued, "In my experience, most Aranians have complex histories and most are wanted by someone in the home country. I and the Knight Council strive for openness and safety for all residents."

"Then why this ridiculous register?" His voice was an angry hiss.

Isandor gave him a sharp look. "Register?"

"The one that requires every business with foreign employees to declare themselves and register with the authorities, so that they can keep operating."

"No, you have that wrong. The register is only for people to let us know their names and where they live so we can warn them in case of trouble with icefire."

"There were three men with a stack of forms asking questions about our businesses, saying that we wouldn't be able to conduct business if we didn't register."

What?

They arrived at the door to the *Dancing Bear*. Through the steamed-up windows, Isandor could see many people sitting at tables, and it struck him how long it was since he had been in an establishment like this, and how much you could learn there. At least it was busy enough to give him confidence that the food would be decent.

Isandor pushed open the door, letting out a waft of humid air, laced with the scent of cooking and the murmur of many conversations. By the skylights, he was hungry.

They found a table in the far corner, next to the entrance to the kitchen. It was probably one of the least desirable spots, since waiters were moving past with trays and dishes.

Isandor took off his cloak and hung it over the back of the seat before sitting down. Marek took the position with his back to the kitchen, so that all the waiters had to squeeze past him.

"Tell me about these men and their register of businesses," Isandor said.

Marek met his eyes with a searching look. "Are you serious or do you really not know anything about it?"

"There has been no such thing set up by the Knight Council. We issued a call for citizens to register with us so that they could be warned, nothing else."

"There were three guys with arm bands with the symbol of the Knight Council who have been doing the rounds to all the businesses here, and visiting all the guesthouses to check for businesses with foreign employees."

Isandor shook his head. "Not authorised by the Knight Council."

A waiter came and Isandor ordered two mugs of cider. There was no menu, but a waiter had just brought out plates for the next table, and the fish looked good enough, so Isandor ordered two meals.

When the waiter left, Isandor found Marek looking at him with a disturbed expression, biting the inside of his lips.

"Were either of those three men familiar to you?"

"I've seen the Chevakian before, but wouldn't know his name. He had a local with him and the Aranian handled the forms. None of the people I was with trusted them enough to register, except one, a northern Chevakian. He said they just wanted to know his name and where he lived, but that was too much for us."

"It wasn't hard for me to find out where you lived."

"No, but finding every Aranian would take them a lot of time. To have that at their fingertips would be a great resource for a prince looking for men to do his dirty work. In one book, he can see where his supporters are, where his enemies are. Aranian princes are always looking for friends or enemies."

That was true. Isandor studied the man's face. He looked quite sharp, not a common soldier or a peasant. "I don't know who you are or what your function is, but I think we can possibly gain a lot from your cooperation. I sense that you are more than you make out to be and that you're scared."

Marek snorted. "That's not hard to guess. Almost every Aranian is scared if he is not in Arania, or worse, if *she* is not in Arania. Maybe the ones in Arania are scared, too. Hell, everyone is scared of each other, probably even the king. That's why we come here, to lead normal lives and get away from having to look over our shoulders all the time. This register—I did a little investigation. The Aranian man who is involved in it is employed by Ledor of House Mara. Ledor has a second warehouse in Curack, which is a sleepy town more famous for its military training bases. The military is the domain of Prince Denori, who is my—much older—brother."

Isandor stared at him, and Marek laughed, not in a happy way. "It is said that every second man in Arania is a prince. That's not far from the truth. Being a prince is no big deal at all in Arania. My father would not know me, and care even less if he did. My brother considered me a risk, because there was something about me he didn't like, some trivial thing I'd said or done. He consigned me to the Special Service, which is simply a way to make sure I died young. I ran instead. They don't know where I am. Yet. I'm lucky I'm not a woman."

"What about Zaina. Is she a princess?"

"No, she's General Pakori's daughter. He's just a dumb idiot, who doesn't deserve such a smart woman for a daughter."

"How did she get involved with Nayek?"

"Her mother was poor and put her name on the Mothers' register. I presume you've heard of the register?"

Isandor nodded.

"Then she became a well-paid mechanic and applied to have her name removed. Her application caught Nayek's interest, so when he needed to be here, he went to seek her out. Nayek does that sort of thing: he picks out one person who's done something he doesn't like and makes an example of them. From what I can gather, he made several attempts to impress his authority or sexual prowess on her. I don't know how much success he's had."

"What if she killed him?"

Marek laughed, and this time his eyes reflected true mirth. "That would be an awesome twist to a horrible situation." His expression went serious again. "With Nayek out of the running for the throne, my dear brother and his cousin Sferuk are fighting for the top spot. That is going to be one hell of a long and costly fight. That's probably why everyone has been called to Curack: my brother calling in favours."

"What does that have to do with Ledor?"

"Denori is Ledor's main creditor. He financed Ledor's ailing business when it was still the vogue to invest in ocean trade. Now that he's in the race for the throne, he needs his money back in order to buy more men or more land, or whatever his plans are. You only need to look at Ledor's business to see that it's all show. He has nothing he can pay Denori back with. Ledor is a noble, for fuck's sake! They don't know how to make money, they're supposed to already have it at birth—excuse my language." His cheeks coloured.

"I don't mind," Isandor said. "And yes, I've often thought the same." Also Ledor's strange attempts to get more money out of him before finally deciding to flee.

The waiter came to deliver the food: two big mugs of cider and two plates of fried fish and vegetables, still sizzling. The smell was heavenly.

"This *is* a good place."

"Surprisingly, yes."

Isandor picked up a piece of fish between his thumb and forefinger and bit into it. He almost burned his mouth.

"Where would Ledor have gone? Would he have fled to Chevakia?"

Marek shook his head. "He's gone to Curack, that's for sure. A good number of Perian nobles are in Arania, mostly Curack. Some are there of their own will, but many owe my brother something, like money, and if they can't pay, they work for him instead."

So that was where Tamerane had gone. "The women, too?"

"They'd be assigned to some harem for the men's pleasure."

By the skylights, no.

Isandor finished his piece of fish, no longer tasting it, well prepared though the meal was. He could think only one thing: he had to get her out of there.

"Curack is a sleepy town, right?"

Marek gave him a sharp look. "Whatever you're thinking, don't. I have seen the Aranian army, and their resources and sheer manpower exceed the population of this entire country. On top of that, they've got these new weapons that can't be fought. You'd be slaughtered. I'm not even sure Chevakia could win a confrontation. There are a *lot* of angry princes in Arania who don't care if they live or die, and who command men who only want one thing: their names inscribed in the wall of honour after their deaths."

Isandor wanted to ask Marek about the Aranian military bases at Curack, but didn't want to do that in this place where people might overhear it.

They finished their meal talking about more lighthearted subjects, like fishing and the care of eagles, but Isandor knew that as soon as he was alone in his room, he would draw up a plan to get Tamerane back. He would also call a special meeting of the Knight Council and relay all this information. For one, the Knights had to locate these Aranians who were collecting information about their citizens under the guise of acting for the Knight Council.

He asked Marek to remain involved, but the man seemed hesitant.

"I don't want any trouble. I managed to find a decent job that pays me enough to survive, but as soon as I create a fuss, my employer will get rid of me."

"There would be no fuss."

"When high-ranking Aranians are involved, there is always a fuss. My brother knows that I dodged service and that I'm alive. He is suspicious enough that, if he really has a chance to be chosen, he will order all his rivals and detractors killed. I like my life as it is. I don't want to became involved in Aranian business, especially not my brother's."

He told Isandor he worked as scribe and translator for an account keeper business. Isandor knew the business' owners and trusted that they employed people with integrity.

"I can't be seen to be political," he said. "It would attract the wrong kind of attention to me."

"I'm still offering protection, if you're willing to help us unmask these men."

"There is no unmasking them. They're here to do their jobs. They're an extension of the prince's influence."

"Protection would involve moving into the palace or eyrie in exchange for information that may well save your life, or your friend's."

"I'll have to think about that."

They left the eating house. People were queued up outside, so it only seemed fair not to occupy the table longer than necessary.

Isandor was going back on the tram and walked with Marek back to the *Sailor's Rest*. All the shops were dark now, and the only light came from sparsely located street lamps. It had gone fairly quiet, too.

Marek stopped in front of the door to the *Sailor's Rest*.

"I didn't want to say this in there, where I'm sure someone might have heard it, and it would have reached the wrong ears. Much as I think the Aranian army is strong, if there is anyone who can defeat them, it's you and the Knights. They have these new icefire weapons."

Isandor nodded. "I've already seen those." And he had no experience fighting with those weapons, because he had always refused to learn. The old king had done so much *evil* with magic.

"They built them with the help of the families who fled to Arania after the explosion. These nobles—Ledor included—are heavily involved with Denori or the king. They will probably not take your side."

No. They would think that all these modern changes he was making had no place in their country. "Thank you," he said. "The Knight Council meetings are always open to you and, as I said, the palace offers protection to those who help us."

"I will think about it." And then he was gone, into the building.

CHAPTER 10

$\mathcal{W}$HEN IT WAS almost dark, Javes and Tali finally found a place to camp. It consisted of a little hollow between two fields where the runoff from occasional rainstorms had created a gully with rutted sides. There were no trees, only a couple of half-rotted fence posts with slack wire, on which he hung the cloth. It was not a very good tent.

Javes dug at the deepest point of the gully to check for water, but as he had suspected, the ground was bone dry. He filled up the bucket from the water bags for the animals to drink.

He and Tali ate salt meat, and a piece of stale bread each. Rations were getting smaller, and they would have to find or buy food soon, or trap an animal, skin and salt it. Tali said that she had trapped jackrabbits. Javes had a sharp knife for skinning.

Pashtan had always made his own salt meat and Javes had watched him do it. He had a bit of salt, and if the air was particularly dry, you didn't even need to use that much of it.

It did mean, however, that they would need to stay in the same spot for a number of days, and he preferred not to do that in a place without water. And in a place where he didn't feel safe.

The ground under the shelter was hard as rock and it sloped quite steeply, which made for an uncomfortable night.

Javes lay awake, looking at the way the faint light of the sky path and the Great Wanderer made Tali's skin sheen with sweat. He wished they'd find a proper well or a water hole. He'd wash her clothes, because the rank stench of women's sweat disturbed him.

The goats had not found much of interest to graze on, and they lay at the top of the gully, next to the post where he had put the bucket. It amazed him that they hadn't gone their own way. They didn't produce much milk anymore; just enough for a glass or two at breakfast.

The camel wouldn't be so silly as to follow along if he didn't force it to. He'd had to hobble it every night, or it would have wandered off and never come back. He could see it as a slightly lighter blob with humps, nosing bushes at the bottom of the gully.

Something snorted in the night, and all the animals jerked into alertness.

Javes sat up. Trying to sleep was pretty much pointless anyway. He crawled from under the shelter and climbed to the top of the gully. All the goats were standing up, looking in a southerly direction.

The land sloped up gently from here, and Javes could only make out where the ridge ended because below a certain line, there were no more stars.

What were the goats seeing over there? He didn't think bears or wolves were in this area. They were much too far north for sabre lions, and those only lived in dense forest anyway.

But he couldn't shake that feeling that something or someone was following them.

JAVES KEPT an eye out for most of the next day and the day after. They passed through utterly desolate country of jagged ridges, sharp stones, banks of sand and plains with desiccated bushes.

Food was getting low, and at the start of the second day, he unpacked all his bags to take stock of what they still had and how many days they could make it last.

"What are you doing?" Tali asked. She sat with her knees drawn up to her chest.

"I'm seeing how much we have to last us until the next town."

"There is no next town. All of the world is burned." Her expression was haunted.

A chill went over Javes' spine.

While he was struggling to get out of this region, what had happened in Tiverius? Did the doga even know about rampaging Aranians? This was not just a small border raid, was it?

He couldn't contact his parents or his tutor. He didn't *know* what had happened in the rest of the country and he had no way of finding out.

He would have to find a telegraph line that hadn't been destroyed, but as with so many things, traffic to Tiverius was one way. You never knew whether anyone got your message. Even Pashtan never got any feedback from his weather reports.

Maybe Tali was right: all around, the world had been burned to ash. Who said that the devastation was limited to this area?

He didn't dare meet Tali's eyes. She had treated him as an older brother, someone who had the answers and knew the way. The truth was that he had neither.

He was floundering and just as scared as she was, travelling through unfamiliar terrain in the hope of doing something that might be utterly futile. Instead of going to Tiverius, it might be safer to join the windwalkers in the desert.

That thought chilled him.

He repacked all their supplies into the bags and tied them to the camel's saddle. As usual, Tali sat watching him like a shadow. She was so thin and her feet and hands were so disgusting.

"We'll find a spot where we can rest and hunt for a bit. If we make enough salt meat, we can sell it in the next town and buy some other things."

"Like what?"

"Some more comfortable clothes for you would be one thing."

"I like this dress!"

"Yes, but when we come south, it's going to start getting colder. You'll need warmer clothes."

She stared at him as if this was news to her.

"We'll have to cross the highland and the forest. It won't be warm there."

"It's a very long way to Tiverius, isn't it?"

"Yes, it is. It will take us a long time. I hope we can buy another camel, but we'll soon be out of camel territory, and I don't know how many we'll encounter. Are you all right to walk that far?"

"Yes. Why not?"

He didn't ask any further, afraid of venturing into embarrassing territory. He had not seen her use the bloodstained bandage anymore, and he still had no idea what she would have done with it or why she needed it.

"Well then, let's go."

Javes checked the packs and then led the camel away from their campsite. Tali followed, accompanied by the goats.

A narrow path wound through the valley between boulders and sharp rocks, wide enough for one person. It wound between rocky outcrops, through little valleys and mountain saddles. It seemed to be a bit cooler up on the ridges, where the wind was stronger than in the valleys, or maybe that had something to do with the hazy clouds obscuring the sun at times.

By the time they stopped for the night in the shade of a couple of large boulders, the sky was so hazy that the sun was barely still visible. It almost looked like clouds covered the sky. Dusk came early and was without orange colours. The camping spot again had no water, and Javes began to see why all the roads went around this area.

The cloud cover became thicker the next day. Walking through the deserted country was almost pleasant. The dry landscape took on a less desiccated hue when there was no sunlight. Different colours came out. A stiff breeze came up which dispersed the strange and eerie echoing sounds of their own footsteps when crossing narrow valleys.

In the afternoon, Javes led the camel up a mountain ridge, and looked into the next valley . . .

On the flat part of the wide valley stood a bowl on a pedestal like the one where the windwalkers lived. Except this one was falling apart. The bowl was broken, with sheets of metal missing and others rusted, and a section of the rim drooped down.

"What is that?" Tali asked behind him.

"It's a . . ." But Javes wasn't actually sure what it was. As the windwalkers had explained to him, they used the bowl to collect water, but this one sat at an angle and wouldn't hold much water. It didn't look like the pedestal had bent. In fact, he thought it looked more like it had been designed that way.

Unlike the one in the northern desert, this one came with a few low buildings.

The plain surrounding the pedestal was covered in bushes, so they let the animals graze while he and Tali went to investigate.

The low buildings were made from that ancient homogenous stone that Javes had seen displayed in a cabinet in the history department of the Scriptorium. It was cracked and badly weathered. Each sides contained windows, but if they had once contained glass, all traces had disappeared long ago. The same with the door. There must have been a doorframe at some point, but now he couldn't even see where a door had been attached.

Inside the building were signs of people having camped recently, but nothing else except for some rusty patches on the dust-covered floor.

Javes thought it was a decent place to camp, but Tali wouldn't come inside.

"The air is bad in there," she insisted.

At first, Javes was annoyed, but then he found a part where the building had two floors and there was a shelter with open sides on the ground floor. He and Tali mused about what it would have been used for.

"Who lived here, anyway?" Tali asked.

"No one recently. I think this is very, very old."

"Older than Tiverius?"

"Much older. This is as old as the tall buildings in the City of Glass."

And Tali didn't know what the City of Glass was, so he had to explain, like a teacher does to a pupil. Yes, he decided, she could be his little sister. He'd never wanted a sister or thought much about having one, but most of life gave you no choices, and it seemed that life had decided to give him a sister.

When the light turned golden, Javes followed the goats and the camel grazing in the valley. To Tali's question as to what he was doing, he said that animals knew where the best food was and could smell water. Sure enough, the camel led him to a hollow where a bit of green grass grew between the bushes.

Javes managed to dig up some muddy water which he strained through his shirt. While he was doing this, Tali came to him with a handful of prickly fruit.

"What's that?" he asked her.

"Gorra. You can eat it."

That? It was like a cactus.

"You need to peel off the skin, like this." She attempted to break the fruit in half, but her fingers were so thin and weak that she only succeeded in getting spines in her skin.

Javes took the fruit from her, broke it open and found pink flesh inside. It tasted quite sweet. "That's nice. How did you know about that?"

"My grandma would take me out to collect things. She would tell me all about the plants and where to find rabbits and how to trap them."

Javes felt ashamed that he had never asked her, assuming that she was like a little girl at home in Tiverius: preoccupied with the latest hair style and otherwise useless. Tali was *not* useless, and he should put aside his judgement and let her come out of her shell.

If he was thirteen and had seen his parents murdered before his eyes, maybe he'd be a little strange, too. It was just that he didn't really know how to talk about bad things, including asking about her injuries, since they didn't seem to bother her physically. What had those Aranians done to her after they had killed her parents? They wouldn't have . . . no, she was a child. Even Aranians wouldn't have been that disgusting, would they?

But it was clear that *something* had happened. They might have chased her. She could have fallen. But it didn't sit well with him. He didn't know much about these things, but he knew that women would bleed periodically once they were ready to receive a man. Most parents in Tiverius would keep their daughters home for at least another two years, even if they had negotiated marriage. The girls were usually sixteen at first bleeding. Tali was thirteen, so that couldn't be it. She looked older to his eye, though. She was thin, but definitely had started getting a female shape.

They ate a strange combination of fruit and nuts and salt meat with goat's milk. It didn't taste half as bad as it sounded.

In the morning Javes was wakened by a strange smell.

It was raining. It was only a sharp shower, but the sky was still cloudy and the red rock had turned dark brown with moisture. The air was still and humid, filled with a smell of wet stone.

Well . . . that was interesting. Rain was a good thing, right?

Further south, this was supposed to be the rainy season, but rain in the desert was erratic.

They saddled up the camel and kept going, plodding along the path followed by the bounding energetic goats. Every now and then, a few spits of rain would fall from the sky. The wind was quite cool.

Walking became uncomfortable because there was a good deal of wind and the rain continued intermittently, lashing into their faces. In the afternoon, they stopped at a collection of boulders at the bottom of a rocky outcrop. The sky in the north was leaden grey and, if anything, the rain's intensity was increasing.

"I remember getting a rainstorm like this when I was little," Tali said. "The sky went black and it rained for days. The streets in town turned into rivers, and then the whole of the desert turned green. The farmers were very happy because they got a very good harvest, but then the whole district grew a lot of grain and the prices to sell it were terrible."

Javes gave her a sideways look. It figured that as daughter of a merchant, she'd be well tuned to commerce.

If anything, rain would be a nuisance to them. With the wind and the lack of trees, there were no places to string the cloth. Maybe they should have stayed at the shelter.

"I'll see if we can do something with those rocks," Javes said. He might have to build something for a temporary shelter.

There was a narrow crevice between the boulders. Javes squeezed himself through and whoa! He almost fell in a dark pool of water. Opposite the gap, the rock face hung over the pool and over a rock ledge that was a couple of paces wide. A perfect place to stay the night.

He jumped from one rock to another around the pool and reached the ledge. It was uneven, and sloped to the side a bit, but it was a better solution than trying to hitch a tent held down by stones that would only shift and fall over once the wind got hold of the tent cloth.

"Come over here!" he called to Tali.

She peeped between the rocks.

"Bring all our things over here."

"But . . ." She looked at the water. Swimming was probably not a skill children in Ysherra needed to learn.

"You jump over those rocks." He pointed. And then he showed her how he had reached the ledge.

They took the most important saddlebags into the cave. They spread out mats and ate from their diminishing supplies. Water was not going to be an issue, but they were running out of food. He asked Tali if she knew which plants were edible.

She explained about tubers that lay under the ground waiting for rain, and a kind of frog that buried in the sand. There was also wild roccas grain—and everyone in Tiverius ate roccas with most meals—but cleaning it was a lot of work. There was, she assured, plenty of food if you knew where to find it.

"I wonder why people have never built towns in this area."

"It's a desert."

"Ysherra is a desert." In fact, he found the terrain here less inhospitable than the agricultural belt around Ysherra.

Tali shrugged. "Maybe it's because of dust devils?"

"This far south? Have there always been many dust devils here?"

"People say so. But I don't know. The desert is full of windwalkers and they snatch people and those people never come back."

"They don't do that. I've met windwalkers. They're just a tribe of nomads with tents and camels."

"Nah." She shook her head. "Windwalkers are the guardians of the desert. They know we're here. They don't like it, and they will come for us. We'll spend the rest of our lives as windwalkers, because they never let anyone go."

"They let me go back to Ysherra."

"Did you see their faces?"

"Yes." Javes thought about the white patches on their skin. He wondered how much stock to put in the sayings of a thirteen-year-old girl, but whatever was going on with the windwalkers, he agreed with her that they were probably more than just travelling nomads. How had they come by those patches of white skin?

By now, it had gotten quite dark. Raindrops made a faint tinkling sound on the surface of the rock pool.

Javes got to his feet. "Well, I don't know about you, but I'm going to wash myself and my clothes."

Tali gave him an uncertain look.

He turned his back to Tali, undid his pants and dropped them, took off his shirt and climbed down the rocks into the pool.

The water was cool, and the rocks under the surface were slippery. The depth of the pool surprised him. The bank fell away quickly until he couldn't even feel the bottom anymore. He swam into the middle.

"I wonder where all this water comes from?"

Tali sat on her sleeping mat, her knees drawn up to her chest. "The water lives under the ground. It is full of ghosts and spirits of all the people who have lived and died here."

"How many people would ever have lived here?"

"You know that they did. We've seen their houses. We slept at one last night."

"I don't think those were houses. The windwalkers say the bowls are for collecting water, but I don't think that's what they're for, either. They can move on the pedestals and don't always point straight up, like the one where the windwalkers live. I'd like to know what they're for."

"They're made by the same people who made that thing you showed my father and didn't want to sell to him."

"I wanted to buy a camel and I didn't think he would pay me enough for it. Did he tell you what it is?"

"No one knows what those things are."

"When people buy those things off your father, who are they and what do they do with them?"

"There is a peddler who takes the metal to Watya, and then he sells it to rich collectors."

"People from Tiverius?" Javes knew plenty of rich people who collected things—pottery, animal skeletons, old coins, paintings, vases—but he had never heard of these kinds of artefacts being collected.

Tali shrugged. "I don't know. I don't see those people."

Javes sat on a rock on the opposite side of the pool. The rain pattered on his head and exposed shoulders, and made little rings on the surface of the water around him.

He wondered if the people who had made those metal artefacts were the same ones who had built the bowls and the City of Glass a long time ago. He wondered if there was a second City of Glass in the desert where the windwalkers found these things. He wondered what sort of people they were and why they had died. So many questions.

"You want to come into the water to wash?"

Tali shrugged. "It's very deep, isn't it?"

"It is, but you can sit on the rocks over there. You can wash out your clothes, too. I'm going to do that soon."

She rubbed her shin, smearing caked dust into mud. She glanced at the water, and at him. "I'm very dirty, aren't I?"

"Yes." It was probably not polite to say that, but there was no avoiding it anymore. Not while there was water, and he had a bit of soap to wash. "I'll turn around while you get undressed. I won't look. I promise."

He did turn around, and could see through the gap between the rocks to where the goats lay sheltering from the rain against the stone.

The water rippled behind him. "You can look now."

Only Tali's head stuck out of the water.

"It's nice, isn't it?"

She scooped up water in her hands, splashing it over her face. Then she ran her fingers through her hair, but they tangled in the big knot at the back of her head.

"Let me comb that out for you."

She gave him a sideways glance but didn't protest.

Javes climbed out of the water. He set the oil lamp on the ground, poured some precious oil into the reservoir and used his spark lighter to light the wick. The little flame spread a warm glow, reflected by the rock walls. By its light, he retrieved the soap and his comb and sat next to her.

He scooped water up with his hands and let it run over her head. Dust-stained water ran over her back. He grabbed the soap and rubbed it into her hair. Then he rinsed again. Brown water with bits of straw ran over her shoulders.

The knot at the back of her head was huge, and for a long time, his picking at it with the wide-toothed comb didn't make any impression, but slowly, he managed to untangle some of it. He drenched her hair with olive oil which made the combing easier.

"Your hair is very thick."

"It's coarse like a horse's tail."

"I think it's pretty."

"You really think so?"

It fell over her brown-skinned shoulders like a black waterfall. She was rubbing her arms to get rid of the engrained dust. When she lifted her arm, he could see the slight rounding of her budding breast.

He wanted her to turn around so that he could see those gentle mounds. Only see them, mind. He would not touch them. He would not run his hands over her shoulders down her sides to her soft buttocks. He would not kiss those innocent lips.

She was only thirteen, and that would not be appropriate.

JAVES STOOD in the middle of a circle of people, mostly windwalkers without their coverings. There was monotonous music with fast drumbeats. Everyone around him was dancing. They were mostly tribespeople and he knew none of them, except Tali.

She was naked except for a belt with feathers around her waist. In the time since he'd seen her—and how long was that, anyway? He'd just seen her when going to sleep last night—she had aged and she was now a beautiful young woman. Her hips were broad, her waist narrow, her breasts were round and full. She wiggled her hips, low light glistening on her sweaty skin.

She was so full, and so *female*.

Tali stared at him and licked her lips, but she would be too young to understand how she was teasing him. He ached so much. He wanted to throw off his clothes, take her hand, and run into the desert so that they could be alone under the sky path.

The windwalkers were dancing and clapping and stamping their feet in the dirt. Why didn't they leave the two of them alone, so that he could—no that was not appropriate. Tali was a child.

But those hips and those round breasts looked nothing like a child.

She winked at him and smiled.

She rocked her hips.

She turned around and bent over, presenting to him the round cheeks of her buttocks with a soft hair-rimmed secret spot in between.

And Javes rose and came forward, although he knew with all his heart that this was wrong. He took off his clothes. His cock stood up at an angle, dribbling slime down his leg. He grabbed her around the waist, tried to push in, but fumbled, and he was too late, and spilled himself all over his pants. He swore.

Someone called out. "Javes!"

He was half-aware that it was dawn and he was in a cave.

"Javes! Wake up! What are you doing?"

He gasped. Sat up, his chest heaving. His pants were wet.

The dream dissipated.

Tali stood with her back against the rock wall, her eyes wide. Rain was bucketing into the pool.

He stammered. "I . . ." Damn it. His pants really were wet and the distinctive smell of spoot rose around him. "I'm sorry. I was dreaming."

"Oh. Was it a scary dream?"

His face grew hot. "No. Er. Yes. I don't know." He pretended to be busy rummaging through the packs, while the wet patch in his pants grew cold and disgusting. This was utterly, utterly embarrassing.

He crawled to the side of the pool and let himself slide into the water.

Tali laughed. "You're still wearing your pants!"

"Oh." *Well, that was kind of the point.* "How silly of me."

While she laughed, he wriggled himself out of his trousers under water and rubbed the crotch until the offending patch of slime had disappeared. The body part that had betrayed him had shrunk to its usual softness and size.

Well . . .

He would sometimes dream like that about girls his age.

Never young girls, though. There was a name for men who lured young girls into their houses, and married them to spite their first wives. They were called crocodiles. They snuck up under the surface, offered the girl money she couldn't refuse and snatched her under the noses of the legitimate suitors who had much less money and little power. The girl saw the big house and all the servants, the girl's parents saw the money, but all the people in town would joke that the old man couldn't get a decent woman or that the man was too weak-willed to handle a woman of the appropriate age.

He did *not* want to be laughed at, and this was *not* like that. Not at all. It was just his body playing tricks on him.

"Are we going to continue walking today?" Tali said. She was looking at the sky from where the rain still fell incessantly.

A good amount of water was trickling from the rocks into the pool, and already the water level was much higher than it had been last night.

"I think we should," Javes said. It would be cold and miserable, but if they stayed here longer, they risked getting caught in this crevice when the water covered the rocks that they used to jump to the ledge. Tali could not swim.

Javes pulled his pants back on and came out of the water. His pants dripped water and stuck to his legs. He shivered.

He put all the gear in the bags, wondering how they would keep everything dry in the rain.

He helped Tali into the gap between the rocks and handed her the bags.

The camel stood on the other side of the crevice, looking miserable. The air had cleared with the rain, but the stone looked dark. Already, little streams flowed through the valleys.

The saddle was dry, but the camel's fur had collected a lot of water. The poor thing stood with its head down, raindrops leaking from its long eyelashes, looking seriously put out by the weather. The goats seemed no more impressed. Two kids even sheltered underneath the camel's belly.

Javes tied their packs to the saddle and they started walking.

It was as if they had entered an entirely different landscape. The rain had turned the ground and the rocks dark, which made the rocky crags look threatening and ominous. Javes kept looking over his shoulder, only to realise that the unusual sounds he heard were those made by Tali and the animals as they ploughed through the sticky soil, where mud would build up under shoes and hooves until it was a big clump. It was very annoying and tiring.

Once the path rose, the ground became slippery—the top layer was soaked with water, but the ground underneath was still dry. The camel walked slowly. The goats were less careful and slipped often. Their pelts were soon covered in mud.

Javes followed in the camel's footsteps, and Tali came behind.

It rained relentlessly. By midday, both Javes and Tali were soaked to the bone. Little rivers of muddy water flowed through the valleys, and they grew into bigger rivers. This became a problem when they had to cross the odd creek. At first the water was knee deep, but it wasn't too long before valleys became deep, fast-flowing rivers that they had to pick along to find a spot where it was safe to cross. They were wasting a lot of time like this.

Javes began to think that it might be better to find a dry place to shelter and sit out the weather. But they had little food. Maybe Tali could collect some berries.

Maybe it would rain so much that no one would go anywhere for days. The leaden sky was really not looking very promising.

Everything was muddy and wet. It was cold, miserable and even the goats became grumpy.

CHAPTER 11

*K*OTORI STOOD AT his window for a long time.

He thought very seriously about jumping, but he was too much of a coward. It would *hurt* falling down on the stones of the courtyard, in that brief moment before he died. What if he regretted his decision at that moment? If he died in his current disgrace, he would *not* have his name inscribed on the wall of the king's servants, and his mother, his poor mother, would die in shame.

So he just stood there and *thought* about jumping, while the sun sank lower on the horizon and turned the city golden. The view was achingly pretty. He *loved* Kadrish with all his heart. Right now, it was not loving him back.

Someone knocked on the door.

Kotori gasped.

It would be the king's guard, coming to get him to be scolded by the king. For a few heartbeats, he still considered jumping out the window, but then he turned around and went to open the door.

The man in the corridor was indeed one of the king's advisors. He spoke the dreaded words. "His Majesty the king requires your presence."

"Yes, yes, certainly. Let me just get . . ." Kotori retreated into his room, not sure exactly what he needed to get. Not his cloak, because it wasn't cold. Not his books or his maps, because no one was asking for a casting.

So he only opened the cupboard door and shut it again without taking anything out. He wiped bits of fluff off the front of his tunic, and then felt strange and empty-handed without his map and the case that held the stones, so he took them anyway, even if he knew he wouldn't need them.

His knees felt like jelly.

He followed the guard into the corridor and the two of them set off through the courtyards and echoing halls of the citadel to the king's private quarters, which were on the middle floor overlooking the city, harbour and the ocean.

King Orik sat in his usual easy chair by the window, near the open balcony door while the warm ocean breeze ruffled the curtains. The sun was about to sink behind the Mother's Veil—the perpetual bank of billowing clouds that hung over the ocean—and the haze-filtered sunlight lit the king's legs and the adjacent carpet.

"The astrologer is here, Your Majesty," the guard said.

"Thank you. You can go now." His voice was cool, and Kotori couldn't detect any sign of emotion. King Orik was good at hiding his emotions; Kotori had never heard him yell at anyone. The patient, measured voice was what made him so scary.

Kotori bowed.

The king said nothing, and Kotori remained bowed, looking at his own slippered feet. Sweat pearled on his upper lip. He wanted to wipe it off, but he couldn't move until the king said it was all right to do so.

"Rise and sit down," the king said.

Kotori did, scurrying to the couch with bent knees so that his head remained below that of the king while the latter was seated.

He sat on the edge of the cushion. "I have to tend my sincerest apologies for making the mistakes. It all started with my prediction for the prince. I don't know what went wrong with that prediction and why the stars showed me one thing and did the other. If you give me some time, I will find out why this has happened—"

The king held up his hand.

Kotori fell quiet. He wasn't even going to be given the opportunity to offer to make amends. That was bad.

"It is not how you backtrack on your mistakes that matters. It is how you make sure they don't happen again."

"Yes, Your Majesty."

"I care more about the reliability of my astrologer than about the outcome of his mistakes."

"Yes, Your Majesty." Kotori sneaked a glance at the king's face which had remained blank. The man *cared* about his favourite son, and this statement certainly had to be a sign of his fury.

"And how do you propose to do that?"

"I will study to find my mistakes and make sure I don't repeat them."

"You already *have* repeated them."

Ouch. "I was too nervous today."

"And now we have a dead child. It was a girl, too. She could have been one of the great Mothers."

"I'm sorry." Yet he wondered what they would have done if he'd predicted a bad outcome because of his throw. No one liked bad predictions. No one liked it when they came true.

"You will have to do better."

"Yes, Your Majesty." Kotori couldn't see *how*.

"We now have two funerals to attend."

"I'm very sorry, Your Majesty."

The king snorted. "Selwa has asked for permission to retire, and I have granted it. She has served me well and will continue to be an asset to new Mothers in the house." He placed the tips of the fingers of one hand against the fingertips of the other hand. "I will need to replace her."

"Yes, Your Majesty."

"Stop grovelling like that. Stand up and look me in the eye. Own your mistakes and improve."

"Yes, Y—" Kotori straightened, his arms stiffly by his sides.

"That's better. I'm going to tell you what sort of woman I'll be looking for."

"Your Majesty, do you want me to work with the registry of Mothers?"

"No. I don't need any more brats. In fact, there are too many brats in this city already. They just become soldiers and maids. We're drowning in soldiers and maids. We need a very special kind of child from a special kind of woman."

"Oh? Your Majesty?"

He said nothing for a while and Kotori feared that he was going to have to divine the type of person the king needed, and he wasn't feeling his divining skills at the moment.

But the king started speaking again. "You know that we have been using the southern art?"

"I had heard rumours, Your Majesty." He didn't dare mention the word *magic,* because magic was dark and evil.

"They are more than rumours. We *have* been using it, since our war strategists have come up with ways to replicate the machines that produce it. But we're faced with a problem."

Kotori wanted to say *Only one problem?* The way the king used "southern art" as a euphemism for "magic" disturbed him deeply. Magic was dangerous and the southern people of Peria had done away with it for a reason.

"We find that we lack sufficient people who possess resistance to the art. Using the devices we have made requires a certain amount of training, and this is not helped by the fact that once training is completed our men take ill and often die as a result of exposure."

Those were no pretty or heroic deaths either. Kotori had heard that the magic art peeled off one's skin and turned one's insides to liquid. Sufferers would shit out their own blood until there was none left. Which, he had also heard, didn't take very long at all.

"The people who possess resistance are all Perian, but we don't have many of those here. As an added problem, many of the Perian women are infertile. Some Aranian families, though, have southern blood and a measure of resistance. I need a Mother, a young woman with pale skin, raven-dark hair and blue eyes to give me sons who can wield these weapons. Her fortune must be good, because we cannot have any Mothers who are untrustworthy or who will create discontent in the house."

"Yes, Your Majesty. Or, no. No discontent, certainly."

"The women has to be attractive to the eye, young and with a certain . . . inner strength. I tire of young girls taken off the register, too keen to spread their legs. The act of taking a woman is much more pleasurable when one feels it has been earned. I've had trouble getting excited about women who are too meek."

"I understand, Your Majesty." Although Kotori understood

nothing of the sort. He had never been permitted a woman, and found the whole business mystifying.

"Good. Then go and find me a woman."

"But if you permit me a question?"

"Go ahead."

"If I find this woman—"

"When, not if."

"*When* I find this woman, and she becomes with child and the child is born and it is a boy, it will be a long time before he is old enough to wield the weapons."

"Yes."

"And meanwhile our men can't use the machines."

"Yes." And then he said nothing for a while, staring out the window at the Mother's Veil.

"But . . . if the woman you want is not on the register, then how will I find her?"

"Use your imagination. Use the stars." The king turned fully to the window, indicating that the audience was over.

Kotori bowed, although the king wasn't watching—he would probably see him in the reflection in the glass nevertheless—and retreated to the door.

"And, astrologer?"

"Yes, Your Majesty."

"The next time you tell one of the birthing Mothers' fortunes, I want the prediction to be correct."

"Yes, certainly, Your Majesty."

Kotori scurried out of the room into the cool corridor and made his way to his room in the astrology tower.

Mother's Breath, what was he going to do? A *southern* woman, no less, and she had to be pretty, and her fortune had to be good. She had to be fertile and had to birth a child within a year, and then that child had to be a son who could then wield the new weapons—wait. The king wasn't really going to stop testing those weapons while this child grew up, wasn't he?

Kotori knew that Denori was dealing with army projects in Curack. Probably the weapons had been made there. For years, Denori had sent units of men into the coastal mountains, and for years those men had failed to return.

What if . . . no, that would be too ridiculous for words.

But just what if the king encouraged his prominent sons to work with these weapons, knowing that the icefire would kill them? The king had said, on occasion, that the son who would take over from him would be smart, because Chevakians and Perians were smart. What if the king wanted Kotori to play some sort of role in eliminating the men the king didn't like? The king was always very reserved about praising his sons or handing out favours to any of them. What if he liked none of them and wanted Kotori's help to start a new generation before he grew too old. What if the king *wanted* Nayek, Sferuk and Denori to die?

In which case the favourable casting for Nayek's trip had been correct: his death was good news for the king.

No, no, that was too terrible for words.

It was suddenly too hot in his room. He was *not* good at controlling his panic. He strode around his desk, from one side to the other and back again, not knowing what to do, hugging himself. His mind whirled. One misstep and he'd be lashed. He'd be put in the dungeons. He'd be tortured. No matter that he was the king's brother. The king had plenty of brothers.

Down in the courtyard of the citadel, the bell rang for dinner, but Kotori's stomach was so knotted up that if he ate anything it would come straight back out.

He rolled out the star map on the table to check what he might have missed. The Great Wanderer was high in the sky, and no tail riders had crossed its path for at least a month. That was the mark of a time of good news. The Little Red Wanderer that hung over the horizon in the early morning had just completed its backwards loop and was moving in the right direction again. That was also a good sign.

Kotori recast the prediction he had made on the morning of Prince Nayek's departure, when the prince had come to this very room and had sat on the chair over there while Kotori spread the star map on the desk.

The stones landed on the Wagon, the Lion and the Horse. The coins landed on the Horse, the Ship and the Ox. He checked his notes, and it was almost an exact copy of the original casting and contained no omens of bad luck, let alone predictors of the prince's death.

He pulled *The Star Signs and Their Meaning* by Sizek off the shelf, but even when he leafed through the entire book, he found nothing about interference of certain common predictors, or anything that might detract from the good omens in the casting.

He had not missed anything. He was not crazy or inept.

There were only two, deeply disturbing, inconceivable conclusions he could draw: one was that the king wanted his sons to die. The other, equally terrible option, was that the stars had lied to him.

Why?

Why him?

How was that even possible?

Then again, he could never forget what he'd read in that Chevakian book:

The reading of stars, as practiced by the Aranians, falls in the domain of lore, not science. We asked several reputable and well-known fortunetellers to predict the outcomes of various events: elections, harvests, games, not just once, but over a period of many years. They repeatedly failed to predict the same, correct, outcome, and there were even some cases where none of the astrologers predicted the events as they unfolded. This proves that astrology and fortunetelling have no place in a rational world where decisions are based on fact.

Kotori would have put a paragraph like that aside as Chevakian nonsense, except he knew of the study. He'd been one of the astrologers they'd contacted, and he knew many of the others, all reputable people whose judgement he would trust. Chevakian concepts of the correctness of predictions were strange. They had asked about dates that events would happen, like "What weather will we have on the first day of summer?" They did not ask, "Will the weather be favourable for this event that is taking place?" Favourable weather was different from the exact type of weather. Favourable depended on who was asking it. He and other astrologers made predictions for people who specifically asked because they wanted to know. He did not make predictions about the weather alone or for people who didn't care. Chevakians did not understand that difference.

But what if the Chevakians were right and the predictions were all nonsense?

He was no longer able to face the books on the shelves which were laughing at him, with the knowledge hidden on the pages, if only he could find where the right kind of knowledge was. He needed guidance, but since he was now the most senior astrologer in the citadel, where could he get it?

Most of his old tutors were dead, and the ones who weren't had moved into the country, except maybe one, whom he might visit tomorrow.

He got up from his chair.

It was so dark out there already, and now that he thought of it, the citadel had gone very quiet.

No wonder, because it was well past midnight.

Kotori went to open the window to let fresh air into the room. But when he opened the latch and let warm evening air into the room, he noticed shimmering green and purple bands in the sky. They took up part of the southern sky as well as the north.

This was what they called *Mother's Breath*.

He'd seen it once before, when he travelled on a ship along the coast north of Curack. He had never seen it, or heard of people seeing it, as far north as Kadrish.

The Mother was angry with him.

TIRED AS HE WAS, Kotori woke before dawn and could not go back to sleep. He got up when the faintest glimmer of daylight coloured the sky. The Mother's Breath had faded during the night; when daylight strengthened, you would not be able to see it.

Rather than wait for breakfast to be served in the dining hall, he went down to the kitchen to avoid the inevitable commentary about his second failure in a single week.

The cook gave him a bowl of steaming porridge and a pot of honey. Kotori sat in the kitchen to eat it, doing his best not to notice any pitiful glances from the kitchen staff walking on their way in and out of the dining room.

He burned his mouth not once, but twice, in his haste to get out of that awkward situation. His colleagues would miss him at breakfast. They would ask around and they would talk. They would gossip about what the king might have said to him and whether he might have been sent on a special project, one from which he was not supposed to return.

After he finished, he went back to his room and got dressed to go out.

The day would be warm and sunny and already there was a lot of activity in the forecourt of the citadel. A truck had just arrived with supplies for the kitchens, and big beefy men were carrying sacks of flour and beans into the cellar doors.

Kotori walked past them and down the stairs that intersected the zigzag drive leading up to the citadel.

It was a lot busier in the streets of the main city than in the quiet passages of the citadel. Today was fruit market day, and a number of small-time merchants were walking down the street while pushing carts with produce. The usual crowd of shoppers was out as well, and people going on business errands or children on their way to school.

Kotori wove between these people. They stared at his astrologer's gown with the gold stars of the Horse on his chest. They bowed and greeted him or moved out of his way. The reverence felt unearned today. Maybe he should not have worn the gown. But then people would have recognised him and wondered why he wasn't wearing it.

There was no winning this game of reputation and rumour.

He went deep into the old city, the maze of alleys and stairways and passages narrow enough to let through only one man at a time. It was expensive to live here, because there was no access for carts and each item had to be carried in by hand, and some even needed to be disassembled before they could be taken to the stately houses mostly occupied by esteemed citizens and institutions.

One such was the Revalidation house, a rambling establishment consisting of a couple of adjacent buildings joined up into a luxurious care house, or hospice, for the very old and very sick.

Kotori came here often, to provide the souls of the dying a star path to walk on so that they could leave their earthly body in peace and join the Mother.

But today, he had not come for that.

The corner room at the top floor of the building had been the home to the same elderly resident for many years. Regular bouts of pneumonia and the relentless advance of age had so far failed to make an impression on the man. He had no family who wished to visit him, and there were rumours that the dedicated and tireless nurses in the facility would sometimes wish him dead.

His name was Sizek, and he was known all over the world, or at least the civilised world, and the world of people who cared about astrology.

Once, he had been an esteemed lecturer at the citadel, although by all accounts he had not been quite normal even then. That was before Kotori's time—a true indication of how old Sizek was—and the man had been forgotten, was talked about as if he was already dead.

Maybe that brilliant part of him already was dead, Kotori thought, standing in the doorway to the room. Light streamed in through the window. From his standing position, Kotori could see over the roof of the next house to where the sunlight sparkled on the ocean, but the man seated hunched over in the chair near the open balcony doors would not be able to see that.

Despite his advance age, there was nothing wrong with Sizek's ears. He turned to the door and gave Kotori a withering stare that was his normal way of greeting people.

Kotori advanced into the room and bowed a few steps back from the chair.

"Good morning, esteemed Sizek."

The man snorted. A young woman scurried in holding a tray with a teapot and cups and put them on the table. Another tray with pieces of flatbread was already there.

Sizek pursed his lips. "No cakes?"

"The medic says you are not allowed sweet things."

"You know what you can tell the medic to do with these pieces of cardboard?"

"Yes, I know." She bowed and left.

Kotori heard that conversation every single time he visited.

Sizek reached out a veined, spider-like hand and snatched a piece of the bread off the plate. He chewed with his molars, not having any front teeth left.

"What are you doing here on a day as beautiful as this?"

"I'm asking for advice."

"Advice, eh? Advice is only given on rainy days."

"On rainy days we can't study the stars."

"Hmmm. True. You're smart. I like smart people. What's your name?"

"Kotori." They always went through this introduction as well.

Sizek's grey eyes, disturbingly sharp despite his age, studied him. The only hair Sizek had left were some whiskers on the sides of his head, which the nurses would shave off if he let them come close enough.

"Hmmm." His near-toothless mouth worked. "Hmmm. Those princes appoint younger astrologers every day."

Kotori was forty-two, a true brother of the king, although that no longer mattered, since the race for succession had passed to the younger generation.

"So what sort of advice *do* you want?" He picked up another piece of the bread.

"If I make a casting and the omens are all good: the Horse, the Wagon and the Ox, and there are no star tails crossing the sky, is there any interference that will turn a positive reading into a negative one?"

"Hmmm?" Sizek's rubbery lips moved while his gums mashed up the bread. "Interference, eh?" He swallowed. "Interference is a thing brought to us by the Chevakians who want to discredit our predictions. There is no such thing as interference."

"Well, whatever it is, I made two castings for the same man. Both predicted good omens. The man in question is now dead."

"Maybe that is your good omen."

"Him being dead is a good thing? This is Prince Nayek we're talking about."

"Hmmm. Yes."

Kotori felt deeply chilled inside. He didn't know what he would do if it came out that the king wanted his sons dead.

Sizek didn't say anything for a discomfitingly long time.

Kotori prompted, "So, do you think there is any factor that I could have missed when I cast his fortune?"

"Those were the star signs that you cast: the Horse, the Wagon and the Ox?"

"And the Ship and the Lion."

"The Lion is good."

"I know, but the prince is still dead."

"Hmmm. Is there anything else you noticed? No star trails?"

"No. I saw, just last night, that the sky shimmers with Mother's Breath, but that shouldn't have any effect on the stars."

"Shouldn't? Boy, where are your wits?"

"Mother's Breath has an influence on predictions?"

Sizek spread his hands. "The Mother has an influence on everything and her breath no less so."

"Where does Mother's Breath come from, and why are we seeing it here, in Kadrish?"

"Because people have angered the Mother and she is upset."

"What can we do?"

He laughed. "She must be appeased."

"How?"

"I heard Selwa had retired. Give the king a new mother. Find him what he wants. And when you've finished your castings, send some souls to meet the Mother. She must be fed. I hear the prince is bringing lots of prisoners into the country. Select the strongest and healthiest men and give them to her."

Kotori didn't want to do that. He had rarely sent men to meet the Mother. The thought of sending brave men younger than himself to a certain death sickened him. "Is that necessary? The Mother's Breath has broken my ability to make correct castings. She is not going to be appeased by the sacrifice of another life. It has to be me receiving the punishment."

Sizek waved a gnarled, veined hand. "You worry too much about these men. They will gladly go. They'll have their names on the wall."

Kotori shuddered at the thought of that wall, now several blocks long, with long lists of names carved into the smooth stone. All those men had died for Arania, and what had been achieved? King Orik was playing with icefire weapons and the men had no resistance to icefire.

Whichever way his mind turned, he found additional worrying signs. He wrapped up the visit with some talk about the weather and left the hospice.

The only thing left for him to do was to punish himself in hopes of exorcising the demons or bad magic that had taken hold of his art, and cleansing it in the face of his worst failure. He must cleanse himself so that he could resume his work with confidence tomorrow.

That was something too embarrassing to admit to doing, and a process no one must see, so he must do it after dark.

He forced himself through the activities of the day, cringing his way through castings for a couple of rich women, knowing that his words were worth less than the air he breathed to say them.

His eyes were gritty with the lack of sleep, yet he was too awake to rest.

He went down to dinner in the big dining hall and sat at the end of a long table. All around him, people talked and laughed.

Kotori was never terribly good at making small talk. A lingering fear from his time in the children's house was that people would use his offhand comments against him. If he admitted to reading Chevakian texts because of his profession, they might call him a heretic.

After dinner, he took tea in his rooms, as usual; but the book on his knees remained open at the same page all evening.

Finally, when the sounds in the citadel dimmed and the lights went out one by one—except the one down in the courtyard—he deemed that it was time.

With a grave feeling in his heart, he went to the citadel's gymnasium, where he extracted a whip from the cupboard.

He went to his room to exchange his astrologer's attire for plain clothes, and then set off for the cellar of the building through the empty stone corridors where most of the lights had already burned out.

The dungeon in the citadel was a dark place at the best of times. It had no windows and knew no day and night. The air was always humid with a faint tang of wet stone. Kotori entered the large vaulted room. His footsteps sounded hollow on the stone ground that bore the paths of ages of footsteps. Fat squat pillars supported the roof. They stood in perfect rows, so you could never see the whole space in one glance.

In days gone past, it had housed food stores and wine; it had been a torture chamber; and, more recently, it had been a hospital.

Its current use—as morgue—occupied only a small corner of the space. Most of the scrubbed and oiled wooden tables were empty, but a cloth covered a table nearest the door and this was where Kotori went.

He pulled the cloth off to reveal the body underneath.

It had been brought into the citadel two days ago after a journey by cart from the mountains. In death, Prince Nayek was as terrifying as he was in life.

His skin had gone pale and grey, but the red tattoos on his shaven skull had lost none of their angry red colour. The prince wore only his leather trousers. The spy reported to have killed him had stabbed him in the side, and the military camp medic had bandaged the wound, but to no avail. Since the prince had died, no one had bothered to change that bandage; and it was pretty disgusting, with yellowish fluid having leaked through the fabric.

It was custom that a body was buried when the cheeks started falling in, but Prince Nayek's face looked as fresh as it had when he'd been killed by the enemy spy.

Kotori took off his shirt and knelt at the table.

"Master and Mother, see your servant. Master and Mother, accept my repentance."

He dug into his bag and found the leather handle with leather straps. A metal stud was at the end of each of those straps. He rose, the whip's handle in his right hand. He pulled the handle outwards so that the leather straps slid through his left hand until the cold metal studs chilled his palm.

"Master and Mother, witness my humiliation."

He let the echo of his voice die out before he braced himself and lashed the whip across his back. The straps flew with a whistling of air. Leather slapped against his skin. The metal studs bit into his shoulder blades.

He bit his tongue. By the Mother, that hurt.

He lashed out again.

Slap.

He could not restrain a moan.

Fire spread out over his back.

He hit again. Slap—groan—slap—groan—slap.

Tears rolled down his cheeks.

The pain was his punishment. It freed him from guilt and doubt. When the Mother saw his suffering, she would absolve him. As a man, lacking the agony from birth pains, this was the only way he could be punished. He thought of Selwa and how she had screamed while giving birth to the misshapen child. He thought of the blood on the floor—

From somewhere in the dungeon came a sound.

Kotori froze, clamping his shivering jaws. He held his breath, looking around the room. If someone was here, they would see his ultimate embarrassment. He put down the whip and put his shirt back on—ow. The dark shadows of the pillar played tricks on his eyes. It could have been a rat or one of the citadel's many cats.

But it was not.

The sound came again, this time clearly identifiable as a gargling breath.

Prince Nayek had opened his eyes.

CHAPTER 12

*I*T WAS DARK and misty when Isandor caught the tram back to the inner city. The streets along the way lay mostly deserted, and the street lamps showed up as ghostly pools of light. Occasionally he noticed a glimmer of icefire that crept over a wall or a fence or window frame. If the sky was clear—and that happened so infrequently now—he might be able to see skylights. He hadn't seen any for so long.

The carriage with its steamed-up windows was full of people going home from having had dinner in the many cheap eating houses in the Harbour District. He received many greetings, bows and curtsies. It got quite busy on the short ride, but no one took the seat next to him. People kept their distance in a what-is-he-doing-here kind of way. Some kept casting him glances as if they weren't sure whether they recognised him properly or if he was merely someone who *looked* like the Queen's brother.

The atmosphere was so disturbingly *normal.* He had become used to seeing Chevakian and Aranian faces on the street. They were on the tram. They worked in shops. They even worked in the palace. They were good, peaceful people who wanted to look after their families and had no interest in the divide between their countries.

But that veneer of civility hid a dark truth, if Marek was to be believed. And Isandor *did* believe Marek, because the young man had said many things that made a lot of sense, and he said them as someone having fled Arania.

Before today, Isandor would have said that Arania didn't have that much influence in the City of Glass. A good number of Aranians were in the city, but he had never seen or heard of evidence that they were organised in some way. If anything, Aranians tended to eschew anything that looked like an organisation. They went about their daily lives.

But this business with the register disturbed him deeply. Who was collecting this information and what were they going to do with it?

And then all these Aranian princes. It was true that Marek had said jokingly that every second Aranian man was a prince, but even so, what were they all doing here?

A major Aranian prince like Nayek wouldn't have come to the City of Glass for minor business. He would be here to meet influential people. If he hadn't come for the royal family—and he certainly appeared not to have—then it was logical that he would have come for the only other group of people in the City of Glass who were in a position of influence: the nobles. But as far as Isandor understood, the nobles were friends with Prince Denori, Nayek's rival. Had Nayek been killed while trying to steal some of these people away from his half-brother?

Were these Aranians after the nobles because of their business influence or was there more to it . . . like old artefacts from King Caldor, and icefire?

By the skylights. Why hadn't Tamerane said more or given him some hints that would allow him to help her? Her parents' problems were not her problems.

The more Isandor thought about it, during the short tram ride up the hill in the stuffy cabin where it smelled like wet bear, the more bad situations came to mind. The Knight Council might have made a stupendous mistake in ignoring the noble families and writing them off as quaint and old-fashioned.

And it was not as if no one had warned him. Rider Barton had expressed reservations about his involvement with Tamerane. On the other hand, if he hadn't been involved with Tamerane, he might not have known all this—incomplete as his knowledge was. It was bad, bad news, but definitely worth knowing.

By the skylights, he only wanted to marry her.

He got off the tram and walked the last bit up the hill. Golden light glowed from shop windows and hundreds of rooms in the towers that stood on either side of the street. It was getting cold. He hadn't brought his gloves, and he had to stick his hands in his pockets and pull the collar up to his cloak. His breath steamed in the chill air.

From the corner of his eyes, he could see little glimmers of icefire that crept over the corners of buildings, like tiny flames winking into existence and then winking out. He remembered how icefire used to do that all the time. Sometimes you could see big golden strands lighting up the air and disappearing into the ground. He hadn't seen these phenomena for years and there was no denying that it was getting worse.

Whatever kind of place Curack was, he needed to get Tamerane out of there. The thought of Tamerane in a garrison town at the beck and call of some sleazy prince made him sick for all sorts of reasons.

But how would he do it? He'd have to ask Rider Barton, who would probably try to dissuade him from doing anything, and that might be the wisest option. But Isandor was through with being wise and sensible. If he didn't do anything, he would never see Tamerane again, and there was no way he was going to let that happen. Besides, these people were up to something.

Short of bringing an entire army—which he didn't have—what else could he do on Aranian soil? It would have to be a really quick action, but he'd first need to know precisely where she was. He should use Knight patrols and hunters, people on birds who could quickly get in and out without being seen.

How far north was Curack? Did they have long nights that he could use to come in close under cover? Eagles didn't like to fly at night, but some could be persuaded to do it for short distances.

He needed his own eagle, because he wasn't going to let other people rescue Tamerane on his behalf. He wanted to see her face when he came for her. She was his, alone.

If any of her captors used icefire, he could deal with it. He would get his great-grandfather's old books from storage and read up on how to deflect and manipulate it. He'd sworn never to do that, but for Tamerane, he would do it.

Once again, people were manipulating icefire, and this time, they were Aranian.

Ledor was part of it. The prince might be part of it, either Nayek or Denori. The two Knight patrols he'd sent got in its way. Something must be happening in the mountains. There was a second Heart, somewhere in Arania, and Aranians had worked out how to use it. Because—

Then it hit him.

—Because someone from the City of Glass had shown them old literature from the time of King Caldor which described how to use icefire. And who else would that someone be other than people who *possessed* that old literature, on their ancient bookshelves?

Growing up in the Outer City, he would rummage through old second hand bric-a-brac stands for those old books. But in the days of King Caldor, the nobles had all the power. Most of them would have hung onto their artefacts in the same way they hung onto their money, their ancient houses and their beautiful furniture. Family heirlooms. They would not sell the *really important* books to second-hand flea market vendors. If they'd needed to sell items—and they might well have, seeing as few of the nobles had much in the way of income—they would only sell it to people who would pay serious money for it.

People who were hungry for revenge and power.

Aranians, who were still sore over the crushing defeat dealt to them by the Chevakian army many years ago.

Stupid. How could they all have been so stupid?

Isandor turned into the palace gates and walked up the path with the clipped trees on either side.

Warm light radiated from the building, filtered in different colours depending on the hue of the glass plates.

A guard in the post under the overhang of the entrance called out, "Is that you, Your Majesty?"

"Yes, I'm back. Call Rider Barton and Rider Carro. I need to speak to them."

"Oh, I'm so relieved. There was a bit of a panic inside when you didn't turn up for the meeting."

"I had to go out and, unfortunately, it took longer than I anticipated."

"The queen will be pleased."

Pleased however, was not how Isandor would describe the look on Jevaithi's face when he came into the foyer and she ran out of the corridor on the other side. She slid to a halt, her cheeks red, her hair flying. Her eyes blazed with anger.

That one look, that brief moment before her expression became more neutral, cemented Isandor's decision: he'd had enough of her antics.

She cried out, "Where were you? We were all looking for you. The Knight Council meeting was on."

"I know." A number of guards and other palace staff had also come into the foyer.

"Then why weren't you there? You left me to deal with all of it, and I didn't have your notes, and we wasted so much time trying to guess what you would have said—"

"Come." He took her arm with perhaps a bit more force than necessary.

She let out a squeak. "What are you doing?"

"We need to talk." He dragged her down the corridor to their private sitting room. It would never do to have an argument in front of the staff, and heaven knew they'd had too many of those already.

They entered the room. He let go of her arm and shut the door.

She rubbed her upper arm. "I don't see why this is necessary."

"Listen, Jevaithi, I am not the Knight Council. I don't even have an official position with the Knight Council. That position, as I recall, belongs to the queen."

She stared at him, opened her mouth and closed it again. "What is that supposed to mean?"

"You know very well what that means."

"No, I don't. You're being stupid."

"Excuse me? *I* am being stupid? Out of the two of us, who is stubbornly holding onto something that obviously isn't working? Who of us is trying to blackmail friends into doing things they don't want?"

"What are you talking about?"

Did she really not get it, or was she being deliberately dense? He breathed deeply, nostrils flaring, and said in a strained voice, "I am *angry* that you blackmailed Rider Barton into sharing your bed even though you *know* that he is not inclined that way. I am *angry* that you force us into a state of perpetual mourning for children that should never have happened. I am *angry* that you expect me to do all the work and make all the decisions. No, I'm wrong about that. I am not angry that I do the work. I happen to like rebuilding the city, but I'm angry that you assume that because I'm doing this, you have some sort of ownership of me and my relationships."

Jevaithi's mouth fell open. "What sort of relationships? Who with?"

"I don't *have* any relationships. That's why. Because you act like you own me."

"What?" Her face was genuinely puzzled. "When have I done anything of the sort?"

"When I told you about the breeder I'm seeing to solve the problem of succession, you acted like a jilted lover. You're my *sister* and I'm trying very hard to love you, but by the skylights, you're making it hard for me."

She stared at him with wide eyes, like a Legless Lion pup whose life depended on the hunter who had cornered it and had to make the decision to kill it or let it live. "I am doing my duty. That's all I know how to do." Her voice trembled.

Isandor closed his eyes. This always happened. He would raise some issues, and then she'd start crying, and he'd feel sorry for her. And he genuinely *did* feel sorry for her. It wasn't her fault that she'd grown up like this.

A tear ran over her cheek. "I can't help that what I do is never good enough for you. And you're not the only one who has no relationships."

He spread his hands. She always managed to turn around the conversation and make it about herself, too. "Then what? If you want a lover, find yourself one. You have my permission."

"Stop being stupid. You're making a fool of me."

Isandor stared at her, pushing down his anger. At times like these, he so badly wanted to take her by the shoulders and shake her until whatever was wrong in her brain fell into place and she started behaving like a normal, responsible person. But she was the queen and he couldn't do that and, anyway, it probably wouldn't change anything.

"Listen, Jevaithi. I've had enough. Here we are, in times of danger. I've discovered that a lot of knowledge gathered by the old king was passed to Arania, by the noble families that we've been ignoring. They've *helped* Arania produce icefire weapons. Arania is angry with Chevakia and probably with us, too. Two patrols have vanished in the mountains. I'm through with sitting in meetings and doing nothing. You can handle the meetings. I'm going to find out what is going on. I'm going to rescue *my* lover from their clutches."

He turned around, went to the door and made it out of the room. He crossed the hallway to his private room.

Of course Jevaithi came in after him. "Since when do you have a lover?"

"I'll introduce you when I came back with her."

He opened the wardrobe and found his warm tunics, his under-coat and tall boots.

"What are you doing?"

"I told you: I'm leaving. I'll be taking an elite patrol and I'm going to the eyrie to prepare for a few days. My skills are rusty." It would be wise to say nothing about icefire training.

"How long is this for?"

"A few days, maybe more. I don't know. I'll be back."

"But we have another Knight Council tomorrow. Today, I already had to adjourn decisions about unrest in the Harbour District."

"Jevaithi . . ." *One day you're going to have to talk about something other than getting an heir.* "You are capable of making those decisions. Use your brain. Make the fucking decisions."

He never used bad language in her presence, and her expression turned shocked.

"But where are you going? What is going on?"

"I don't know yet, but it's a hell of a lot more important than anything going on in the palace, so if you'll excuse me—"

"No, I won't excuse you. I have the right to know what is going on."

"I'll give a brief to Rider Barton. I understand you know him well."

He could see the anger in her face a moment before she lashed out, before he threw up his hand and grabbed the wrist of the hand about to slap him in the face.

For a moment, they faced each other, Jevaithi red-faced and furious, Isandor meeting her eyes with the most threatening warning expression he could manage.

"Don't." He let go of her hand. "Don't. Ever. Do that to me."

She crossed her arms over her chest. Her cheeks were bright red. "You were making fun of me. Do you think I like sleeping with all these different men?"

"Jevaithi, I don't care. I used to care, but since you fail to understand that you're doing this to yourself, I can't help you anymore. That is the mistake you make. We, you and I and the council, can solve everything. If you would just let us help you."

"And that is *your* mistake, because there are certain things that only I can solve."

And they were back to the old subject. Isandor picked up his cloak. "Whatever. Suit yourself. I'm done. Look after the council while I'm away." He turned at the door. "Oh, and before I forget: when I come back, I intend to get married."

He went into the corridor and shut the door behind him.

Of course he heard the door open before he had gone far.

Jevaithi called out, "What's this about? You can't just leave me alone to deal with everything here."

"Yes, I can. I think I should have done it earlier. Have fun." He strode down the corridor.

"Hey! Listen to me. I'm the queen. You have to listen to me." She pulled his shirt.

"And I am the king, and no one fucking listens to me. Behave yourself and stop making a scene. I'm telling you this once, and won't say it again. Whatever we've been talking about in the council is about to be overshadowed by something big and evil. I'll give a brief to Rider Barton and he can put his knowledge with my fears and raise it with the council."

"Who is this woman you want to marry?"

"Tamerane of House Mara. She is smart, intelligent, she deserves better than she gets. I love her."

"Don't you love me?" The tears were running over her face.

Thousands of responses came to him. In his anger, he really wanted to say *Not if you behave like this* or *Why don't you just grow up?* But he knew how she'd gotten this way, and there was no point in saying those things.

He wanted to say, *Why don't you start doing the job you're supposed to?* but that would just lead to more crying about her inability to conceive, and that was not the job he was talking about at all.

He wanted to say, *Why don't you just go to your room and stop pretending that you can run a country,* but that was unfair, because she did try, occasionally, and when she did, she actually did quite a decent job.

Or he could say, *Can you just tell me what's wrong, then we can deal with it and move on,* but he'd tried that so many times already, and it only led to incoherent sobbing.

He didn't think Jevaithi herself knew what she wanted or what could make it better. So he just blew out a breath to calm himself. "I do love you, but by the skylights, I suggest you start doing something very soon that justifies my love."

And then he strode out of the hall, trying to cut himself off from Jevaithi's wails. It was very hard to keep going, not to turn around and console her and tell her it was all right. Things were *not* all right, and the only one who could fix it was Jevaithi herself.

As he went around the corner someone caught up with him and put a hand on his shoulder.

"Well played." It was Rider Barton.

"I don't know about that. I don't know anymore."

"It was necessary."

They walked silently for a while.

"How much did you hear?" Isandor asked.

"Most of it."

"I'm sorry about mentioning you."

"It was fair. Everyone knows where I stand." And then a sharp look. "Are you serious about marrying Tamerane?"

"I have never been more serious about anything in my life. If you're worried about her family, I think it is time we engaged the nobles to find out what's been going on with them. I don't think we'll like what we'll find. Come."

He led Rider Barton into his study, where he related all the things he had learned from Marek, and other things he suspected based on Marek's story. Rider Barton's expression went dark.

He blew out a breath and shook his head. "A business register? Just for the sake of tracing their wayward citizens? What for?"

"Aranians have strange, controlling ways. Poorer Aranians go into binding contracts with rich and influential people. It seems that the influential people, when they want more influence, go through all the promises made to them and reel when in. While I'm gone, you should see this young Aranian man and let him point out to you suspicious activity linked to Arania."

"Certainly. Any insights he can help with would be great. We'll get right into it."

"I'm going to need a bird," Isandor continued. "I want one that's not too nervous about flying in the dark."

"You can use mine."

"No, I want a dedicated bird, possibly a young one. I've got a few days to break it in. I want to plan this well. I also want a couple of good Knights to come with me. I leave in three days. Give me a good team."

Rider Barton nodded and put a hand on Isandor's shoulder. He had never been a man of many words, but it had been a long time since Isandor had seen that expression of satisfaction on his face.

It was time for action.

CHAPTER 13

THE EAGLE THAT Zaina had used to escape the Aranian camp did not know the way home. Either that or it wasn't interested, or it wanted to stay close to its mistress, Rider Jeito, who was still captured in the Aranian camp.

It went up to a cave high in steep the side of the mountain peak where it was cold and draughty, and from where, when the weather was clear, Zaina could see the camp.

She was dependent on the bird's stubborn resolve. It would sometimes let her ride its back and soar over the valley, but would always return to this dratted cave. Zaina didn't know how to control the bird and it, and the two other birds who had come with the expedition, were probably secretly laughing at her.

She could not climb down the mountainside. Oh, she had tried, but the rock face was just too steep and she had none of the gear that mountaineers would use: ropes and hooks and picks.

The eagle did bring food, of a kind: dead deer or goats or smaller birds that it had caught. Of course there was no way to make a fire in the cave, so Zaina picked at the carcasses with her dagger and cut out the bits that didn't look too obnoxious and ate them raw.

Of course she had plenty of rocks to sharpen her dagger, and even more time to contemplate what to do with it once she finally got off this fucking mountain. She could see the lowest tip of the glacier where they had been captured. She could see the camp in the valley beyond. A lot of convoys had arrived since she had been sitting here, and she tried to imagine the things that might be going on at the camp.

Prince Nayek dead. They would have found him soon after she fled. There would have been an uproar.

The prince was unlikely to be in direct command of any of the units—because the major princes usually hired armies, but didn't fight in them—but the commanders and the generals would have been trying to please his every wish in the hope that he would look favourably upon them once he was on the throne. Since that was not going to happen, they would be looking for the next person to support, whoever that was. Maybe more than one person. There would be a major reshuffling.

The other members of the expedition would have been questioned about her—this was where it got hairy. The thought of those honest people suffering for what she had done, and for her argument with the prince, made her feel sick. Daro was a good kid and Rider Tomason an honest man who didn't deserve any mistreatment. And then Rider Jeito . . . Zaina didn't even want to think about it. She admired Rider Jeito, even daydreamed about her. But no matter how strong she was—and her speed and strength were legendary—she remained a slight woman on the wrong side of middle age. There was no way she could fend off a couple of soldiers, once a commander had decided that she should be tortured or raped.

"You're just punishing me for that, aren't you?" she said to the eagle. "You're going to let me sit here and watch."

Although if the eagle were punishing her, it would have left her behind in the cave to die.

The bird sat down on the uneven ground. Zaina had spread out the blanket that covered the saddle and the leather pouch so that she didn't have to sit on the cold rock. She dragged the blanket over and sat down, leaning against the eagle's side. They spent a lot of time like this, dozing. The eagle's body was warm.

Often, it would tuck its head under its wings, but today it remained alert. It looked down at the camp, where its master suffered in captivity, its orange eyes constantly moving.

The other two birds had not shown as much loyalty. Zaina spotted them flying high over the mountain every now and then, but they didn't come near, not even when she whistled.

"You want me to free her, don't you? You want me to pay for the bad thing I did and turn it around."

The eagle glanced at her briefly.

"If only I had some help, because I can't do this alone. I'm not stupid enough to think that I can fight armed men by myself with no training. If only you'd take me somewhere I could find help. You could take me back to the City of Glass. I could warn the king."

The eagle, of course, said nothing. It was a very one-sided conversation.

The early night settled over the land. From her high perch, Zaina watched the sky flash with fire and slowly fade to red, purple and blue.

The green and purple bands of skylights came out. Stars twinkled in the sky.

Zaina dozed off, knowing that she would have to do something to get off that mountain.

SHE WOKE up when it was still dark. The eagle's muscles were tense. It was wide awake, making soft, alarmed noises. Zaina sat up.

Something in the valley *glowed*. It was hard to see what, because a layer of mist usually settled over the valley floor and this night was no exception.

A couple of points of light glowed under the mist, giving the valley an eerie appearance.

Whatever was that?

There was a small sound from further down the mountain.

Zaina crawled to the edge of the cave and looked down. The two other eagles sat on a rocky outcrop, sitting with their heads down, tails up and wings slightly spread as if about to take off. Zaina had not seen the birds for a few days and she filled with hope that someone might have noticed them and followed them, especially since one of them still wore its harness.

Zaina whistled.

One of the birds did take off. It glided on huge wings underneath the mouth of the cave. Jeito's bird chattered at it. The other eagle replied with a long cry. It sounded muffled and mellow in the dark.

"Come here," Zaina called.

The eagle glided out of sight. Oh, damn, where did it go? She leaned forward. The moon was a very small speck above the horizon, soon to vanish completely, and it gave no light. The two bands of the sky path glowed weakly, and the skylights still shimmered green.

All of a sudden, a gust of wind made her hair fly. Zaina gasped and retreated into the cave, when great wings flapped above her and the other eagle landed on the ledge next to her. Jeito's eagle rose, arched its neck and hissed at it, feathers raised. The other eagle hissed back before both birds smoothed their feathers and went back to looking at the mist.

Zaina pulled the leather saddle and pouch from underneath the blanket. She approached the new eagle. It let her come close enough to grab the leather straps of the harness. She attached the saddle to it and hung on because the saddle was all she had. She inserted the blanket and stepped into the stirrup and swung herself onto the bird's back.

It was a little awkward, but the bird didn't move.

"Come on," Zaina said, patting the feathered neck. How did one get the bird to fly? Jeito would just climb on her bird and then it would take off.

The bird started preening its feathers.

"Come on, go." She pulled the reins, tapped the bird's flanks with her heels, but all that got her was a disdainful look with those penetrating orange eyes.

"Yes, I have no idea what I'm doing. Come on, help me, if you want me to save your masters."

Jeito's bird arched its neck and uttered its stuttering cry, and the bird she was sitting on replied by putting its head down and angling its beak up and replying with a cry of its own. It leaned forward when it did this, and Zaina had to hang onto the metal hoop that stuck out at the top of the saddle—

And then all of a sudden both birds launched into the air.

Whoa! Zaina almost fell off.

But—maybe—would this be the time she finally got out of that fucking cave?

Any other place would do. Even the trucks. She could gather all the remaining fuel into one vehicle and drive it back across the mountains.

But the third eagle joined them, and then the eagles flew in the other direction, over the valley that held the Aranian military camp. Another field of tents had been added in a valley that had been out of Zaina's view from the cave. She spotted a couple of trucks, too, and wagons. A light dusting of snow coated the ground. The snow was wet, which made the wheel tracks show up as dark stripes. It also showed up the footsteps of a group of men who were still gathered on the hillside on the far side of the camp.

The eagles kept quite high, and the fluffy clouds that hung over the valley occasionally obscured her view, making it hard to see. What was going on at that gathering, what was on the wagons that they had brought and what were those men doing in that field of snow? By the look of things, they'd set up a fence surrounding a square piece of land. Most men were standing outside the fence, but a few were inside it. Zaina could see no animals. The men faced each other as if in a fighting ring, but they were too far away from each other to be engaged in a fight. A square object, about knee high, stood in the snow between them. It was a very strange setup.

Her eagle flapped its wings and turned sharply.

For a brief, dreadful moment, Zaina was afraid that it was going to take her back to the cave, but it flew past the mountain into the next valley.

Zaina didn't know how to steer the eagle, and she could only hope that it was going somewhere useful. The other eagle, Jeito's bird, that had imprisoned her in the cave was flying above her, with its feet tucked up against its belly. It gave a shrill stuttering cry and turned to the south.

Zaina's eagle followed, flying into the perpetually dusk-tinged air; the third trailed behind.

They came over the glacier, and Zaina could see the broken truck still on its side in the stony creek bed. The other trucks were all gone. Well, damn it. Just as well she had no control over this bird, or she would have sent it back here and would have been stuck worse than she had been in the cave.

The land rose up underneath her. She could see the tracks made by her expedition when they had come down the glacier. She could see the saddle of the pass, where they had camped. And beyond that, she could see glimpses of the southern plain.

The eagles flew in that direction.

IT WAS EXTREMELY cold at the height where the eagles flew. Zaina had decent clothes, but her hands grew so cold even inside the gloves that she had to wriggle her fingers. Her feet were cold, too.

The birds had cleared the last of the mountains and now flew over the southern plain. She knew that the ocean was to her right, because she recognised the huge bank of clouds that always hung over the water, billowing high into the dusky sky. In Arania, they called it the Mother's Veil.

Ahead, the usual mist rose from the bay, obscuring the location of the City of Glass, but she thought she could see a faint glow of lights in the mist.

She was in luck. The eagles were going to the City of Glass, to the eyrie hopefully, and soon, because if she had to hang on any longer, she was going to fall off.

The birds glided low over the city.

She could see the little rocky island just outside the mouth of the harbour and longed for the comfort of her workshop—except it wouldn't be comfortable, because Aranians would be looking for her, especially the men who worked for Nayek. Her old room wouldn't be safe, either, and besides, the inn owner had probably given it to someone else. She would barely be able to look king Isandor in the eyes after having led Nayek to the expedition, leading to the capture of the rest of the team. Some of the team members would be dead. By now, they might all be dead, and for what?

But she could do nothing to steer the eagle. It was flying inexorably towards the moment that she would have to tell her story—and be punished? That was how things went in Arania. The bringers of bad news got the blame.

The eagles knew the way home. They circled around, flew low over the bay and turned back to the tall buildings of the city, heading for the open side of the top floor of the eyrie.

Zaina's eagle landed first. The force on Zaina and her ice-cold hands was so great that she lost her grip on the top of the saddle. She slid over the eagle's wing onto the hard floor.

Ouch.

A young Knight came rushing forward. "Are you all right?"

Ow, ow. Her hands hurt from hitting the ground because they were so cold. Her legs were so numb that she couldn't get up.

A lot of other people were rushing into the stable. The air was filled with voices.

"Look, that one is Jeito's bird."

"Where is Jeito?"

"Who is this woman?"

"Where is the expedition?"

"Where is Rider Tomason?"

They all crowded around.

A Senior Knight helped Zaina to her feet. "Who are you? You're Aranian?"

"I was on the expedition. I'm a mechanic and I was with them to look after the engines. I managed to escape." Zaina's face was numb from the cold and she could barely talk. "They've been captured. I don't know if they're still in the camp. The eagle . . . it roosted for a couple of days in a cave and I couldn't see anything." She was embarrassed that her voice wavered. She had been certain that she'd die out there.

"Calm down. Let's go to the palace. I'll call the council."

Zaina's mind was going *Nooooo*, but she knew she couldn't hide the truth, a truth that included her history with Nayek that could no longer remain untold.

Two Knights helped her out of the stable room and down the stairs into the official part of the eyrie, where the senior Knights had their offices and where the dorms were.

A female Knight gave Zaina some generic non-uniform clothes, because hers had been frozen and were now soaked through. The outfit consisted of men's clothes, and the trouser legs were much too long for the only pair of men's pants that fit her butt. She needed to stuff them in the top of her boots before she could walk, and that was just as well, because the boots were also much too big. She was finally starting to get sensation in her feet again.

The Knights accompanied her into the palace garden. The queen's coach stood under the overhang of the entrance. No one was in the foyer or the hallway. A lot of doors were open, showing rooms without people.

"It's quiet here," Zaina said.

"Half the council has gone. The king has gone."

"Gone? Where to?" Her heart jumped. She didn't think that anyone else in the Knight Council would give her the time to explain before they accused her of treachery—in which they might be right.

Well, that was not to be helped now.

The people gathered in the Council Chamber constituted not even half the Knight Council members. Many seats around the table were empty. Where was everyone? Where was the king?

Jevaithi sat at the head of the table.

Zaina met her eyes and bowed.

"Do sit down," Jevaithi said. Her voice sounded prim.

Zaina did, conscious of her too-big clothes.

She knew little of the queen. People in the street spoke of her in a reverent way, as if she were a goddess. Her appearance was waif-like, dreamy, with flaxen hair and elfin-like blue eyes. She was pretty, in a delicate and fragile way.

Jevaithi started the meeting with an introduction. "We are here today because one member of our latest expedition has returned. She brought with her the three eagles that were with the group. I have invited her here to share her story."

A man in the corner was busily scribbling.

She asked Zaina to state who she was and why she had gone on the expedition. When speaking about her Aranian background, Zaina could hardly look the Knights in the eye. They would all think that she was a spy and was the cause of the expedition's misfortune. And she hadn't even known the true purpose of the mission.

Jevaithi then asked Zaina to tell her story: how they had left and where they had run into trouble. Zaina couldn't bring herself to mention the night-time visit by Nayek and that she had known that they'd been followed from that point onwards. She had assumed that Nayek was there for her, but looking back, she wondered why she had been so short-sighted, and while she spoke, she felt increasingly bad about having kept quiet. In truth, she should have told Isandor about Nayek when she first came to the meeting in this very room. That would have prevented a lot of trouble.

The Knights listened to her story, but their faces remained eerily unemotional.

The Supreme Rider Barton, however, seemed to understand at least part of what was going on.

He asked, "You *did* know this prince, didn't you?"

"I was fleeing the Mothers' register." And she explained having seen her own mother suffer in General Pakori's house, why she had left and how she had tried to have her name removed, and that she had thought Nayek was after her.

Through all of this, Jevaithi sat staring at her.

"I don't know why he came after me in particular, I honestly don't know. I agreed to come on the expedition so that I could get away from him, because I didn't think he would follow me."

"But he did?" Jevaithi asked, her voice too gentle for the situation.

Zaina nodded, looking down. "He told me to sabotage the expedition."

A Knight said, "The expedition was unmasked because of your connection to him."

Zaina cringed. "Maybe, but I didn't know that I knew that I was going, and though he might have asked me, I swear I never sabotaged anything." She put her hand on her chest and looked up. She would not be accused of that type of treachery.

Another one of the Knights, a stern, humourless-looking man, said, "Why didn't you tell Rider Tomason about him?"

Zaina looked down. "I couldn't do anything else. He was going to take me in his mothers' house and he kept talking about how he was going to . . . defile me. You don't understand the determination of these men. They cannot stand the thought of ever being outrun by a woman. The faster you run, the more they chase you."

"Was that why you killed him?" asked another knight, quite young.

Jevaithi put her hand flat on the table. "I think that is quite enough. Stop questioning her like this. Can't you see that she is no traitor?"

Silence.

The cheeks of the Knight who had asked the question coloured, and he bowed his head to the queen.

Zaina said, "No, I'll answer the question. Have you ever killed someone?"

His cheeks went even darker. Zaina guessed he probably hadn't. She guessed he was not a regular member of the council, because he did seem rather young.

"You don't think when someone is chasing you." All the uncomfortable memories from Nayek's attempts to pin her down made her shudder. "Anything that you do when your life is in danger comes from inside." She put a fist on her chest. "You can try to reason about it afterwards, but at the time, your mind is running wild, and the only thing you want is for that disgusting man who is much bigger than you to stop trying to shove his dick up your backside. Yes, I shoved the knife between his ribs, but it was between me and him, and the matter is finished now. It had nothing to do with the rest of the group."

In the uncomfortable silence that followed, she met Jevaithi's eyes, and the queen's expression was strangely intense. Chilling, even.

Rider Barton cleared his throat. "Well, as far as I can see, they've attacked a peaceful group outside their borders. If that is not an act of hostility, I don't know what is."

"And that camp," said another Knight. "That's not formally on Aranian soil either."

Council members around the table shook their heads.

They went into a lengthy discussion about the location of the border, and both the Perian and Aranian views on this. Apparently, most of the mountains were under dispute.

Zaina was nodding off during that conversation. She hadn't realised just how cold she'd been while on the back of that eagle, and the warmth flooding her body made her very sleepy.

Next, the council discussed what their response should be. Rider Barton declared that they were forced to respond, even if only to counter the act of hostility towards a non-hostile team. They'd send a substantial retrieval mission.

The stern man, who Zaina learned was Rider Carro, pleaded for caution. "We already have a rescue mission out. We cannot risk engaging Aranian troops on two fronts, because we don't have enough people in case either of the two missions lead to further conflict."

"We cannot let this go unanswered," Rider Barton said, and more Knights agreed with him than wanted to remain cautious.

"Do you think it is necessary to engage them in conflict?" Jevaithi said.

Rider Barton said, "Whether they want to have a conflict or not, that's up to them. We'll go to that camp and demand the release of our people."

This was the consensus of the meeting, and all the Knights left with tasks to fulfil to make it happen, with promises for more meetings about who would go and what they would take.

People were getting up and leaving the room.

A hand of panic clamped around Zaina's heart. What would she do? She could go back to the workshop, but had no idea how many of Prince Nayek's supporters would wait outside for her. She had nowhere to stay. She could ask Marek, but he had issues of his own that she would do well not to get involved in. She didn't entirely trust her other friend Eshtar not to make a move at her if she went to him for help. She was so tired, and had no possessions, and only a little money left. She hadn't received all of her payment for the expedition, but asking for the money while things had gone so badly wrong partially through her fault seemed a little crass.

When the Council members got up, she couldn't bring herself to leave the room with them. It was warm here. She could go to sleep on the floor. She'd do any kind of work for a roof over her head.

"Zaina, that's your name, isn't it?" The voice was gentle and female.

Zaina turned around. It was Jevaithi. No one else was left in the room, save for the maid at the door.

Zaina had noticed on previous occasions how Jevaithi managed to make looking uncomfortable into an art form, how she always held her left hand under something, like a draped shawl or vest as if she was super-conscious about her fake hand.

Zaina pushed herself up. "I'll go now, Your Majesty. I'm sorry for nodding off. I was just . . . really tired."

"Are you all right? Do you have somewhere to go?"

Zaina breathed out heavily. "I have nothing left. All my possessions were in that truck." Including her mirror, the only thing she had that belonged to her mother. *That* hit her like a kick in the gut. She desperately fought her tears.

"We've got plenty of clothes that you are free to have."

"Thank you."

Jevaithi let a small silence lapse. "Do you have any people to take care of you here? Or do you want to go back home?"

"No! I refuse to call that place home." The response had burst out of her before she'd had the chance to consider if it was appropriate to be said in front of the queen. Her cheeks went hot. "I'm sorry . . . I didn't . . ."

"It's all right. I understand why you wouldn't want to go back. But do you have any people to help you here?"

Jevaithi's voice was so gentle that Zaina almost burst out in tears again. Here she was, all about prickles and crawling away in a hole for self-defence, and this beautiful creature actually wanted to help her. She should be ashamed of her behaviour.

When Zaina said nothing, Jevaithi continued in her gentle voice, "That story you told about the Mothers' Register and how you were chased by the prince disturbed me deeply."

"I'm sorry. I didn't intend to upset you."

Jevaithi would have grown up in a protective home, with good education, so far removed from Zaina's reality that she'd even doubt most of Zaina's story, and Zaina was getting quite uncomfortable with the queen's close attention. It wouldn't be long before she said something stupid. "Look, I'll find a place. I'll be fine." Not that she knew where. She couldn't go back to the workshop, because Nayek's friends would be waiting for her. She didn't want to set them on Jadan as well.

"No, you won't. You can stay in the palace and do jobs for us. My *brother* won't mind."

Whoa, some issue there. Was that why the king wasn't here? He didn't seem that petty to her.

Jevaithi signalled to a servant at the door. The woman came forward.

"Give Zaina a bed in the servants' quarters. Give her warm clothes and tell the guards to assign her to the grounds teams."

The woman bowed. "Certainly, Your Majesty."

Zaina rose, was about to turn to the door, and hesitated between wanting to run and wanting to throw herself at Jevaithi's feet. "Thank you so much, Your Majesty. I haven't deserved any of this, but I appreciate it. I will work hard."

"Jevaithi."

Zaina frowned.

"Call me Jevaithi."

CHAPTER 14

$\mathcal{L}$ANA CRAWLED BETWEEN the seats, but the man had already seen her.

He called out to his mates and two of them came into the bus, too.

"Go away, leave me alone!" Lana crawled away from them, but she already sat with her back against the side of the bus, and there was nowhere to go.

He grabbed for her foot, and she kicked at him; but he managed to get hold of her ankle and pulled her across the wet and disgusting floor.

"Hey, let go of me. Viki! Viki! Help!"

The man laughed. He grabbed her arm.

Lana tried to hit and kick him, but he dragged her forward. Her shin painfully connected with one of the benches in the bus.

"Viki, Viki, help!"

He dumped her on the front seat, took off his jacket and wound it around her head. Then he tied the sleeves around her upper arms so that she couldn't move.

"Help! Help!"

It was dark inside the jacket and stank of stale sweat.

The man picked her up again, slung her over his shoulder and went down the steps of the bus. Lana's backside hit the side of the door.

She called out, "Viki! Help! Put me down!"

The man walked across the muddy ground. Lana heard nothing except the squelching of his footsteps, no voices, no sign of where Viki and the bus driver were. She thought of the yell and the splash she'd heard. She felt sick. What had happened to Viki? Where was this brute taking her?

After a while, she heard other male voices. The man who carried her spoke. Lana didn't recognise any of the words. They were definitely Aranians.

He slung her onto something wet and smelly and warm—the back of a horse, judging by the way it moved under her weight. The man tied a rope around her feet, and then climbed up into the saddle that poked into her side.

The men chatted and laughed while the horse plodded up and down hills and occasionally through water. Lana's backside was getting very wet with the rain.

In the dark jacket, Lana had no idea where they were going. She pleaded for the men to take it off, but that only earned her a slap across the buttocks and a few words in Aranian.

They rode and rode.

Where were they going? What were they going to do with her? Lana had heard all kinds of terrible things about what Aranians did with women. A feeling of panic gripped her.

What about Viki and the driver? They would see the tracks from the horses and come after her, right?

How could she warn her father? Why had she been so stupid to want to travel anyway?

After quite a while, the horse slowed and stopped. New male voices joined the ones she already knew. The man behind her slid from the saddle and pulled Lana to her feet. Her legs were stiff from hanging over the back of the horse and she almost lost her balance. A rough hand steadied her and then pulled the jacket off her head. The chill air made her shiver.

She was in a shed with an open side in which stood three trucks. Crates and boxes were stacked up along the back wall.

Through the open side of the shed, and in between two trucks, she could see rain-sodden stubble fields. The air was misty and grey. It was probably late afternoon.

The man guided her to one of the trucks, a freight vehicle with its back door open. He pushed her up the little ladder that led into the cargo hold.

Inside, a good dozen brown-skinned wide-eyed faces turned to her, all of them belonging to women. None of them spoke, but they shuffled aside for her so that she could sit on the hard floor of the truck bed.

Lana sat, drawing her knees up to her chest, shivering. She was wet and cold and filthy. All her belongings had remained behind in the bus, including the spyglass that she had spent so much money on, and her notebook.

She met the eyes of the woman next to her. She was very young, a girl almost, and had a head full of bushy hair. An older woman next to her looked like her mother.

The Aranian shouted at them from the back of the truck. He climbed on the canopy and let down the cloth that covered the opening. It got very dark in the cargo hold.

"Is it still raining?" asked one of the women in a low voice. She was perhaps the same age as Lana, and had a narrow face, sharp eyes and long curly hair that she wore in a ponytail at the back of her head.

"I think so," Lana said. "I had a jacket over my head so I couldn't see very well."

The man yelled and banged against the side of the truck. The mother cringed and put an arm around her daughter. Another woman pressed her finger against her lips. The young woman who had replied to Lana scowled.

Lana's eyes had become used to the low light. She studied the other members of the group. They appeared to be local women, dark-skinned and dark-eyed, most of them in peasant dress. They were probably from Watya or Tamyra or surrounding hamlets.

A group of men talked outside, and after some discussion they got into the vehicle. Someone opened the boiler and tossed in some wood or firebricks. Lana could hear the chunks hitting the side of the boiler.

The door shut, and the man walked past the side of the truck. He climbed into the cabin, talking to the men who were already there.

The truck started moving.

"Where are we going?" Lana asked, judging it safe to talk.

"Nowhere good," said the mother.

"We're being sold as whores," said the woman with curly hair.

The mother scolded, "Shhh, Nashi. Hold your tongue. You frighten my little girl."

The young girl was crying.

Nashi lifted her chin. "I can hold my tongue, but that doesn't change what they do to women in Arania."

"Shhh."

"What shhh? It's been happening all along. They only take the women. No one says anything about it. No one raises it with the district representative because, oh, the Aranians will stop coming and might stop buying our stuff." She sniffed and pulled her knees up to her chest. "But all right, be my guest and pretend you never knew. We'll all be whores anyway."

Lana shivered. From what she had heard, Nashi might well be right. "What about the men who were on the bus with me?"

"If you didn't see them at the farm back there, they are probably dead. And to be honest, that's probably the best way for them to be."

A woman at the back said, "Oh, shut your mouth, you scarecrow."

Viki dead? Panic gripped Lana's heart. Up until now, this had felt like a situation that, given a chance, she could escape from. "You're saying that's been happening all along. Since when?"

"Months." Nashi's eyes burned.

Another woman added, "At least since the dry."

"Why didn't you tell anyone?"

"And who should we tell? Who do you think will listen to us, some dumb villagers from the north? We even had trouble getting people in Watya to help us with putting in the water tanks. Do you think any rich councilman with guards would listen to poor dumb villagers and would be willing to bother the people in Tiverius about it?" She gave Lana a fierce look. "You don't look from here. Where are you from?"

"I'm a meteorology student." Lana was going to tell her who she was and where she came from, but she shuddered at the thought that the information would find its way into the hands of their captors. She knew about the way Aranians treated their women. If they knew who she was, they'd make a deal out of it and maybe even blackmail the doga and her father.

"A student? Are you, now? Who has time to be a student?"

"I am, and I'm studying for the benefit of everyone." Lana was getting a bit annoyed with Nashi's tone. "I was here with my tutor. We were on the way to Ysherra. To *help* the district."

Nashi snorted. She looped her arms around her knees. "Well. That would be a first."

"You really have a chip on your shoulder, right?"

A woman behind Nashi said in a soft voice, "Be quiet now. She is from Tiverius, and she'll get us all into trouble."

"Any more trouble than we're in already?"

Several women called at the same time, "Nashi!"

She scowled, and rested her chin on her knees. And because she clearly could not stay silent, she asked, "Who ever goes *to* Ysherra anyway?"

"We were going to see another student in Ysherra. His name is Javes."

A woman at the back said, "The lad I've seen with Pashtan?"

"I guess so." She didn't know what Javes' tutor's name had been. "He was studying dust devils."

All the women laughed.

Nashi said, "No one is dumb enough to study dust devils. If you come close enough to study one, you die."

"Do you know what they are?"

"They're evil magic, that's what they are."

"Shhh," another woman said.

Nashi whirled around. "What now? Are you afraid that she can't handle the thought of *magic?* There's been magic in these parts for many years—"

"Be quiet, Nashi. These people are not like us, and who knows what they'll tell their bosses and who will come here to lecture us about it, or cut off our water."

The woman Nashi eyed Lana. "I think she looks smart enough to be able to handle the truth."

After that, no one said anything for a while. The truck had gathered speed, although the road was very bumpy. Lana's backside hurt, but there was not enough room in the back of the truck to stretch her legs.

The women were mostly silent, staring numbly into the void, but

Lana learned a few of their names. She also learned that Nashi came from the town of Tamyra, on the road from Watya to Ysherra. Tamyra was, in Nashi's words, an oasis, because it lay on the bank of one of the main feeder rivers for the Aramys River, and this river was seldom dry. Nashi's mother grew medicinal herbs, which Nashi's sister sold at market; Nashi herself paid visits to people too old or sick to come to market to consult her sister about which herbs buy. "Sometimes, the people are in so much pain, they ask me for poison to end their lives. And if they're too frail to recover and have ugly growths all over their bodies and going into their mouths and they can't eat, I give the poison and watch them go to sleep. Sometimes, people ask me, usually rich people, if I can give the poison to someone else, and I tell them if they ask me again, I'll tell the district representative. Sometimes mothers want herbs for their little ones, and I give the children tea or potions, or I'll rub ointment on rashes or cuts that have gone bad. Sometimes mothers want the calming tea when they're giving birth, and I might help the midwife, or help the mother when she can't afford a midwife."

She was, in short, a medico in absence of a formal education. That made Lana re-think her opinion of Nashi. This was harsh country, a long way from Tiverius.

Lana said, "Whatever is going to happen to us, we must help each other and stay together. Does anyone speak Aranian? I speak it a little bit."

Several women said that they knew a few words.

Some didn't know any at all. Lana suspected that out of the group, her knowledge was probably the best, which didn't bode well.

They talked about where they were being taken for a bit, but no one knew what was going to happen, only that previous women who'd been taken away had never come back. And yes, they did think that the district's representative, Shara, who was a supporter of her father's, knew about it, but nothing had been done. Lana felt ashamed on behalf of her father.

The women were all from the poorer section of Watya, apart from the vocal and outspoken Nashi who was from Tamyra, and two other women from Ysherra, the mother and daughter, who had apparently travelled to Watya to meet a prospective husband for the daughter.

Most had been captured in the evening or morning when walking along the river flat with their washing.

For a few days they had been staying in the farmhouse where Lana had joined them. The soldiers had treated them fairly and had never attempted to lay a finger on them.

"That's not necessarily good, though," Nashi said. "These are lowly soldiers. They need to get permission from a superior to have a woman—"

"Or many women," said someone else.

"Yes. The rich men have huge harems. The point is that the soldiers won't be allowed to touch us. They keep us as gifts for the rich men. They love exotic brown girls."

"You really have a very bleak view of our future," said the mother from Ysherra.

"If you have heard any other experiences, you're welcome to share them."

"I have heard that the rich Aranians get foreign women to work in their kitchens and laundries. If you behave and don't create too much trouble, then they give you enough freedom so that you can escape."

Nashi gave her a sharp look. "What is that supposed to mean?"

"Keep your mouth shut and do as they say. Stop talking back to them all the time. You're just creating trouble for us. I have a husband and I want to go back to him."

A few others nodded.

Nashi rolled her eyes.

Most of the women just said nothing and stared ahead. Nashi dug out a little pouch from under her clothes. She shook some of the content—shiny black seeds—onto her hand and put them in a handkerchief which she pulled from a pocket. She rolled it into a little parcel, which she gave to Lana.

"What is it?" Lana took the bundle of cloth, feeling the smoothness of the seeds inside.

"Eat one every three days. Make sure you bite it through before you swallow. It tastes absolutely terrible, but these will keep you from becoming with child. If you're lucky, for long enough for the rich man to lose interest. That's when you can escape."

"Thank you." Lana tucked the little bundle in between her chest and her breast wrap.

※

THE TRUCK STOPPED to refuel and fill up with water. The men opened the back and let everyone out for a short period. They made sure that each woman was kept separated from the others and they yelled every time the women tried to make conversation. Lana really needed to pee and was annoyed that a soldier came with her and watched, but he made no attempt to bother her.

The second time the truck stopped, it was dark. Lana had been dozing, leaning against the woman next to her, whose head rested on Lana's shoulder.

When the truck screeched to a halt, everyone woke up.

A soldier opened the flap and opened the tailgate which let sharp cold air enter the stuffy cabin. He yelled something in Aranian, which she presumed to mean, "Get out."

Lana accepted his hand to jump from the cabin. Considering that they had kidnapped a truck full of women, these men treated them surprisingly well, which was an odd thing to say about kidnappers. Lana agreed with Nashi that this might not be good news.

The truck stood in the middle of a village, under a single street-lamp that stood in the square.

They were at a small farming village where all the houses except the one across the street were dark. A man stood with his hands in his pockets in the light of the lamp, watching the women. His breath steamed in the light.

The road was paved and the building style of the houses—with cement and thick walls of natural stone—looked really unfamiliar. At the edge of the pool of light were some trees, pines like you would sometimes see in Tiverius.

"Where are we?" Lana asked Nashi. It was the first time that Lana had seen Nashi standing up and, wow, she was really tall.

"In Arania. See the crest on the building there?"

Lana had noticed it, above the door: a shield with two horses facing each other and crossed lances underneath. "What does it mean?"

"That's one of the royal estates."

"Have you been here before?" It surprised Lana how well informed and well travelled Nashi was.

"Here, no, but I've been in Arania. Some of the herbs you can't get in Watya, and I travel to the markets at Tereya or Beishan to buy what we need."

"And no one stopped you at the border and wanted to see papers?"

Nashi gave Lana a blank look. "Who is supposed to stop us?"

"Isn't there a border post with guards?"

"I've never heard of such a thing. Would they really be standing there for the one or two people wanting to cross every day?"

"But that means Aranians can easily come into Chevakia as well."

"Of course they do. They've done this for years. They're usually merchants and often they sell something; or they buy things, like the metal artefacts that the windwalkers bring us. They're very keen on those."

"What sort of artefacts?"

"You haven't heard about them?" Her tone was almost condescending.

"No. I might be stupid in your eyes because I'm from the big city and I obviously don't know anything, but I could mention more than a hundred things that you've never heard of."

Nashi gave Lana a sharp look. Lana guessed Nashi was probably not used to anyone talking back to her. She could just imagine Nashi being a very, very bossy healer, dictating how and why people were stupid about the way they did things. But Nashi wasn't stupid either. If anything, she was bossy because she was smart. So her expression softened. "It's about really ancient things that windwalkers find in the desert. The men all go stupid over these things. Supposedly women are not supposed to touch them because that's bad luck. They're artefacts from a time long ago and I bet they don't want women involved because they're pretty things and the men are afraid the women might like to keep them or decorate our houses with them."

"What do you mean from long ago?"

"Really long ago, before the start of time."

Lana remembered her younger days when she had travelled with her parents to her mother's place of birth. She remembered seeing the tall buildings and the grotesque molten glass sculptures, and the walls and floors from fake stone. She remembered her mother's foster son, king Isandor, talking about the old civilisation that had built the towers. "Are these artefacts as old as the ones in the City of Glass?"

She gave Lana a blank look, but was clearly too proud to admit that she had no idea where the City of Glass was.

They went back into the truck, where Lana told Nashi about the City of Glass, and Nashi asked hundreds of questions and other women kept making shushing noises. But who could sleep anyway? Eventually, Nashi fell quiet.

Lana still couldn't sleep. She worried about her parents and about Javes and Viki. If Ysherra was dead, then Javes would be dead, too. If she hadn't seen Viki before being taken off the bus, he was probably dead, too. She just hadn't seen what happened to him because she had the jacket over her head.

She kept seeing a guard delivering a letter to her father saying that she was missing, probably dead, and that he would have to take that news to her mother. She would die of heartbreak, and then her father would be alone.

The tears streamed over her cheeks, but she did her best to make sure the other women didn't hear her cry.

THIN STRIPS of light peeped through the gaps between the canvas on the truck canopy when they stopped again. This time, when the engine stopped, there was a lot more noise outside.

The man came around and let down the flap at the back, giving Lana a view of a courtyard with blocky sandstone buildings on one side. There was a lot of activity on the paved yard, with people walking in and out of the building.

It was a station, she realised when the distinctive chug-chug of a train echoed over the courtyard.

The men helped all the women out and handed each of the women a small parcel wrapped in brown paper. Lana got hers. It was heavy and a bit moist and, when she ripped the paper, contained two slices of heavy, black bread with a white substance in between.

It smelled really strange, but Lana ate it anyway. The white stuff was some kind of cheese, but it was sweet. The bread stuck to the inside of her mouth, which made it hard to swallow. The other women complained about it on the way into the station.

A lot of men were on the platform, obviously having arrived in the train and on their way to somewhere. They all had identical packs, but didn't wear a uniform. Yet they looked like soldiers. They acted like soldiers.

The women, including Lana, were made to climb into a carriage and sit on the hard wooden benches. The carriage contained a number of other women who had obviously arrived in different groups. They were all Aranian and looked at the group of Chevakian women with suspicion.

Lana could understand little of what people were saying, and she was disappointed that she could only read a few signs. Obviously astrological Aranian was not the same as the conversational modern language. And here she was thinking her Aranian was passable.

No one in the carriage spoke much while they waited for the train to start moving. The guards patrolled the door, casting searching looks over the passengers—the vast majority of them women—in the carriage. Some women still filed in, giving the guards a chip or piece of card at the door. Some even appeared to have packed. Others knew each other, nodding and smiling to other women as they found seats.

Very strange.

"They're women who have been requested on the register," Nashi said. "They travel to Kadrish to take up their positions in whatever harems they've been consigned to."

"How do you know all this?"

"What is there to know? Everyone knows this."

"But . . ." Lana raised her hands in frustration. She certainly hadn't known. She didn't think anyone in Tiverius knew this. "Why don't you *do* anything about it? This is slavery."

"These women think it's an honour. Their lives in Kadrish will be better than in their home villages."

"But not ours."

Nashi laughed. "No, not *ours*. But for many women, this isn't so bad."

"Why has no one told Tiverius?"

"We don't *want* to tell Tiverius, because if we're not careful they'll subject us to some silly legislation before they'll do anything about the awful weather, the dust devils, or the trains they've promised for so long."

And of course they still thought that meteorologists controlled the weather. Lana didn't want to go down that path. The guard at the door was already giving them warning glances.

The train started moving with a lot of hissing and clouds of steam.

Lana leaned back in her seat. Her eyes felt gritty with the lack of sleep, but she didn't want to sleep because she didn't trust anyone here and didn't want to miss an opportunity to escape if one arose. The scent of sweat rose from her clothes and the strange breakfast sat heavy in her stomach.

The other Chevakian women seemed similarly numb. Too tired to sleep, too worn out to cry.

The landscape outside was deceptively pretty, with rough peaks of red rock and wooden valleys under what looked like a cloudless day. It was dry, inhospitable terrain, but was pretty from the window of a train.

For most of the morning, the train travelled through this landscape. Occasionally, there would be a little village in a valley, usually with a river and fields of crops and roads.

Twice, the train stopped: once for refuelling in the middle of nowhere, and once in a large town full of blocky stone houses. A large domed building protruded from the roofs. That had to be the temple of the Mother.

After midday, the terrain became flatter and, if Lana's feeling was right, they were going down.

By the end of the afternoon, Lana caught some glimpses of something she had only seen a few times in her life: blue water stretching to the horizon.

The ocean.

Nashi had been right: they were going to Kadrish, which lay on the western coast.

Sure enough, by the time the light was turning golden, the train turned a wide bend, and brought the city into view.

Lana had heard about Kadrish, mainly from her uncle Milleus and her father: that it was a cruel place, that the people were barbaric.

She had not expected it to be pretty.

The soft yellow light hit the gently undulating land that

surrounded the city. The ocean was deep grey with two islands offshore in the distance. A huge bank of clouds hung over the western horizon. Lana had read that this was a permanent feature called the Mother's Veil.

The houses of the city clung to the hillsides, sometimes punctuated with white marble towers with many levels and, in the distance, a hill on which stood a large building with a dome, surrounded by smaller domes.

That had to be the infamous citadel, where the king lived. Her uncle Milleus used to describe it as "a place where fops and whiny assistants walk around in dresses that look like they came out of a child's dress-up box."

But the cluster of buildings, too, looked pretty with its golden domes and many towers. Clearly, Arania valued pretty architecture, unlike the straight and blocky buildings in Tiverius.

From the train window, she could see into alleys and yards of the city. The streets were tidy, the houses adorned with coloured mosaics in patterns of flowers. There were little temples and bushes full of dark pink flowers that hung over white-painted walls.

People wore colourful gowns and jewellery, and adornments in their hair.

The train slowed and slid into a large hall where it came to a hissing stop.

In between the clouds of steam, Lana could see a lot of people on the platform.

The Aranian guards in the carriage were yelling at the women. Something about guards and being presentable. The Aranian women gathered their bags.

Lana had nothing to collect. Her suitcase still lay in the luggage compartment of the bus that stood in a flooded creek in Chevakia.

The first of the women filed out of the carriage, and Lana followed down the little steps and onto the tiled platform. Strangely, she worried about how people would see her: tired, filthy and smelly.

There were a lot of soldiers on the platform, carrying bags with sturdy shoes dangling from the side and rolled-up sleeping mats on top. At a shout from a superior, they made a path for the women to walk across. Some of the men even bowed.

Next to Lana, Nashi snorted. "They worship women as vessels for their seed to grow."

Lana touched the little parcel of seeds in her underclothes.

The air was warm and humid, and had an unfamiliar tang that didn't exactly smell pleasant, but Lana was glad to be out of the train, even if she was extremely tired and worried. The idea of being in a train and having no control over where she was being taken did not sit well with her.

The guards led the group of Chevakian women out of the station into a street where houses towered on both sides. Unlike Tiverius, there were no yards, and all houses were built so that they leaned against each other, with no space in between.

The place was pretty, and the people looked healthy and proud. So different from how she had imagined Kadrish to look.

The guards marched the group into a wider street that led up to the building on the mound that Lana had seen from the train.

"That's the citadel," Nashi said.

Yes, Lana had figured as much, and also that it was where they were going. From close up, the conglomerate of buildings looked even more impressive.

The soldiers led the group through a forbidding gate that gave access to a courtyard and then up a broad stone staircase. By now, most of the women had fallen quiet and were looking around with wide eyes. They came out into an arched foyer, where a thin man with a note pad waited for them.

The soldiers got the women to line up. That man came past, barking, "Name?" at each of the women.

When the woman said her name, real or fake, he would scribble on the pad in Aranian characters, look at the woman in question as if she were an animal for sale, and scribble some more.

Lana gave her name as Mala, and the man spent longer examining her than looking at the others. He separated out a strand of her curly hair, spat in his hand and wet her hair—ew. The curls went straight. Then he dried her hair with a handkerchief and it went curly again. More scribbling ensued. While he moved down the line, he kept looking at her.

Lana knew that she looked very different from the other women. She took after her mother much more than her father. Her hair was almost black, her eyes blue, her skin pale with a smattering of freckles. She looked Perian. Even in Chevakia, that would occasionally get her comments.

The thin man with the notebook had finished with the last of the women. He said something and gestured.

The guards led the group into a corridor.

At the end, warm light radiated from an open door.

The room on the other side was quite large, with an arched ceiling. Soft benches stood scattered around the room. An in-ground bath in one corner was filled with steaming water, and trays of bread and fruit stood on the low tables.

The man with the note pad showed wardrobes with dresses. Two room attendants stood on either side of the door.

The door closed.

"See, I was right," Nashi said. "We're being prettied up for the whore market."

"Just to be clear, I can understand every word you say," said the bath attendant. Her voice sounded prim.

"And I don't care," Nashi retorted to her. "Because I'm right."

"You are given the time to bathe and new clothes so that the astrologer can decide which is the best purpose you can serve."

"How about: none. How about we go back home?"

Lana gave Nashi a sharp look. She didn't think this was the best way to make a favourable impression. Not that she wanted to be seen favourably, but she wanted to be seen as compliant so that she could find her own way to get out of here. It was a long way back to Tiverius, and she wanted to be sure she had the means to make it before she attempted.

The women bathed and changed out of their disgusting clothes into the offerings in the wardrobes. Lana ended up with a light blue gown because, according to the bath attendant, "It accentuates your eyes."

They washed and combed each other's hair and ate from the bread and fruit on the tables.

Nashi didn't like it. She sat in the corner on one of the benches, still in her old smelly clothes.

Lana went to join her.

"You should eat and get changed."

"I'm not wearing any of their clothes or eating any of their food." She spoke loud enough for some of the other women to turn around and stare.

"Shhh. No, I don't feel like it either but, unfortunately, I have to eat, or anything I'll try to do will be useless."

"But look at those women. They get some dresses and they're happy with their lot. They don't care. You're smarter than that. Why are you wearing their clothes?"

Lana let her eyes roam over the women in the room, still in the bath or reclined on the couches, eating. One or two were already asleep. She guessed that for most of them, this was a luxury greater than they would get at home, and that the life they had in Watya was not all that great either.

She didn't think any of them were *happy*, just relieved that they were still alive and exhausted. She turned to Nashi. "Listen: I swear we *will* escape, but we need some time to plan and find out the best method; meanwhile, we can't draw too much attention to ourselves. Eat, get changed and pretend you're one of the others. It's not good to be singled out here."

Nashi blew out a breath through her nostrils and finally went to the bath.

CHAPTER 15

KOTORI STIFLED a scream. He clamped his hands over his mouth and reeled backwards across the stone floor in the cellar. He crashed into one of the stone pillars, and nearly knocked himself out when the back of his head hit the stone.

For a long time, nothing happened, other than that the prince's chest clearly *moved*. He was staring at the ceiling, but his eyes blinked.

Kotori's heart thudded against his ribcage. He alternated between wanting to run and a desire to get help, knowing that if he came to the guards saying that the prince had risen, people would think he was mad.

The prince ran a hand over the disgusting bandage that hid the stab wound in his side. He lifted his head.

This was impossible. The prince was dead. He had to be a ghost, except all Kotori's tutors had insisted that ghosts didn't exist.

The prince opened his mouth, letting out a rasping whisper.

That was it. Kotori backed towards the door. His bad luck was complete. Not only could he no longer read the stars, but his attempt to punish himself brought the dead back to life. He should remove himself from this world before things got any worse.

The rasping voice continued.

Kotori was almost at the door when he realised that the prince was speaking real words.

"Water . . ." he said. "Water, please . . . water."

183

Well. Kotori checked himself.

Ghosts weren't usually thirsty, were they?

"Are you really alive, prince Nayek?" Even to Kotori's own ears, his voice sounded high and nervous.

"Fuck if I know. Give . . . me water."

While trying to get his mind around the question of whether something that didn't exist could or could not be thirsty, Kotori went to the cabinet beside the door. All kinds of macabre implements for the preparation of bodies for embalming, a privilege of the rich, were inside: knives for cutting open dead bodies, bowls for catching blood and intestines, big needles and pig intestine thread for sowing skin back together, long hooks for removing brains from skulls through the dead person's nose.

On one of the shelves, he found an old teacup. The edges were chipped and the inside covered in brown stains, as if it hadn't been washed out in years. Disgusting, but it was the only item that he would consider putting drinking water in, even for a man who was supposed to be dead.

He filled it with the ladle from the reservoir of rainwater in the corner.

Then he wasn't sure how to approach the prince or even how close it was safe for him to come without being contaminated by dark magic, in case the prince was a ghost.

But Nayek could barely lift his head, let alone a cup of water, so Kotori tried to put the cup to his parched and cracked lips—shuddering all the way. A lot of the water missed his mouth and ran along the sides of the prince's neck onto the table. Prince Nayek's tongue looked like a piece of leather, all brown and swollen.

"Fuck you . . . give me the water."

Kotori resorted to pouring a tiny bit of water into the prince's open mouth. That way he didn't have to touch the body.

After a while the prince got tired, and his eyelids started drooping.

Kotori put the cup down. He knew he would have to go upstairs to get help, which he dreaded deeply.

People, particularly the other important princes, had already adjusted to Prince Nayek's death. The ground had shifted; battles for the vacant spot were in full swing.

No one in the citadel would welcome this news, save perhaps for

Selwa, Nayek's mother. The king always called Nayek "a rude bastard", Denori and Sferuk would not appreciate that their battle for the favoured spot had turned out to be futile, and neither of them liked Nayek because "He's too soft on the Chevakians." The king's favouritism had leaned towards Sferuk lately, anyway, even if Nayek had kept the ear of the king's advisers, who were not in favour of another war.

"We've got the weapons that will defeat the motherless bastards," Sferuk would say, even if those weapons would also kill a good number of Aranian men.

Arania had plenty of men.

It did not need any more princes. It definitely didn't need any dead princes to come back to life.

Kotori eyed the giant gutting knife. He could pick it up, take the bandage off the prince's wound, drive the knife into his heart to make sure that Nayek was dead, and stick the bandage back over the evidence. No one would ever know.

But Kotori was too much of a coward to kill a man, certainly one who was defenceless.

He could put the cloth back over Nayek's body and hope someone embalmed him before noticing that he wasn't dead.

No, that wasn't his style either, even if this would cause so much trouble for him and everyone else in the citadel. It might well be that someone would decide to kill Prince Nayek, but at least that person wouldn't be him.

He was a coward.

Kotori heaved a sigh.

His life hung together with bad news.

He picked up his whip and slowly climbed the stairs to the ground floor, his fear and pain fighting him all the way. Even the slightest whisper of his shirt against his back made his skin burn like fire. He was a physically and mentally broken man, and spreading the news about Nayek would only make his situation worse.

While he'd been in the dungeon, the corridors had gone darker as lamps ran out of oil. His footsteps sounded even louder than they had before.

A nurse sat in the emergency room of the citadel's hospice. She gasped and clamped her hand over her mouth when she saw him.

She rose. "Oh, astrologer, what happened—"

"It's not about me—"

"But look at your back."

Kotori glanced at his shoulders. The marks made in his skin by the metal studs on the whip had wept spots of pink-yellow fluid through his shirt.

"It's not about me," Kotori said again, although the warm air from the fire in the big sick room made him dizzy and he felt certain that spewing would be in his future.

"Yes, it is about you. You look like death warmed over. Come with me."

She pulled his arm and guided him into the treatment room.

A heavy scent of disinfectant made him feel even more ill.

"Listen to me," he said—

—And then suddenly he sat on the floor puking stringy bits of slime mixed with yellow globs over his hands, and each time he retched, the pressure set his back on fire.

"Look at you," the nurse berated him.

She helped him to his feet and made him lie face down on a treatment bed. She took a pair of scissors and cut the shirt off his back.

While he lay there, with his face pressed into the mattress, trying very hard not to spew again, he told his story.

The nurse vanished briefly. Kotori could hear her talk to someone else in the hallway, and this was followed by quick footsteps as, he presumed, the other person gathered a team and equipment to fetch Prince Nayek from the cellar.

They arrived when the nurse was putting the finishing touches on his back. "There," she said. "Now keep still and try to sleep for a bit. The salve will soothe the pain and help the wounds to scab over."

But tired as he was, sleep proved impossible. She'd left his back uncovered and even the slightest breeze burned over his skin.

Besides, the nurses had brought Prince Nayek into the room with a lot of noise and many visitors. The King was there. Selwa was there. Every time the prince moved, he broke out in bouts of swearing. He swore a lot in between, too.

Over the course of the rest of the night and very early morning, Kotori learned, by putting together the pieces of conversation, that the supposed spy who had stabbed the prince was a woman off the

Mother's Register, and that the prince had been caught with his pants down.

The king found it funny, and that earned him more swearing.

"I'll kill the fucking bitch," Nayek said.

"Where is she?" the king asked.

"She escaped with one of those fucking birds, but we still got the other members of her spying team as prisoners."

"*Southern* prisoners?" The king's voice turned from amused to interested.

"Yeah, why?"

"Men, women?"

"Mostly men. One woman."

"Have them brought here."

"All right, but . . ."

"Bring them here, and I will lend you some of my guards to protect you in this room."

"What happened to *my* guards?"

"Denori took them."

"What the fuck . . ."

"You were dead for over a week."

"The fuck I wasn't."

"We all thought you were."

"And that means everyone divvies up my fucking stuff, right?"

"Your language does not do you favours, son."

"The fuck it doesn't. See if I fucking care."

The king pursed his lips and rose. "It's up to you, son. If you don't want the guards, I won't send them."

"No, I want them, please. Denori will have my arse if I don't get the time to recover."

"Then I advise you to moderate your language and your ways, son."

Nayek snorted, but said nothing. His father was the king, after all, and he had a big say in who would be his successor. The king left, and Nayek broke out into a string of swearing that did nothing except drive the nurses from the room.

The guards came a bit later. Denori came as well. Kotori could hear him at the door, but the guards wouldn't let him in.

A nurse helped Kotori sit up for breakfast. His back hurt like blazes, but the woman said he'd be allowed to leave later in the day. Nayek was far weaker and would have to stay at least another week. Kotori did his best to ignore the prince, because he felt in no state to answer questions about his castings. He didn't know if the punishment had any effect on his ability to cast properly, but he didn't feel up to testing it. Not here and now, where the prince was so close and Kotori couldn't flee to safety.

A medic came to look at his back later in the morning, and he said that Kotori could go back to his rooms. He also sent a boy to Kotori's quarters to get clothes.

When Kotori returned to his private rooms, a courier had brought a letter. His heart jumped. More trouble?

But it wasn't as bad as could be. The letter was from the Mother's House. Apparently a group of peasant girls had arrived in the citadel and they needed to be assessed for their suitability for various jobs. As far as astrology went, this was a low-risk job. No one would keep too close an eye on the fortunes of a handful of peasant girls.

But going down into the reception wing meant he had to dress in his astrologer's robe, and his back was still very tender. He put on an extra shirt, in case one of the wounds started weeping again, and struggled to don the robe over the top.

Phew, it was hot with all those clothes on, but it was not to be helped. He collected his star map and the box with the stones and went downstairs.

As usual, the selectors had brought the women and girls to the large audience chamber in the reception wing. Sometimes the king would hold minor parties in this room, but mostly it lay vacant. It was not nearly as pretty and opulent as the large chamber on the other side of the citadel. In fact, this room was rather dark and dank, with no windows and only oil lights in a multitude of sconces on the walls. Even in the middle of the day, it was a place of darkness, a place that hid imperfections in the human form in a multitude of confusing shadows. Kotori never understood why he had to judge the perfection or otherwise of women in a room as terrible for the purpose as this, but it was not his place to question.

The guard preceded him into the room, calling out, "All stand for the king's astrologer!"

Kotori entered the room.

The women were all standing—not that he thought that any of them had ever sat down—and the air was sweet with the rose perfume which he'd come to associate with these events. The citadel would provide clothing and would bathe and dress the women, discarding any of the clothing they had worn, like the women's previous identities.

The secretary told him that they had arrived on the train earlier that day, and they came from the far east. Kotori liked that. No families to deal with, no questions from whatever houses they were born in.

They were lined up in two rows on either side of the door. He guessed there were about thirty of them, and they all wore dresses in that distinctive style that marked new arrivals at the citadel. The king's dressmaker ordered them by the hundreds.

He stopped and looked from one to another. They mostly *were* peasant women, or at least looked to be such. None of them were ugly, but they weren't pretty either, with their hands showing the signs of hard work and their faces the signs of sun exposure. They were plain, very plain.

Most of them bowed their heads when Kotori studied them and their appearance. They would be good for working in the kitchens or the laundry, looking after the children or tending to the king's gardens. He didn't see any outstanding beauties in this group, at least not to his right.

"These ones can go downstairs," he said to the guard, and turned to the women on the other side of the door.

Now *they* were different. Several had dark skin and dark eyes. One was strikingly tall. She carried herself in a proud manner and did not bow to him. Her penetrating gaze made him uncomfortable, as if she knew that he was a fraud and had trouble getting his predictions right. As if she could see the welts on his back through the layers of fabric that were starting to make him sweat.

"What is your name?" he asked.

She didn't answer.

"Do not be rude to the king's astrologer," a guard said.

She gave the man a blank look.

"We are Chevakian and most of us don't speak your language," another of the women said in a strong accent.

And she was—oh, wow, a fiery beauty with raven dark hair in a mass of curls and southern blue eyes. And oh, the figure of her!

"What is your name?"

"Mala."

"Do you have a family name?"

"In the City of Glass, we do not have family names."

"The City of Glass?" He turned to the secretary. "Where did these women come from?"

"They were collected in the border area near a town called Watya."

That was still a long way from the City of Glass, but—Mother's Breath, he remembered the king's task: find a southern woman to replace Selwa.

He stepped back and looked her up and down. She was not too short and not too tall, because it would never do to present the king with a woman taller than him. Her hips were broad, her breasts firm. She had a well-defined chin. The king would always tell him that he wanted women with strong chins.

The look in her eyes was clear and intelligent. She might be a little fierce, but that was all the rage lately. The fruit that was the hardest to get tasted the best.

Yes, oh, yes. This woman would please the king.

Kotori went to the table, put down his case and spread the map on the table. The woman looked on with a curious expression. He opened his case and took out the coins and stones.

That penetrating gaze of hers made him nervous. Kotori turned away from her. He must concentrate and do this properly, not let his nerves show so that, again, he would make a fool of himself. He'd punished himself. He was done with that.

If the casting was good, she would move straight into the Mothers' House and the king would be very happy with him. He would have redeemed himself of the terrible miscasting with Selwa, and whatever mess was going on with Nayek.

He breathed deeply—

"What are you doing?"

He let out his breath and turned to her. "I'm trying to concentrate."

"You have a star map. It's from midwinter when the Great Wanderer is high in the sky."

That surprised him. "Are you an astrologer, too?"

"I study astronomy. Astrology is nothing but lore and myth. It is interesting, but we cannot take it seriously."

And yet he was going to use astrology to determine her fate and everything about her stance and the clear look in her eyes showed that she knew this, and despised him deeply for it.

He turned away from her again.

"So, what are the star signs you're looking for and what do they mean? I understand the Wagon means progress and the Horse means good deeds and noble minds, and that the Chicken means hard work. Who decides this and how do you interpret meaning?"

"I cannot tell you in an afternoon. This is why astrology is a life-long study."

"A lifelong habit of making things up. Do you just tell your superiors what they want to hear? What do you do when you get it wrong? Or do you make your predictions so vague that they can't possibly be wrong?"

Kotori kept his back to her, attempting to ignore her, but his heart was hammering and his cheeks burned with embarrassment. Her words stung like scorpion bites. *Do you just tell your superiors what they want to hear?* He saw his hand moving the stones in Selwa's room.

His younger self would have gotten angry. He might even have ordered a guard to slap her, although one did *not* mistreat someone who would be a Mother.

The guards were probably wondering why he hadn't ordered them to slap her, except he knew it would have no effect. This woman would rather die than cower, and she outclassed him in every way. The king would adore her and she would very quickly be an impor-tant woman in the Mothers' House. The fact that she humiliated him did not matter, if she excited the king. The fact that Nayek was still alive might be destabilising for the king's position, and the king needed to display his continued virility.

So he breathed deeply and cast the stones and coins—

—And two of the coins rolled over the map. One tipped on its side and landed in the Eagle. The other rolled around and around and fell on top of the first coin. And the emerald—Mother's Breath—it had landed right on top of the Great Wanderer.

What in the world did all that mean?

The Eagle was a rare star sign, visible only for part of the year low on the southern horizon, and it was usually obscured by the clouds of the Mother's Veil. When it was visible, extreme things happened: the Great Citadel Fire had been during one such period. King Orik had been born during another.

And then a stone landing right on top of a wandering star was unheard of. The last time that had happened, he had cast the ruby on top of the Small Red Wanderer. That was a very bad omen, even if the child that he had made the casting for had been born speedily, without trouble, and was still happily alive.

What was this supposed to mean? The Great Wanderer was the king of the skies. It stood for leadership and strong personalities. He couldn't send the king a woman who had leadership ambitions.

She was looking at him, and he met her eyes, knowing that the stones spoke true. This woman would help the king . . . or she would kill him.

Mother's Breath, was there no end to this nonsense?

Kotori stared at the cloth. Unlike in Selwa's room, many people were watching and he couldn't just shift the stones a little into the next, more convenient, star sign, arguing that they would have fallen there anyway had he not been so nervous and cast them improperly.

"That's a star sign I can't remember," the woman said, leaning sideways so that she could see around him. "What does that mean?"

"When were you born?"

She replied, and her birthday missed the visibility of the Eagle by two days. But a line drawn from the Red Sister—where the Ruby had landed—to the Great Wanderer had been pointing at the Eagle. Was that a good or a bad sign? What about the sapphire, which had landed neatly between signs, and the third coin, which lay inside the Lion?

Those were good signs, weren't they?

Except the sapphire could spell bad news if it was too close to the Horse.

Then he remembered that the Chevakian calendar was a week ahead, and so she *had* been born in the sign of the Eagle.

His head hurt.

Boy oh boy, what was he going to do? The signs were that either she would lead Arania to doom or great glory.

The king would punish him if he found out that he had passed her to him with these omens.

But the king would punish him even more if he saw this woman around the citadel, lusted after her and wondered why Kotori hadn't brought her to him.

Was there *anything* that would go right for him lately?

With trembling hands, he gathered up the stones and put them back in the case. He felt ill, ready to faint. "She was born in the sign of the Eagle. This is an extraordinary occurrence. She comes with me."

CHAPTER 16

THE STRANGE CONVERSATION with the queen played through Zaina's mind several times in the next few days.

The guards allotted her a bed in one of the female dorms, full of kitchen and laundry maids who viewed Zaina with a good deal of suspicion. Zaina, in turn, didn't know what to say to them, and so they settled on keeping out of each other's way.

The Knights were preparing for the expedition, and although most of that work was done at the eyrie, Zaina got called on to do the jobs that the Knights *weren't* doing now that they were preparing for the mission.

This meant maintenance work and caring for the animals.

She looked after horses because the stable hand figured that she, being Aranian, knew those. But the palace stables also contained a handful of big white fluffy dogs and, of course, the famous white bears that pulled the queen's coach at the very back.

At first, the handler wouldn't allow her to go in the pen with them. But then he was called on to take the eagles for fitting the metal spikes that extended their talons, and he needed her to take over, so he introduced her to the bears.

They were scary big, coming up to her chest. They had very good noses, the handler told her, and the two curious bears in the stable demonstrated their noses by sticking them over the top of the fence.

Underneath the white fur, the animals' skins were black, and their noses were black, moveable and wriggly.

Zaina let the animals sniff her hand. Their noses were wet and cold.

"You have to watch them. If they get cranky, they can bite your hand off," the handler said.

"Thanks." Zaina withdrew her hand and wiped bear slobber on her jacket.

"Animals seem to like you, though. I heard the Knights say that you have that gift. No adult eagle would have let you ride it otherwise."

Zaina remembered how Jeito had seemed to subject her to some kind of test, up on the pass. The memory made her miserable. Jeito had been her hero and she didn't know if she could ever make it up to her. Yes, she should have told Rider Tomason about Nayek, but she had been too much of a coward.

The stable hand showed Zaina where the feed was and Zaina spent most of the rest of the day mucking out stables. Towards the end of the day, the stable hand came back. He led the bears out into the yard and tossed Zaina a brush.

To keep the fur clean, the animals needed to be brushed every day.

The bears liked this, and it was a glorious job. Weak sunlight just peeped into the courtyard over the roof of the servants' quarters, brightening the day. The bear leaned into whichever part of its body Zaina was brushing. It angled its head so that she could reach the top of its head. It flicked its ears whenever the brush touched them. Big handfuls of soft fluff came out. A young boy was collecting this—for making felt, apparently.

Zaina had been brushing for a while when she got the feeling that someone was watching her. At first she thought it was one of the guards outside the entrance, but no, it was Jevaithi, a pale face behind a ground floor window.

Zaina tried to keep working, but it was distracting and disturbing. Was Jevaithi keeping an eye on what Zaina was doing because of the past problems she had created? Or was she doing something wrong? But the stable hand would have told her if she were.

The pale face remained behind the window.

"Yeah, she does that a bit," the stable hand said when he noticed Zaina looking at the window.

"Isn't she really busy?"

"When you're the queen, you can be as busy as you want."

True.

Then Zaina asked, "Why does she just sit there staring? She can come out here and talk to us."

The stable hand snorted. "Her dress will get dirty."

Perhaps. Zaina was not familiar with the world of dresses, and she thought the reply was a bit mean-spirited. "It seems kinda . . . lonely in there."

"You said it."

Zaina cast one more glance at the window, but the bear needed to go back inside so she untied the reins and walked it into the stable.

When the servants and other assistants were seated around the long table in the cramped and humid kitchen, Zaina asked them what Jevaithi did during the day.

She got some laughter in response, and a kitchen hand said, "You know she's obsessed with producing an heir, right? That doesn't happen by itself."

That produced more laughter.

"Where does she eat?"

"In her room, usually," the kitchen hand said.

"All by herself?"

"At the moment, yes. Otherwise with her brother. Sometimes they have guests. His foster mother lives in Chevakia. It's been a while since I've seen her, though."

"She's very ill," someone else said.

Zaina thought about the lonely face behind the glass. Why didn't she come out and talk to people? They would like that. She would seem more human to them, and they wouldn't make all these silly jokes.

OVER THE NEXT FEW DAYS, the pace of activity increased. Zaina spoke to Rider Barton twice about the layout of the camp and the surrounding land. He had quite detailed maps of where all the mountains were. The road was drawn in as a solid black line.

"It's badly eroded," Zaina said. "That's why we went down the glacier."

"Except the glacier isn't very stable, especially at the bottom."

True. Going down that way had probably been a bad choice. Zaina wondered what would have happened had Rider Tomason not made that decision. They might have skirted the camp and might have gotten past without being detected by the Aranians.

Nayek would still be alive, chasing her.

Killing Nayek hadn't taken her off the Mothers' register. It probably had only made the remaining princes keener to teach her a lesson.

She shuddered.

He asked her to draw a map showing where the rest of the expedition members were likely to be held.

"Did you see any members of the first expedition?"

"I didn't, but I was taken aside as soon as we came to the camp, because Prince Nayek knew me."

His face remained unemotional, but Zaina was sure that he didn't like her replies. She didn't know much of what went on in the camp, and the other prisoners could have been taken elsewhere for all she knew. Or they could have been killed.

She told him all of what she had observed from the cave in the mountain, including the light that had alarmed the birds.

He nodded. "This is why we're sending only specific Knights. The fact that you can see icefire means that you probably have some resistance to it."

"Was that icefire? There seemed rather a lot of it."

"There used to be a lot more. I'm told that one used to be able to see arcs reaching into the sky at the City of Glass. I can't see it—I belong to the Pirosian clan—but it doesn't harm me either. Unlike the Chevakians who can't see it but who are harmed by it. If you can see it, you've got Thilleian blood and that means that you have resistance. We always thought that the ability to withstand icefire was restricted to the City of Glass, but there are even Chevakians who have very weak resistance."

"What would the Aranians be doing with icefire?"

"We can only guess, but we can start investigating by sending people who are not affected by it."

The bottom line was that the Knights knew too little about Arania, and Zaina, having grown up poor, couldn't tell him what he wanted to hear.

The group they were sending was a combat unit of Knights in full gear.

The focus shifted to the eyrie.

Zaina was asked to oil and polish harnesses and mend saddles. She fitted saddles on eagles and cut and filed their talons so that the vicious metal talon-extenders, that had arrived in a neat case with felt lining, fit over the top.

She fed and groomed the birds. Eagles enjoyed being rubbed and combed a lot. The wax made their feathers shine and they loved it. They even helped rub it by tilting their heads upside down and rubbing the top over their backs while all their feathers were fluffed up. They looked like giant feather balls when they did this. It was a hilarious thing to watch.

Meanwhile, the Knights met on one of the ground floor rooms at the eyrie. Zaina could see them when she walked past. There were about twenty people in the room, most of them seated on wooden benches. Many were older, experienced Knights whom she had watched at shooting practice. They used short, squat crossbows and their aim was deadly.

Zaina had stood at the door looking into the room, where the Knights were shooting at shapes of animals and people for target practice.

She had been notified that the group would be leaving in the afternoon.

"What do you want me to do?" she asked Rider Barton. He was going to stay at the palace, but would be spending most of his time at the eyrie.

"You can refer to the queen and ask her what needs to be done. So many of us aren't here that there is probably a lot of work."

That was what Zaina feared. Jevaithi had not shown herself, or at least not that Zaina noticed, but she dreaded being in the half-deserted palace with Jevaithi watching her, because how could she work like that?

How could she talk to Jevaithi without referring to her stalking?

You know how you're always watching me when I work in the pens? Do you know that's really annoying?

But one just did not say things like that to the queen.

And meanwhile, Zaina was thinking of risking a return to the city and the workshop. She missed the work, she missed Jadan and the others, and the simple fact that engines that came in for fixing didn't come with politics or secret stalkers. Life was so much simpler back then.

THE GROUP of Knights left from the top floor of the eyrie late in the afternoon. It was a strange time to be leaving, but Zaina had been told that the Knights owned a camp at the foot of the mountains where they would stay overnight and discuss further plans. The sky was almost dark, and clear as it rarely was in Arania, especially near the coast, where the mist and clouds of the Mother's Veil always obscured the view to the west. There were never any pretty sunsets.

The Knights led their eagles to the mouth of the top floor, mounted their birds and launched into the air. The eagles swooped down, so the Knights usually disappeared from view straight away before rising back on lazy wingbeats. There were more than twenty-five of them, the best hunters and most ruthless fighters.

Zaina hoped that they could free the others in the camp and could do so without any major injuries or worse.

When she turned around to go back to her work, she found Jevaithi behind her. Zaina had known that the queen was in the eyrie, of course, but had assumed that she had left earlier.

Elfin-like and gentle-looking, but lonely. She lifted one corner of her mouth at Zaina, but Zaina could only see those blue eyes and wonder what Jevaithi wanted from her or thought about her. She almost certainly looked down on her, and might even consider her a traitor. Maybe that was why she was watching.

One thing her mother used to say a lot: "If you think or feel a certain way, tell someone, because they can't smell what you feel."

She crossed the room to where Jevaithi stood, and knelt at her feet.

"You Majesty, I have many shortcomings, but being a spy or a friend of Kadrish isn't one of them. I am sorry for not mentioning the prince when I came here before the expedition, but that was because I was too terrified of him. I'm sorry that I'm a coward." She bowed her head. "I like it in the City of Glass, and want to be able to stay here with an honest heart."

Jevaithi made a small noise and for a moment Zaina thought she might laugh. But then she said, *"You* are a coward?"

"I am, Your Majesty."

"I told you to use my name. Please get up, because you're much braver than I, or many of us. Don't let me see you cower again."

Zaina rose but kept her head bowed. "I am at your service. I may be from Arania, but my heart lies in the City of Glass. Many of my friends are here and I would not betray them."

"Thank you. We can use people like you. You are a strong woman."

"Please tell me what you want from me, because I noticed you've been watching me and it . . . unnerves me." Her heart was thudding.

"It does?"

"I'm sorry." Zaina looked down. Why was this so awkward? "Well, I . . . better feed the bears before it gets too dark."

"Do you want any help?"

What? "Help?"

"I'm not just a pretty girl wearing flimsy dresses."

Well . . . the dress she was wearing now would certainly fall under that category. "It's not really necessary."

"What if I said I *wanted* to help?"

"I couldn't say no."

"Would you want to?"

What sort of question was that? "It would be up to you, but if you really want to work in the stable, then that dress is not going to be suitable."

No, she knew. Jevaithi was going to stand there and watch her work. What had she done to deserve this?

On the way out of the eyrie, Zaina managed to convince Jevaithi that her dress was not suitable for work in the stables. Maybe Jevaithi meant "work" meaning the stable hand did the work and she watched, but if she said "help" and "work", Zaina was determined to get her to work. She wasn't going to have anyone stand there watching her work, not even the queen.

So Zaina went to the stables alone. The bears were waiting for her. She gave them the stale bread from the kitchens that she mixed in a tub with chunks of fish. It looked all pink, bloody and disgusting to her, and the smell was not much better, but the bears liked it.

Her task, when the bears finished, was to collect the empty trough and clean it out. She dragged the smelly, fishy food trough to the entrance of the stable, the paved area where the stable hand would wash the horses. She dropped the trough and went to find a bucket of water and when she came back to the trough hauling the heavy bucket, someone had turned up.

Zaina did a double take because she didn't know if this person in a too-big set of overalls was a young man or a woman. And then another double take because it was Jevaithi, and Zaina couldn't believe how thin she was.

"I wanted to work," she said.

Zaina debated saying, "If I give you a broom, your arms might break." But that would be distasteful because Jevaithi only had one hand, and her fake arm looked thicker than her real one. So she said, "The work is quite heavy."

"That's all right. I'm fine with that." She took the broom.

Now it was Zaina's turn to watch. To her surprise, Jevaithi did appear to have some experience cleaning out stables. She didn't wrinkle her nose at the smell. She wasn't afraid of the animals either. The dogs nosed her pockets, and she scratched them behind their ears.

For a while, they worked in different sections of the stables. Once, the stable hand came in and gave Jevaithi a wide-eyed look.

"Your Majesty, let me do that." He held out his hands to take the broom from her, but she clamped it to her chest.

He bowed. "As you wish." He backed off and scurried out of the stable.

A horse chose that moment to snort loudly.

Jevaithi chuckled. "They're not used to seeing me here."

No, well . . . there was a reason for that. Didn't she have more important things to do, especially now that everyone was gone?

"I learned how to look after and milk goats in Chevakia. Not many people know that, and even fewer believe it. It was when we'd fled the Knights, just before the explosion."

"You *fled* the Knights?"

"It was in the time of Rider Cornatan. I was sixteen."

Now Zaina put the broom aside and looked into Jevaithi's eyes. Something about Jevaithi's voice made Zaina pay attention.

Jevaithi no longer looked like a waif queen. Her hair had come undone from working, her cheeks were red and there was a dark smudge across her forehead.

"I knew nothing when I was sixteen, except fear."

"Fear?"

"Yes." Jevaithi leaned against the fence. The horse on the other side nosed the back pocket of her overalls. "I don't know what you think about me, but I'm guessing you think I'm a spoilt rich girl."

Zaina's cheeks glowed. That was exactly what she'd thought.

"Rich I am, maybe, but the money is not mine to do with as I please. I care little about money, anyway.

Only a rich person would say that. If she were poor, like Zaina's mother, like Zaina had been, you cared about money. It was often the only thing you cared about.

"I bet you're thinking that's easy for me to say, because I'm rich."

Well . . . Zaina's cheeks glowed more brightly. She wished Jevaithi would go and talk to someone else. It wouldn't be long before she could no longer restrain herself and said something insulting or stupid or something else that got her into trouble.

"You remember what I said on the day you came back to the palace?"

"Not really." There had been a lot of talk about many different things that day.

"I said, after the meeting was finished and everyone was leaving, that your story about the Motherhood register touched me."

Yes, Zaina did remember that. She had thought it a strange thing to say but had assumed that Jevaithi said it out of politeness.

Jevaithi went on in a soft voice, "The Aranian Motherhood register reduces women to vessels for children of powerful men. It is an instrument to repress women, their opinions and their influences. When a woman is expecting, she is considered weak. She is also considered of no value, other than to the man whose child she carries."

Zaina frowned at her. She guessed all that was true, but what did that have to do with her?

"Women can be bought and traded, and they constantly live in fear of their lives. That's how it goes, doesn't it?"

Zaina nodded. "Pretty much."

"In the City of Glass, we have the opposite problem, with the same outcome. We have poor fertility and women are bought so that they can produce children for those couples who can afford it."

"But women here have a choice. They get paid, and are often well off."

"All women, except one."

Zaina met her eyes, her heart thudding. What was she telling her and why?

"When I was sixteen, all the senior Knights were jostling around me to determine who was going to be the first in my bed. My mother died when I was six. Isandor is my brother, but I didn't know about him. I was afraid every day. Rider Cornatan—" Her expression grew distant. "Rider Cornatan threatened me with rape at least once every day. He would say this when I didn't listen, when I talked back to him, when I asked too many questions."

"Sorry. I thought . . ."

"You thought a life of luxury meant no hardship? I was a prisoner in the tower, because Rider Cornatan controlled where I went and how or when. He controlled who I met there, and he told me what to say. If I didn't say when he wanted me to, he threatened me. This is why the motherhood register story touched me: because I understand what it is like to flee men who want to use you. I want to make sure you understand that. A veneer of riches is no guarantee that bad things don't happen to you."

She set her broom down and strode out of the stables without waiting for Zaina's reply or meeting her eyes. Zaina stood there, helpless. She debated running after Jevaithi, but that would be *wrong* because the queen was . . . the *queen* and no matter that she seemed vulnerable, she was still untouchable, much more than her murdered lover Xalia, who came from a well-off house, had ever been. And even that line of thought disturbed Zaina deeply.

CHAPTER 17

SOMEWHERE IN THE MIDDLE of the afternoon, Javes and Tali came over the crest of a hill to find a decent-sized town in the valley before them.

According to Pashtan's map, which Javes had last pulled out two days ago, the town was called Lekata, and it lay on the northern bank of a seasonally flowing river.

That season was well and truly in, and the river showed in the distance as a huge ribbon of silver that embraced the town in a snake-like curl. The town lay on a low hill and Javes guessed that if the rain got any heavier, there was a good chance that water would cut across the plain on the northern side of the town, turning the town into an island in the middle of a raging torrent.

From a distance, Lekata looked like a regular northern town with blocky houses made from pale pink stone. He remembered coming through towns like this on the bus from Watya and thinking that Ysherra could not possibly look any less inviting.

Ysherra had proven him wrong.

Lekata was probably three or four times the size of Ysherra, not as big as that dust hole Watya, but definitely a sizeable town.

They had to decide whether to push on or stop for the night. Fortunately, nature had provided an overhanging rock ledge under-neath which someone had put a bench so that casual walkers could sit here to enjoy the view. They took a short break there.

Javes was so tired that he could lie down here and sleep and probably wouldn't wake up for two days. Tali sat with her knees drawn up to her chin. She was shivering and her lips were blue.

"Do you want to rest here or keep going?" Javes asked.

She shrugged.

Behind her on the rock wall hung a sign that stated *You are now in the district of Lekata.* That would be the doga district of Lekata, as opposed to the district of Ysherra that they had just left. Javes had also noticed how the road had widened and even looked *paved* further down the hill. Cute signs, benches, paved roads. There was the northern disadvantage right in your face.

"Are you cold?" he asked Tali—a silly question, but her continued silence bothered him.

"I don't feel so well," she said after a while.

No, he didn't feel well either. Fatigue gave him a headache, and the fact that his stomach was quite empty didn't help. Tali, however, had not looked well since they started on this journey, and even before. He remembered the happy young girl who had agreed to look after Pashtan's goats when he went to find the windwalkers, and wondered where that girl had gone.

He didn't know if it was normal for girls of her age to be this skinny. One part of him wanted to help her, and the other part was unsure that he *could* help her, and was afraid that if he got too close to her again, those embarrassing feelings would return.

They each sat on one end of the wooden bench. Javes looked for some scraps of salt meat in the bag. It was almost empty, and the salt had attracted moisture from the air. The meat was no longer dry and chewy. They finished the last bits in the bag.

"That's it. We're going to have to keep going. We've got nothing left for breakfast." In all honesty, he wanted to cross that plain between their position and the town before it flooded.

The rain had stopped briefly, although it definitely didn't look like they'd seen the last of it. The camel and the goats took the opportunity to grab mouthfuls of grass from the side of the road as they walked at a brisk pace.

"What is that town?" Tali asked.

"It's called Lekata."

"From the sausages?"

"I don't know. Do they make sausages?"

"They do. They're very hard and dry."

That was pretty much the description of everything produced in this region.

They reached the paved section of the road. A few carts passed, but nothing that you would call major traffic. Yet, seeing those carts, and seeing the donkeys plod along the road, gave Javes a calming feeling. The road was still open, and farmers went about their normal business. The town was not a ruin of burned buildings. With a bit of luck, they should be in and out of the town by nightfall.

Pashtan's map didn't show a railway into the town, but they might find another mode of transport to a larger town that did have a station.

The telegraph poles beside the road also looked extremely *normal*. Javes even found a weather station at the bottom of one of the poles.

The station was undamaged and had a signal, so he decoupled the telegraph wire from the barygraph and tapped a very quick message in code:

SONORICS AND ARANIAN ATTACKS IN YSHERRA AND ELSEWHERE. AM NOW IN LEKATA. RETURNING TO TIVERIUS BY CAMEL. JAVESIUS HAN DEMERIAN.

There. If anyone still read these messages, or cared about him, that would keep them busy. He replugged the barygraph in and cast a quick look over the readings. There were no dust devil spikes, but in the past few days, the sonorics level had risen to eighteen motes per cube, and whichever way he looked at it, that was much too high for any normal level in Chevakia.

Well, the barygraph was connected to Tiverius, and would be sending through these measurements, so he was sure that they knew this already. It wasn't up to him to worry about it.

He closed the little door to the weather station and they kept going.

The road wound through increasingly densely farmed hillsides.

The olive groves were green and healthy, the branches laden with fruit, still green but about to turn black. There were no farmhouses, so the owners were probably well-off enough to live in town, and the town was probably worth living in.

Tali talked a bit about selling milk and buying a cart. Javes let her talk. He was happy that she seemed to have come of her shell, even if he didn't think they could get enough milk quickly enough for such a purchase because the goats had been malnourished and not milked regularly enough, but he let her talk.

They came over the crest of the last hill and had a view over the town. The road was clear, although water already lapped at the fields on either side.

Lekata was a market town. The northern road was not the only one to lead into it, but all roads led to the market place.

And it was extremely busy. People were on foot or pulled hand-drawn carts. They rode horses, or sat in donkey-drawn carts. They carted sacks of grain and beans, cages with chickens and long, narrow baskets that contained one live pig each.

Javes' camel got some jealous and odd looks. Tali had tied the goats back in the harness, and they were not particularly happy with that situation, because the stalls were full of items that caught a goat's interest.

A lot of people on the street had come from further away. They rode carts loaded with many possessions: boxes, crates, even mattresses and tables and chairs. Entire families hung around these carts.

Women were haggling over bags of beans or loaves of bread. Men were inspecting or fixing carts, or sat at eating houses smoking over tea while the women worked.

Children ran wild, out of the control of their parents; but some, those whose parents didn't *have* a cart and who had arrived on foot, lay sleeping on the ground.

Other families were trying to sell their possessions.

As Javes and Tali made their way around the market place, many gazes followed them: from the teahouses, from the stalls, from the upstairs window of a house.

"All these people are watching us," Tali said in a low voice.

"They're just jealous of our camel."

The beast in question regarded all the activity with a look of typical camel-like disdain.

Javes first went to the animal pens. Two of the kids had grown sufficiently to be sold. They were both billy goats, and their horns had started to grow. Since it looked like the goats were going to make the trip to Tiverius with them, Javes didn't want two extra billy goats to deal with. They gave no milk and created trouble.

For some of the money he got, he bought beans, because they were more nourishing than grain. He bought a bag of salt meat and a little jar of fragrant olive oil. They might be travelling, but that was no reason to eat poorly. He also bought a simple jackrabbit trap so that they could supplement their diet.

From a family selling their housewares, he bought a little pot stove that would run on wood, firebricks, rubbish or oil. He also got some soap, a collapsible tub and a blanket.

There was far too much jostling over the carts for sale, and the prices were hideous. Javes wasn't sure why people were obsessed with donkey carts. They were too vulnerable.

He checked the animal pens, but there were no camels for sale. He hung around for a bit at a pen with a couple of scruffy ponies, but he didn't like the look of them either. Besides, Tali couldn't ride. If he had another camel, he could just tie it at the back of his camel, and it would follow. They were out of luck in the camel department today.

They were about to leave when Javes spotted a small stall where a man with a grizzled beard sold swords.

Javes stopped to look. The weapons were old and rusty and had probably last seen action in the Aranian war.

A sword was too big and he didn't know how to handle one, but a dagger might be a good thing to have. Their journey would be long and the feeling that they were being followed had never gone away, although he'd seen no evidence and it was probably his paranoia playing tricks with him. Nevertheless, it would be good to be able to defend himself, even if only against camel thieves.

"Is this all you got?" he asked the old man.

The man gave him a searching look. "Are you looking for collectors' items like these or useable weapons?"

"Why would I want to buy a weapon if I didn't intend on using it? These swords are too big."

"They're ancient artefacts, not for battle."

"Where would I find useable weapons?"

The man pursed his lips. "There's a strange fellow who has a shop in town, but he's not cheap. He doesn't have as many swords—because swords are military-issued weapons and soldiers hand them back in when they leave the service—but he's got daggers, traps, knives, whips, guns and crossbows."

"I like the sound of those."

"Be prepared to part with a lot of money."

Javes didn't *have* a lot of money, but decided to check out the shop anyway, so they left the marketplace and wrestled their way through the tide of people to a street that ran from the market square to the bridge that ran over the river.

Even though it would be a while before it got dark, the light went gloomy. A few specks of rain fell from the sky. They would soon need to find a place to stay for the night, and they would have to leave town to do so, because Javes had no money to waste on a guesthouse.

Ah, there was the shop.

Javes stopped and studied the various weapons in the dusty shop window. People streamed by, casting grumpy looks at him or the camel or goats because they were blocking the way.

Javes wasn't sure what he should get. As the old fellow had said, the prices were pretty steep, but it didn't look like the owner sold a lot, which probably meant that he could be made to negotiate—something he had learned from his merchant brothers.

He didn't like the powder guns. They were not very accurate, took a long time load, and carrying the powder around was a risk.

But that crossbow that lay on a shelf at the back of the display looked very good to him. It was made of smoothly-polished hardwood, stained bronze. The slide had a base of metal, and it came with a handful of bolts that were fairly short, but had serrated heads. He had never seen a design like it.

"Can we go?" Tali asked.

"I want to have a look in this shop."

"Then go into the shop. You've been standing here forever."

Javes wasn't used to this tone from her. "What's up with you?"

"I'm tired and hungry."

Yes, he was tired and hungry, too. They had the essentials of what they needed and they still needed to find a place to sleep before it got dark; and with the rain, darkness was going to come early today.

He had no money to buy a weapon and it would probably be

better to move on, but he'd had no money for a camel either, until one came his way by chance. And the camel, that haughty beast with the droopy lips that got up every day and walked without complaining—well, mostly so anyway—was the most precious possession he had ever owned. He would not have had the camel if he'd decided early on to stop looking for a camel because camels were too expensive. If he had, he'd still be trudging around with Pashtan's fixed-up cart.

So he decided to hell with this moody, complaining girl, and went into the shop.

As soon as the door shut and cut off most of the noise from the street, the owner scurried out a door behind the counter. He was a man on the wrong side of middle age with eyebrows so long he had fashioned them into horns. He was thin, a good deal taller than Javes, and wore a dark suit jacket with gold buttons.

He bowed. "How can I help the sir?"

Javes stuck his hands in his pockets—and found a sizeable hole in one of them—and thought very hard of his oldest brother who had the inborn ability to get money out of anyone. "I don't know that you *can* help me."

That was exactly something that Belo would say.

"Oh? Is the sir looking for something in particular?"

Javes eyed the shop's wares displayed on many shelves. The fellow didn't just sell weapons, but also other items of sophisticated male interest: pipes and intricate tobacco boxes, reading glasses, pens, leather-bound books, clocks and even an Aranian star chart. From here, he could just see the top of the crossbow and behind that, through the window, Tali's sullen face while she waited outside with the animals.

"Business been good lately?" Javes fingered the hole in his left pocket and hoped nothing of importance had fallen out during his trek from Ysherra.

"I've been getting lots of interesting new stock." Which wasn't exactly answering the question, but the shelves *were* well-stocked. Probably because many people had been leaving town and had needed the money to do so, leaving him with lots of things to sell and no one to buy.

"Hmmm. I'm from Tiverius and I'm buying unusual pieces for

collectors. In particular, collectors of weapons. I noticed the crossbow in the window."

The man nodded, his expression eager. "That is indeed a collector's piece."

"How so? Tell me about it." It was a game, imitating Belo's voice. Seeing how far he could get. He decided in his mind that he'd be willing to give up one of his windwalker treasures in exchange for the crossbow, probably the piece he'd found in Arukat's house. Then he would have his meagre collection of coins and maybe one of the goats available if in the next few days he found a farmer who wanted to trade a camel. He would have to pay a farmer in coins, because a farmer would not know the value of the ancient artefact, let alone where to sell it.

The man went to collect the crossbow from the window.

The back of his jacket was made from different, considerably thinner, fabric than the front. Was this because it would be too hot or because it saved money?

He pulled a piece of velvet from under the counter, spread it out on the counter top and put the weapon on it.

Close up, it was, in one word: formidable.

The shop owner went into a longwinded story about how there used to be a craftsman in town who made these, not just weapons, but other items of extreme sophistication and beauty. The fellow had died ten years back, and his three daughters had been fighting over their father's legacy ever since.

Javes didn't really care about the story. It was getting dark outside. For a few times in a row, he'd heard a deep rumble that sounded suspiciously like thunder. Tali stood under the overhang of the shop entrance, her arms clamped around her body. She looked angry and impatient.

"Look. The weather is not improving. We need to be on our way. How much?"

"Well . . ." The man looked put out. Maybe he had hoped for a whole afternoon of negotiating over tea and cakes or something.

"Tell me how much, because I don't have much time."

"The original price I had on it was six hundred foxes."

"That's ridiculous." Javes turned around. "I'm wasting my time here."

"But sir, I reduced it three hundred."

"That's still ridiculous." Javes opened the shop's door.

Tali looked up at him, and the expression of relief on her face disturbed him. This was a bit more than her sullen impatience. He mouthed, *what?*

She glanced to the other side of the street.

A good number of dusty people with mountains of possessions strapped to carts were making their way through the street, all in the direction of the bridge, the direction where they needed to head as well.

But on the other side of the street, in a little alcove stood a man, or at least Javes thought it was a man. He was dressed in a long robe with a hood pulled over his head. As if he sensed that Javes was looking at him, he turned around. His eyes met Javes', eyes so pale that they were almost without colour. The skin on the man's face was almost white.

A wind walker. A chill went over his spine. He turned to Tali. "Was he bothering you?"

"He's just staring at me. He scares me. He's a magician."

"There are no magicians."

"He is a magician anyway. They rob from the dead."

"He's a windwalker."

"Yes. A magician. I told you so. They bring bad luck."

Javes didn't know what to do. The man wasn't bothering anyone, he was just staring, and Javes hovered in between ignoring him and going up to him to ask what he was doing here.

Behind him, the shop owner had also come to the door. "Sir, sir. I'd be willing to sell the weapon for two hundred." Then *he* saw the windwalker across the street and let out an audible gasp.

"You know this man?" Javes asked.

"No. But he's a creepy character."

"Why don't I believe a word you're saying?"

The shop owner didn't reply. He stared at the windwalker, opening and closing his mouth several times, like a fish on land.

"Wait here," Javes said to Tali. While she protested that the man scared her and he couldn't just leave her in the street, Javes grabbed the poor shop owner by the upper sleeve and dragged him into the shop.

The man's eyes were wide. "What is your game, playing with windwalkers?"

"I'm thinking you know him better than I do. What is your relationship with him?"

"He is . . ." The man glanced aside to where the windwalker still stood in the alcove, watching the goings-on in the shop. "You're not who you say you are, aren't you?"

"I'm asking *you* a question. I *am* from Tiverius, if you must know."

The man glanced aside again. "He is known as Shen Mani. He trades old stuff."

"You mean artefacts from ancient times. Like this?" Javes took the globe from the pocket of his vest.

"No, no, not like that. Please, sir, leave now."

"It's just getting interesting."

"No, no, you don't want to meddle with this character. Please leave an old man in peace."

"Why don't you tell me—"

The shop window shattered. People in the street screamed and ran.

Javes ducked. He'd let go of the shop owner's shirt, and the man crawled on hands and knees behind the counter. Javes grabbed the first weapon available—which happened to be the crossbow on the counter. He clicked the bolt in and pulled the slide back. It armed with a smooth click. "Tali, come inside!"

He couldn't see her. Javes ran into the street. Tali had fled further down the street with the animals, pushed out of the way by the tide of fleeing people.

Several beefy men had cornered the windwalker, who raised his hands to protect himself. His hands were white-skinned with extremely long fingers. There was glass all over the shop display and surrounding area, and no sign of a weapon.

Javes ran across the street and wormed himself between the beefy men, likely farmers on their way home from the markets. One man pushed the windwalker against the wall while another searched his pockets.

The man kicked out and the third farmer elbowed him in the ribs.

"Stop, stop," Javes said. He pointed the crossbow at the windwalker's head.

"Whoa! He takes no second measures," one of the farmers said.

"Do you know this character?" another asked.

"I *think* I've met him before." Only last time he'd been covered from head to foot in cloth and he hadn't even seen the man's eyes, but he had the same thin build, and the windwalkers at the camp had said that the man travelled around a lot.

"What have you got to say for yourself, you magical piece of shit? Speak, or he'll do unkind things with that weapon."

"All is as intended." The windwalker's dry voice sent a chill down Javes' spine.

"Stop talking gibberish. At least uncover your head when you're talking to an honest citizen." The man yanked the hood off the windwalker's head.

And all the men gasped.

The windwalker had no hair on his head, but his scalp was covered in fleshy growths as if his head belonged to some disgusting creature that lived only beneath the earth. The growths varied in length from elongated warts to long fleshy lobes thick as a man's finger that looked like tentacles. The ones from his neck reached to his shoulders. Even his ears were covered in growths. In amongst this monstrosity, his near-white eyes looked disturbingly normal.

Javes felt sick.

"Who are you and why were you following us?"

"I gave it . . . for safekeeping. It's not yours to sell."

"What? The globe? No, you gave it to me in exchange for robbing the body of my tutor. If that was you, if you are the same person that the windwalkers call Karlen." Now he understood why even the windwalkers had never seen his face, and wondered if the white patches on windwalker skin broke out into fleshy growths with age.

"You . . . don't understand."

"Then enlighten me, because I'm fed up with being followed over this stupid thing. If your story is good enough, I might even give it back to you."

"All right. No need to point that thing at me."

Javes lowered the crossbow. The man's expression said it all. This globe was why he'd followed Javes, and maybe . . . maybe even what the Aranians were looking for.

The beefy townsmen backed off.

"Are you going to be all right, young sir?" one asked.

"We'll be fine, thank you. I know this man."

The three continued towards the bridge, swept up in the human tide of refugees that made its way out of town. Javes and the windwalker remained in front of the shop.

CHAPTER 18

AUTUMN HAD FINALLY come to Tiverius, and it had come with a sharp snap of moist air and a cold wind that swept clouds across the valley. Sady knew they were too far from the deep low-pressure system that had just about rained itself out over the northern desert, but he felt as if the clouds and occasional spit of rain were part of the system anyway. The city's weather stations even showed a very slight, if in no way significant, elevation of sonorics.

For the past few days, his desk had been full of messages about the flooding. Half of Watya was still under water. The bridge at Lekata would probably not hold out. The road across the river was already flooded in other places, where simple fords led across the riverbed that was dry most of the time.

There had been no reports from Tamyra and Ysherra, and he assumed that the northern desert was awash with water. Reports from people in the region said that when the big rains came, the entire desert floodplain disappeared under a slow-moving sheet of water and, because of the topography, all that water had to pass through the Aramys River at Watya. That was when underground water tables were replenished.

He understood why there had been no word from Lana and Viki in Ysherra—it was very likely that in the deluge the telegraph poles sagged and took the line down with them—but he didn't like it. So he didn't fidget and he tried not to worry, even if Loriane made much less of an effort to conceal her worry. He was her steadying hand and her guide. He couldn't allow his worry to show.

And it was busy at the doga and busy at home, where he asked Farius to organise the repainting of the sitting room and the upstairs hallway so that it would be nice when Lana came home. He also spent a lot of time talking to Loriane about her children. He sent off the letters, and they discussed what they should do to meet those interested in seeing her.

Sady said he wanted to travel to the City of Glass, to which Loriane said that she didn't think she was up to the long journey by train.

"Who needs the train when we have balloons?"

She smiled, but her smile quickly faded. "Don't you need the balloons to keep an eye on the Aranians?"

"I'm sure we can use one."

"Really?" Her eyes shone.

Sady knew: she wanted to see her home one last time. He should make it happen. So he spoke to the medic, who didn't like it, but he suggested he'd pay a nurse and junior medic to accompany them on the trip, and the prospect of going to the City of Glass with her became an expedition and an obsession.

But no matter how much he wanted to, stepping away from his position as Proctor became increasingly hard. He'd led the country through the previous crisis, his advisors said when he brought up the subject for the umpteenth time. People would want him to lead it through this one.

"But I am an old, tired man. I *want* to retire and enjoy what time I have left with my wife."

It was a selfish reason, especially since all previous proctors had to be forced to resign and would have stayed in the position until they died, if the country had let them.

The trouble was also that the doga had no clear alternative. Traditionally, proctors had come from the ranks of the military, but General Selidas was too young and, as yet, uninterested in politics. Thankfully the temporary head of the Meteorology Department, Rodius, was uninterested in politics as well. Viki wouldn't do it, because Sady had already asked multiple times, and the central Chevakian senators were passive as usual, and no one from the outer districts inspired any of the factions in the doga enough to stand behind them. If Sady stepped back, they'd probably end up with some interim leader who lasted less than a year and who would be thoroughly uninspiring, while behind the scenes, rifts deepened and factions made stabs at each other under water. The country could not afford that to happen right now.

So he gritted his teeth and kept going, but he asked for an extra administrative assistant, because he wanted to spend more time organising his trip.

Meanwhile, some reports about the damage done by flooding came in from the northern towns. Watya was tougher than it looked and had weathered this many times. The telegraph line came back two days later, sending a flood of backed-up weather reports. The line to Ysherra was still out, and so was Tamyra, a town on the road to Ysherra, that did not usually suffer major flooding. From memory, the mountain ridge that stretched into the desert to Red Hill came down to Tamyra and most of the telegraph poles would be sitting on rock.

He didn't like the absence of data from Tamyra, but there was probably some logical, weather-related reason for it. For all he knew, a post or two had been hit by lightning and finding a replacement and getting it installed was probably not the first priority of the people in the town.

So he set aside his worry and continued to work.

He was about to go home for the day when a junior worker of the telegraph office came to see him.

"I thought you might want to see this, Proctor."

The young man deposited a sheet of paper on Sady's desk. It said,

SONORICS AND ARANIAN ATTACKS IN YSHERRA AND ELSEWHERE. AM NOW IN LEKATA. RETURNING TO TIVERIUS BY CAMEL. JAVESIUS HAN DEMERIAN.

Sady's heart missed a beat. Javesius, or Javes, was Viki's student in Ysherra. Ysherra had come under attack from Aranians? Tamyra, too? Where was Viki? And where was Lana?

Sady picked up the paper and went straight to the General's office, only to find that the general had gone for the day. So he ordered a messenger to find the general and ask him to come to Sady's house.

Sady found if hard not to say anything to Loriane at dinner. He didn't want to worry her unnecessarily. Viki was smart, and they'd probably stayed in Watya when the weather turned bad. It was likely that access to telegraph messages out of Watya was restricted to emergencies, and private citizens, even esteemed senators, would have to wait.

Farius came into the kitchen to notify Sady that the general had arrived and was waiting in the library when Sady had just about finished dinner.

"Any problems?" Loriane said.

"Assessing the situation with the floods."

Oh, how he hated the way she looked through him. She *knew* there was bad news.

Sady went to the library, where the kitchen staff had supplied the general with tea.

"Did you hear about the message?" Sady asked.

The general nodded. "We heard about the attacks through a different channel at the same time. According to our source, there have been attacks by Aranian rogues throughout the north, including Ysherra, Tamyra and even just outside Watya."

Sady's heart jumped. "Have you heard from Viki at all? He's in that area."

"Wouldn't he contact you rather than me?"

True. Sady tried to calm his fast-beating heart. Lana was all right. Viki was smart and would stay out of the way of danger.

"What are your thoughts about these developments?"

"I've already sent our troops stationed in that area up north to investigate the situation. We currently have units in Watya and Lekata."

"They haven't seen this young man on camelback? It seems to me he has an interesting story to tell and we should bring him to Tiverius faster than a camel can walk."

The general shrugged. "If he keeps following the road, he'll pick up the railway line soon enough and he'll come home that way."

"Yes, but won't the trains be full of people fleeing the north?"

"Possibly." The general looked worried. He would remember the deluge of refugees pouring into Tiverius after the disaster in the City of Glass. He would have been too young to have been in a position of influence back then, but he would remember it. "I've placed immediate orders for a couple of additional units to go up north. With your permission, I will also call up the first reserve division of veterans."

"Do you think that's necessary?" Sady's heart jumped. Many young men spent a few years in the military when finishing school before going onto a civilian job. The first division included those who had served in the past five years who had the most recent experience.

"We have an extremely long border to patrol. The fact that the Aranian camps are in the central region means that we have to keep a decent presence here; even if we don't *think* they will do anything, we can't afford to be complacent. We simply don't have enough men to effectively patrol both the northern and southern regions as well. And on top of that, to assist with the handling of any refugees."

"Makes sense," Sady said, although he felt ill. This was altogether not going in a direction he liked. "Is there anything at all we can learn about the Aranian motives?"

"Besides two princes fighting out their rivalry over our heads, probably not."

Sady blew out a heavy breath. "All right. Call up the reserve division. Make it clear to them it's for humanitarian purposes."

"I can't make that promise," the general said. "And I don't like lying to my men. We *hope* it's for humanitarian purposes only, but events may turn out differently."

After some discussion about authority to command the use of trains and the best locations to station balloon divisions, the general left. As Sady escorted his guest to the door, he realised with growing dread that there was no way that he could retire gracefully in the current climate. If he stepped back now, he would be a coward. He had to see this through.

THE NEXT DAY, Sady chaired another closed session of the doga. This was an unscheduled emergency plenary meeting during which he gave the general the floor.

More news had come in from the north. It seemed that Arania had used the cover of the weather system to push across the border. The general didn't have evidence of organised activity: the Aranians had not, by his accounts, taken possession of any of the towns they had attacked, but had left a trail of destruction. Ysherra was badly hit, as was Tamyra. Refugees were flooding into Watya and Lekata and the army was sending trains.

The general spread out a map that showed the activity of the Aranian raids to be concentrated in the north.

Shara, who was the long-time senator from that area, asked him if he had any figures on the number of people killed, injured and displaced, and he did not.

A southern senator wanted to know how many Aranians lay in wait in the desert and received a volley of laughter in response.

"You do *not* go into the desert after rain," Shara said. "It becomes impassable."

"But people *do* live there, don't they?" The senator didn't give up so easily. "I've heard of people called windwalkers. They wouldn't have been aiding Aranians and supplying them with the knowledge to survive?"

Sady didn't *think* so, but oh, his worry spiralled out of control. They had *known* that the border patrols in the north, and the far south as well, left much to be desired. Somehow, everyone had been too busy to give that issue real consideration. Because no one cared about a stinking hot desert and wild, impassable mountains anyway, did they?

They might all have been so terribly wrong.

How could he reach Lana? How could he get her out of there?

After that meeting the various committee meetings about day-to-day affairs seemed irrelevant. Sady wanted to go back to General Selidas and ask him specifically to send a team of men to find Lana and Viki and return them to Tiverius.

The news of both the weather and Aranian attacks spread through town, and Sady could no longer keep it from Loriane. Even while she was housebound, nurses came to visit her to talk about the subject of women's health, and she would hear about it sooner rather than later.

When he did, she repeated what his conscience had been telling him: that Lana was with Viki, and that Viki was sensible and would stay away from trouble until it was safe.

Still, he found it hard to sleep, and noticed that Loriane didn't sleep much either. He rose early to bring her breakfast and made his way to the doga for another day of meetings. The weather was suitably threatening, with low clouds chasing each other over the city. It was so dark that even the lights in the main foyer were still burning.

"Oh, proctor, a courier came in with a parcel for you. I told him to put it on your desk, but he said he wanted to speak to you about it, because he had some documentation. He's gone out to get breakfast and will be back soon."

The parcel on Sady's desk was about the size of a shoebox and was wrapped in plain brown paper. The handwriting on the front was unfamiliar. It was stamped *Watya*.

Sady's heart did a flip.

He inserted trembling fingers under the seal and ripped it. He peeled the paper off the box, and opened it. Inside lay a dirt-stained, water-warped book: Lana's notebook.

Blood roared in his ears. For a moment, he thought he would pass out.

Lana. No, no, no, no. Lana!

Then he noticed the man who stood in the doorway.

His voice wouldn't cooperate so he waved him into the room. "Shut the—" He had to clear his throat. "Shut the door. Sit down."

The man sat on the edge of the seat opposite the desk. He wore a plain military uniform.

"What happened?"

"A unit of ours found this next to a bus stuck in the mud on the road between Watya and Tamyra."

Sady stared at the book. He didn't *want* to hear the rest. He wanted to die. No, he wanted to go home and give Loriane poison that would gently put her to sleep before killing himself.

"Next to the bus the unit found two male bodies. One was the driver of the vehicle, the other—from the description given, I suspect this to be Vikius han Marossi, Chief Meteorologist."

Now Sady looked up, fighting black spots in his vision. He whispered, "Lana. What about Lana?"

The soldier shook his head. "The patrol commander realised that there had been a third person. They combed the area, but didn't see her. They found footsteps leading up to a ridge and lots of hoof prints from horses."

Horses. Aranians used horses. "My daughter has been taken hostage by Aranians?"

The man pressed his lips together. "At this point in time, that looks the likely scenario."

Hostage. Hostage was not killed. *Hostage* meant that she was somewhere in Arania, maybe mistreated and having to go through unspeakable things, but *alive.*

Viki, though . . . what was he going to say to Viki's wife and his ten children?

How was he going to tell her that he'd done his best to protect her husband? He had *not* done this. He had assumed that Viki was invincible, infallible. He had travelled many times before and did not need protection.

How was he going to look Viki's wife in the eye and answer her questions on what he was doing to punish those responsible?

What was he going to say to all those refugees once they arrived in Tiverius?

How was he going to face Loriane?

How was he going to get Lana back?

Sady rose from the desk. By now, he was trembling so much that he had to place both hands on the desktop to support himself.

He called in his assistant from the foyer.

The young man's eyes widened. "Proctor, whatever is the matter?"

"Call General Selidas and his immediate advisers into my office. Call the legal department. Oh, and the speaker of the doga."

The man's mouth fell open. "But that is . . ."

"A war council. Yes."

CHAPTER 19

OF ALL THE THINGS it could be famous for, Curack was most famous for its miserable weather: a grey blanket of clouds that rose from the ocean and from which, on most days, a fine drizzle would come down, not enough to be worthy of the term "rain", but enough to make the cobblestones slippery and clothes clammy, and to make it impossible to keep anything dry.

It also made rooms perpetually dark and gloomy, especially the office of the harbourmaster. That large harbour-front building with south-facing windows never saw sunlight, and sunlight itself was sparse enough in Curack.

From the upstairs window, Tamerane could see the ghost ships arrive: big wooden vessels with large sails that came out of the mist, steered by a crew of a mere three men.

On the deck, there would be rows and rows of man-shaped and man-sized bags. They were usually well closed, but sometimes you could see a pair of shoes sticking out.

Of course, she wasn't supposed to see this, and definitely wasn't supposed to look, much less ask questions. The two soldiers, near-mute hunks of muscle and flesh who sat on either side of her desk, made sure of that.

So she drew diagrams and made her calculations and spread all of them out over the desk, and pretended she hadn't seen the ship. She pretended she couldn't smell the searing of burned flesh every night.

And she also pretended that she hadn't noticed that she'd made a mistake on page two.

No one would know.

By the time the General found out because his precious icefire machine stopped working . . . well, she'd figure out how to deal with it. Prince Denori would probably rape and kill her if he found out that she'd made deliberate errors, but he had left for Kadrish two days ago. General Pakori was an older man and seemed more of the hanging or shooting kind, but she also guessed that, with the Aranian obsession with mothers, he would be hesitant to kill a woman, and wouldn't kill her father because he wanted to foster relationships with the nobles from the City of Glass and you didn't do that by killing people.

She was playing with fire, but counted on the proverbial climate to be wet enough for nothing to burn. She could not simply obey orders she received. That would be akin to murder, and there was enough death in this place already.

She couldn't stop looking at the ship that had moored at the quay opposite the window. A couple of burly men had been waiting with a cart, and they were now loading the bodies onto the tray. When it was full, it would leave for the incinerator in the next bay, and a new cart would come.

Father had said that these were prisoner ships from Kadrish, and that the Aranians sent their criminals out to sea where they were killed and then moved to Curack for burning. She wondered what leader would just send his people out to sea and order his men to hack them to pieces. The body bags were frequently stained with blood.

One of the guards rose and went to the door. Tamerane couldn't imagine why anyone would want a job like theirs: to watch a frumpy girl do endless calculations. They were not supposed to talk to her or to each other. She'd tried making them smile or laugh, or making them angry, but it was as if they were made of stone.

She took a clean sheet of paper from the drawer, but from the edge of her vision, she spotted movement on the deck of the ship. One of the bags moved, and sat up. First a pair of feet came out, then legs and knees. Then the person wriggled himself onto his knees and pulled the bag off his head.

He was a lanky youth with dark hair. Did she see correctly that he was wearing a Chevakian military uniform?

Her heart thudded in her throat.

One of the burly men on the deck of the ship had seen him. He shouted to his mate and pointed. The Chevakian man ran to the front of the ship, weaving around the bodies, and jumped over the railing. He landed with a splash in the icy water of the harbour.

For a heart-stopping moment, the surface smoothed into its normal, oily state, but then the water rippled and his head bobbed up, a good number of paces away from where he had hit the surface. He struck out for the opposite side of the harbour, in front of the harbourmaster's office.

By now, a couple of Aranian guards had come onto the quay. They started running along the harbour front, but it was quite a distance around the harbour, and the man was almost at the steps.

The two guards in the office with Tamerane looked at each other. The one who Tamerane suspected was the senior shook his head. He glanced at her. The words remained unspoken, *If we leave her, she'll cook up some plan to make us look stupid.* They didn't say them, because they had found out that her Aranian was quite good.

Well, it wasn't Tamerane's fault that they'd been dumb enough to leave her to get that horribly sweet Aranian tea, and she'd used the opportunity to raid the harbourmaster's medicine cabinet for something that might help her father's crazy heartbeats and sweats at night, and had accidentally found a big supply of lurid toys that she'd quickly stuffed back when she heard the men returning but that had avalanched out of the cupboard when they went to check it.

Just the fact that she had caused them and their master embarrassment—a woman, no less—had been the subject of a lot of hilarity.

The escapee climbed onto the slippery, algae-covered steps. He ran, dripping wet, across the quay and vanished out of Tamerane's field of vision, she guessed into one of the alleys that led through the old and crowded part of town.

The guards arrived on the quay a bit later. They walked around, checking hiding places, still breathing heavily from their run.

At the ship, a man shouted and pointed across the water. The guards vanished from Tamerane's view, shouting and banging on doors.

The two burly men at the ship's deck were opening all the body bags to check that the occupants were actually dead.

Tamerane could not stop looking. No, the prisoners had not been hacked to death. They'd been burned. All exposed skin had peeled, and their limbs had blackened.

Tamerane tried to focus on her work, but she kept seeing blisters and loose flaps of skin.

Arania was a terrible, cruel place.

She hoped the Chevakian soldier escaped. She *wanted* him to escape and tell the world about the atrocities Aranians inflicted on prisoners.

Someone knocked on the door. One of the guards opened it and went into the hallway, speaking in a low voice to another man. He came back, but said nothing.

Her guards didn't speak in her presence because she could not be allowed to hear anything.

A group of guards now gathered on the quay. Tamerane hoped this meant that they hadn't caught the Chevakian. The guards in the room said nothing, and she worked, making calculations, using the old books from the Brotherhood of the Light, which had been an underground organisation in the City of Glass during the reign of Rider Cornatan.

He had forbidden all material that explained and advocated the use of icefire, and although he had done many evil things, Tamerane agreed with the ban. Icefire could be used for good things, but it could be used for so many more evil things. So far, none of the things that Aranians wanted to use it for were good, starting with the fact that icefire was dangerous to Aranians. She had to find a way out of here. Every night, she went to sleep thinking about Isandor and his soft arms, and of the throbbing she felt in her stomach at night, hoping that she could find safety before her pregnancy started to show.

AT THE END of the day, Tamerane wrapped her books in a blanket in a leather satchel, but still the paper always felt slightly moist, and it bore marks of spotting and browning. And because Aranians used black rock for making fires, most books were stained with soot.

It annoyed her that people could be so careless with books, but that said just about everything about Aranians. They didn't care, and she didn't understand why her father cared and why she had to be here—oh, she understood about her father's debt, but failed to see *why* he had even signed this stupid deal in the first place. Prince Denori was a jerk of the first order and didn't deserve her father's support.

She hated this place and she hated the people, and couldn't even complain because, as a family, they were better off than many, Aranians or Perians alike.

So she clutched her books, sheltering the satchel from the drizzle with her coat and her hair and walked, hunched over, through the narrow streets of the town. Her footsteps echoed against the walls of the houses that lined the streets. Thank goodness she had brought her good boots from the City of Glass, because everything sold in the shops in town was ill-made and poor of quality.

It was a stiff walk uphill from the town administrator's office in the middle of town to the slightly run-down house that the Aranian army had allowed the family to use. Tamerane had never put much stock in physical training, but she was getting lots of it. That, and the fact that the food was terrible, made for her dresses loosening around her thighs. The cushion on her stomach refused to budge, but she was fairly certain that had a different reason.

She reached the house and pushed open the front door, to be met with the musty smell of the carpet in the hall. Noises indicated that her mother was in the kitchen.

Tamerane shed her coat and shivered in the clammy air.

It was warmer in the kitchen, where a fire roared in the furnace, and where a couple of pans stood on the hotplate, blowing clouds of steam towards the ceiling.

Tamerane dropped herself into a chair at the table that stood in the middle of the kitchen. Her mother sat in the chair in the corner doing embroidery while the maid stirred a steaming pot.

"Your father is in the study," her mother said.

"I know, but it's cold there and I'm hungry." Tamerane put her bag on the table, opened the flap, took out the blanket and unfolded it to take out the books. She spread them on the table.

Her mother shook her head. "I wish you wouldn't leave those books in the kitchen, dear."

"These books are our heritage from Peria. They are being ruined by this dreadful weather. I only bring them in here to dry them out; otherwise they'll end up with brown spots all over them. You know that some of the books in Father's study have mould growing on them?" Those were Aranian books, and she didn't care about them. She believed there were precious books in the library in Kadrish, but she had not seen one of them in this dreadful place.

Her mother shook her head. "One day, those books will be the death of you."

Tamerane knew that her mother didn't mind the books so much, except she didn't understand them, never having experienced the joy of study herself.

Tamerane reached out for the fresh loaf of bread on the table.

"Be patient, dear, and wait for your father."

Tamerane withdrew her hand but, by the skylights, her stomach was so empty, she felt faint; and fainting would never do, because her parents would be suspicious, and they'd . . . who knew what they would do, or what her father's Aranian masters would do, if they knew she carried the child of the Perian king.

"Have there been any letters for me?"

"Your father took the mail. He should be able to tell you."

Tamerane rose from the table. Yes, she got the hint. *Go and see your father now.* Except she dreaded any conversation with her father these days, fixated as he was with giving the Aranians what they wanted.

She left for the cold clammy hall and went to the front room.

A fire burned in the hearth, but it wasn't big and warm like in the kitchen. The black rock stoves were not half as good as the firebricks, besides making everything sooty, but black rock was cheap and available everywhere in the mountains around Curack.

Her father sat at the desk, but because it was a fair distance from the fire, it lay outside the reach of its warmth. He wore a thick coat and kept his left hand inside his glove, while writing with his right. He was writing a letter in Perian on the family's official stationary. Tamerane had seen some of his correspondence. It mostly begged other nobles to join them, because "you'll be free of the restrictions by the new Knight Council."

"Did you see the general?" he asked without looking up.

"Briefly." Tamerane thought of the stern figure of General Pakori of the garrison that was stationed just inland from the town. He would sometimes visit her in her little office, and tell her of his demands. Bigger machines, more powerful icefire strands. He didn't let her come to the garrison, and she wouldn't write to him, so he had to lower himself to travelling into town to see her personally.

From everything he did, every word he spoke and every disdainful look he gave her, she got the impression that he thought that women were good only for one thing.

"What do you think? Can it be done?"

"Changing the settings on the machine, yes. It's got a good lot more capacity before it blows up. But I'm wondering how many men he's prepared to lose for this. Even if *we* change the settings, he'll still have to put the thing on a balloon and he'll have to get a pilot who is resistant to icefire." If she sounded belligerent, that might just be her intention.

"They'll probably want us to do that," her father said, his voice blank.

Tamerane nodded. *Us* meaning Perian young men, who had been born with a resistance to icefire. The Aranians didn't divulge what they wanted these death traps for, but Tamerane was sure General Pakori intended to fly the balloons with their deadly load into Chevakia and kill as many people as possible there without having to rely on Prince Sferuk's army. Because he worked for Prince Denori.

Prince Sferuk had started his offensive in the north of Chevakia, and prince Denori had to step up his efforts with the icefire weapons he had long promised, but were simply not ready yet.

Both projects were about impressing the king so that he would choose the victor as his successor. They were not about conquering land or cities. They were not about the citizens or even the soldiers. Likely, those soldiers would die, and what was more, they'd be happy to do so, as long as they got their name engraved in the wall of honour.

It made her sick, but she and Father had already fought so many arguments over it that she knew it was pointless trying to sway him.

Likely he *did* object to the Aranian tactics, but he was too proud to admit it, or too afraid of the consequences.

"There was a letter for you," he said.

Tamerane's heart jumped.

He slid it over the desk. The front bore her name written in Aranian in unfamiliar writing. She let out her breath again, since this was obviously not what she hoped. Not that she *really* expected Isandor to write, or rather, that she expected him to risk her position by writing to her, but she *wanted* to hear from him. The last thing she saw at night when she cried herself to sleep in her cold bedroom was the shock on his face when she told him she couldn't marry him. She longed to tell him and the world that she was pregnant with his child. She'd wanted, no hoped, her parents would be proud of her, would present her to him in the wedding ceremony. They'd end up selling all they had to the Aranians instead. All those old things that had been handed to her father when he inherited the house. Those old books that annoyed her mother so much. All that knowledge that was specifically Perian, and Tamerane hadn't even studied all of them yet.

Tamerane slid her finger under the letter's seal and ripped it. The letter inside was an invitation for her to visit the famed Astrology library in Kadrish, with a list of books they held. The librarian was, he said, *honoured to teach you Aranian ways.* She bet he would be honoured. She didn't want to go there for their silly predictions. She wanted to go because of the quality of their maps and because of the books they were said to have in languages no one could read.

Well . . . she sighed. When coming here, she had assumed that she would be working on star charts and knowledge of the skies.

How dumb she had been.

Soon after arriving, she had been told what they really wanted her to work on. Icefire: how much was needed to kill a person or to destroy a building, and how to increase the production of it by the crude machines fashioned by the Aranians after old books taken by her kinsfolk from the City of Glass. Death and destruction, because the use of these machines would kill Aranians as well as Chevakians; and no matter how often she told the general that these machines would slaughter his army, he still wanted her to work on them.

So this letter from the Astrology library came as a bittersweet memory of the innocent work she thought she'd be doing.

Father glanced at her, raising his eyebrows.

She said, "Nothing important. It's about a question I asked."

"Oh."

He seemed disappointed, and she didn't ask him more. She so badly hoped that he had a good heart and didn't like any of what they had been forced to do; but if that was the case, he was so good at acting that she'd begun to doubt her faith in him. She'd had trouble going against her father's wishes precisely because he always meant well, even if she disliked it. But now, she could no longer believe that he didn't know the implications of what they were doing here: making mass-murdering machines.

The bell for dinner rang in the kitchen.

Her father broke the uneasy silence by pushing his chair back over the plain timber floor. "Let's have dinner, then." His voice was mock cheerful.

Tamerane followed him into the kitchen, where they shared a dismal meal in uncomfortable silence punctuated by her mother's attempts at chatter. Tamerane wanted to argue, she wanted to shout at her father to stand up for the family and what he believed in. But of course the maid was Aranian, and she could not be allowed to hear any of the family's discussions, because she would report it to her master.

So Tamerane remained quiet, but oh, she was biting her tongue. How could her parents let themselves be bullied into silence?

Because it had been so cold in the room, Tamerane had to use the outhouse. Frequent trips to the outhouse was an annoyance related to pregnancy that she had forgotten about, and it was getting pretty bad, too. That was in addition to her breasts feeling hard like rocks, and the way she felt ill every time the maid cooked her fatty bacon for breakfast. How long could she keep her condition hidden? Already her mother commented on the fact that she was always hungry.

She let herself into the dusky back yard, shivering against the moist, biting wind. It was dark between the house and the wall. She had to mind where she put her feet on the paving, slippery with moss.

A dilapidated shed stood to the side of the narrow yard, and as she walked past, she heard a noise inside.

What?

She stopped and took a step back so that she could see into the shed's open door. The shed contained buckets and mops and a few barrels of salted fish and some beer—both were Aranian delicacies that Tamerane could not appreciate in the slightest. The house belonged to some military hotshot, who used the back yard and upstairs rooms as a store for purchases, like liquor, that he could not store at the barracks.

Ground squirrels would sometimes come into the shed and make a mess with sticks and grass that they hauled in and splinters of wood that they pulled off crates or wool that they pulled out of stuffing of saddles or other items in the shed.

She stepped inside—and as soon as she came into the door, an ice-cold hand shot out of the darkness and grabbed her over the mouth. Her captor—a tall man—dragged her away from the door. She squeaked and tried to kick him, but he was too strong.

He held her in a strong grip, but froze in that position, one hand on her mouth, the other arm around her body, pinning her arms by her sides.

"Be quiet, and I won't harm you." His voice sounded quite young.

He had, she realised, spoken Perian. She stopped struggling, and he relaxed, allowing her to look over her shoulder. She recognised him: it was the refugee from the ship, complete in his Chevakian military uniform, wet and dirty.

Very slowly, he let her go, backing away. "See? I mean no harm. I need food and blankets."

"Who are you? I saw you escape from the ship in the harbour. Where did you come from?"

"It's a very long story."

Yes, and she still needed to pee. "Wait here." She had an idea.

Tamerane went back into the house. Her father had gone back to his cold room, but her mother was still in the kitchen with her embroidery.

"Do you have any bandages I can use? I just got my bleeding."

Her mother directed her upstairs, to the linen cupboard against the wall in the hallway that held towels and cloths. She took a couple out for good measure, and pulled two folded down blankets off the top shelf. Next to the cupboard was another cupboard that contained the owner's store of pickled vegetables and fish. She took out a couple of bottles—heaven knew what was in them—and carried the lot down the stairs, through the hall and into the shed.

After a quick visit to the outhouse, she went back into the shed, where the poor man had wrapped himself in the blankets.

She learned that his name was Zeiro. He was half-Perian, had grown up in Fairlight as the son of a railway worker and served in the Chevakian army out of Watya, which was in northern Chevakia. He was with the balloon unit and had been captured when their balloon had ventured too far to the west into Aranian territory.

"There was a really bad storm and we got blown off course, straight into an Aranian military camp. They took us on the train to Kadrish, where we were made to work in a quarry. Most of us there were Chevakian soldiers. It was hard work and we got no news from outside, but we weren't treated too badly. I don't know what changed, but one day, soldiers came and took us to a big shed in the harbour. We were made to go onto a ship and set out to sea, all of us locked up in cages on the deck. Not long after we set sail some kind of lightning hit the ship and all the men on the deck started screaming and dying. It was awful. Their skin was peeling and their insides just turned liquid and came out of their backsides."

"It didn't affect you?"

He shook his head. "I might have got a little red, like sunburn, but nothing more."

Tamerane was sure: this was icefire. "Did you see where it came from?"

"I was too busy surviving to see that, but it wasn't obvious."

"Did the crew bring any crates on board?"

"There were a few boxes, yeah, but I couldn't see what was in them."

Sure enough. They had taken an icefire machine on board and executed all the prisoners, and this man happened to have been resistant, by virtue of his blood. "What happened next?"

"Everyone died. The whole deck was covered in bodies. The crew came to unlock the cages, carried the bodies out and put them all in bags, and took the cages apart. I played dead, because I saw them kill a man who was still alive. They put me in a bag as well, and I held still until we came here, just letting myself out once or twice at night when no one was on deck. Then, when we came here, I ran."

The feeling of sickness she always had when working on the icefire science grew into a sense of revolt. She helped make these things. She should *stop* cooperating with the Aranian schemes. Her father should stop cooperating as well. They should go home, warn the Knights, warn Chevakia and, together, do something about it.

"Please," she said. It was cold in the shed and her jaw was shivering. "Please, do you know a way to escape? We could find a way out of Arania together."

He shook his head. "I can barely survive. I don't know where we are and I have nothing except the clothes I wear."

CHAPTER 20

IN THE NEXT few days, Zaina kept going over Jevaithi's words, trying to figure out why she had confided in her, specifically. Maybe it was because everyone else already knew the story, or she thought, in light of the massive destruction of the explosion, that complaining about being threatened by the very people who were meant to protect you was irrelevant compared to the death and destruction that other citizens of the City of Glass had suffered.

But Zaina couldn't ask.

Jevaithi didn't come back to the stables, and Zaina didn't spend as much time there anyway, because she got called away to do engineering jobs and spent more time at the back of the building, and at the eyrie to help with the Knights' preparations. Weapons needed to be cleaned and checked. Powder guns were finicky things that required a lot of fine-tuning. This was not Zaina's specialty, so she wasted time learning the details.

She liked coming to the top floor where the eagles were, and the Knights didn't seem to object. Jeito's eagle was bored, she was told, and it seemed to enjoy her visits where she brushed its feathers and scratched its head.

"Why don't you join the Knighthood?" a young stable hand asked her one day.

"Me? Could I?" She had never thought about it. She had her workshop—where she still hadn't been since she returned, although she had sent Jadan a message.

She should check on the workshop, and yes, the idea of joining the Knighthood was strangely attractive. More than anything, it made her feel that she might finally be *safe* from Aranian persecution.

But the Knights certainly wouldn't want her, an Aranian traitor whose only concern was herself.

Still, the suggestion niggled at her for the next few days, until it was swamped by the sheer amount of work, followed by seeing off the heavily armed group of Eagle Knights who would hopefully retrieve the members of her exploration team from the Aranian camp.

After they left, it grew even quieter in the palace. The Knight Council was at less than half regular strength and meetings were kept short. A couple of Legless Lions got into the storeroom at the back of the palace, and made a mess there, which Zaina helped to clean up. The stable hand also decided to take three new horses for measurements to have winter jackets made for them, so Zaina helped him manoeuvre the nervous animals through the streets of the city.

Zaina finally found some time to go to the Harbour District four days after the mission had left.

She felt nervous about going out there by herself, even if she knew that Nayek couldn't ever come to haunt her again. His immediate helpers had probably been distributed amongst the other princes, and they would have different plans that did not involve chasing her, she hoped.

Once again, she walked along the familiar streets, past the *Silver Gull*, the *Dancing Bear* and all the shops.

She could see the open door to the familiar workshop from almost a block away and sped the rest of the distance up the hill.

The two young mechanics were working on what looked like a brand new ship's engine that stood on a couple of trolleys.

One of the boys turned around when Zaina came in.

His eyes widened. "Zaina! You're back!" The other mechanic also looked.

Jadan came out of the office. "We were worried about you."

Her familiar, thin, boyish face almost made Zaina cry. She ran across the workshop floor and swept Jadan up in a hug.

"What happened? Why are you back? There were some Aranians here who wanted to know about the injury you had and where you had gone and who I told about it. I didn't tell them anything, but they took me out of the city and were going to beat me up, but then the king and Rider Barton came out of the sky on birds and rescued me. The king came back here to look at your administration. He wanted to know about your contacts with the city's nobles and—"

"Slow down, Jadan. Explain what happened."

They went into the tiny office—which was much tidier than when Zaina had used it—and Jadan told what had happened and how the king had visited twice.

Well, that might be part of the reason that Jevaithi was keeping an eye on her. It made sense.

Then she asked Zaina about the expedition, and things got a bit awkward. While Zaina admired Rider Jeito, Jadan idolised her, and hearing that she was amongst the captured made her turn pale. Zaina didn't think that Jadan could cope with hearing that it was her fault.

They moved on to business and the running of the workshop.

"I'll be staying at the palace until I'm sure that it's safe to come back and that I'm not going to put you in further danger."

Jadan nodded. Zaina hated it how scared she looked. Jadan was her pupil, her protégé, and she deserved to be safe. They were all in this together: Zaina, Jadan, and Rider Jeito.

By the time Zaina left the sky was almost dark, despite it's being only afternoon. This sunless winter was really getting on her nerves.

Zaina walked through the Harbour District, letting the familiarity wash over her.

She sat down on the steps to the harbourmaster's office, closed at this time of day, and watched the activity around the ships.

Her thoughts threaded back to the similarity between Jadan and Jevaithi that she had noticed. Both were thin, boyish. Zaina suspected Jadan of eating the male parts of the Tusked Lions in order to keep herself looking like a boy, something Jevaithi would never have been allowed to do.

But where Jadan was a blossoming flower waiting for a butterfly to land on it, Jevaithi had been circled by hornets all her life. She had never known the sweet innocence of young love from another woman. She might not even realise what a beautiful thing that was. Xalia hadn't known either.

Zaina could remember that first kiss they had shared, in the pouring rain at the back gate to Xalia's house. It still gave her the shivers.

Poor Xalia.

"Zaina."

She turned aside to the direction of the voice. Marek stood on the quay, a tall figure with shoulder-length dark hair in a stylish coat and high boots. He looked . . . different from the lanky and fidgety man who had been her friend, somehow prouder, more confident.

"Marek, is that you? Wow. You look . . . different."

"You haven't been away that long. What's different about me?" He spread his hands. His smile was still the same. "I didn't know you were back. Want a drink?"

"Sure."

They went into the familiar ground floor room of the *Silver Gull*, where not much had changed. Marek walked through the crowded room, and even greeted a few people. *That* was definitely new. He didn't seem to be as fearful anymore.

"So, how have you been?" Zaina asked. When they had sat down.

"Good, good. Busy."

"You? Busy? What with?" He'd take odd jobs every now and then, but nothing that required him to give out more details than his first name and, consequently, only things that paid like shit.

He smiled and said no more of it. Typical Marek, secretive as hell. He was probably afraid that she was going to take his well-paying job off him.

She asked, "Where is Eshtar?"

"He went home, after hearing about the big storms in his home-land. He wasn't getting any replies from his family, so he went to check on them."

Yes, Zaina remembered how Eshtar used to cherish the letters he got from home. Out of the three of them, he'd been the one most connected to his folks. She also remembered hearing some stories about the storms, although any interest she might have had in the subject was overshadowed by her own predicament.

Once upon a time, and it felt impossibly long ago, she had corresponded about engines and old artefacts with a man called Shen Mani in that region. She wondered what had become of him.

Marek told her how one day, soon after she had left, the king came to seek him out.

"The king himself?"

"You heard it. He was interested in the involvement of Aranians in the city."

"What did you tell him?"

"I answered his questions. Did you know that the Knight Council asked for a list to be made of foreigners in the city, but this 'register' of businesses with foreign employees is an 'initiative' of some of the more inventive Aranian minds in the Harbour District?"

Well . . . that was . . . not completely unexpected. "Is that why Nayek had so much interest in the city?"

"Probably. But I've discovered something else. The Aranians who started this 'register' don't work for Nayek. They work for Sferuk. Nayek was here to spy on his rival's activities. He always had a lot of business interests in the Harbour District, because he likes business and money. He was aware of Denori's activities in the military sphere, with buying favours from the nobles, but he might have been upset by the boldness of Sferuk's attempts to control the Aranians in the Harbour District through this register. These were people Nayek would formerly have considered his."

"Nayek is dead. I killed him."

Marek took in a deep breath. "Well, I don't know. There have been some very strong rumours that he was very close to death, but didn't die."

"I put a knife between his ribs. His blood ran over my hands."

He nodded. "That doesn't always kill a person."

A chill went over Zaina's back. She thought she'd be free from Nayek. She hadn't checked whether he was dead or not. He hadn't come after her. He'd collapsed on the ground in the tent. She'd heard rumours that he was dead, so she'd assumed that he was dead.

But if he wasn't . . . he'd be sure to want revenge.

Marek said, "I've been thinking a lot recently, and the visit from the king made me realise that we cannot remain passive and we cannot hide forever."

Zaina shook her head. "We can't hide at al. Wherever we are, someone will find us. Especially if Nayek is still alive." She shuddered.

Marek, too. If he was on the run from Denori's army, then he'd be running forever, especially if Denori considered him a potential rival, and he'd only put rivals in the Special Guards. Marek had to be a prince. Denori would follow him to the edge of the ocean and probably even beyond.

"There is only one way we can stop this," Marek said.

"How?"

"We must help the local authorities stop Aranian infiltration."

"You mean become a spy for the Knights?"

"Not necessarily a spy, but we must be active in giving them the information they need in order to get rid of the Aranians. I spoke at length to the king. I have since been involved with Supreme Rider Barton, who is a deeply respectable man."

Zaina thought of the discussion she'd had this morning with the stable hand in the eyrie.

Yes, it was true that she loved engines, but her workshop would never be successful if she had to be constantly on the run or fear being discovered.

She said, in a low voice, "I was asked why I didn't sign up for the Eagle Knights."

"What did you say?"

"Nothing really. I didn't know what to say. It seems a little . . . weird to me to serve in the army of a country where you weren't born."

"But you want to stay here, right?"

"Yes. I guess so." Although she'd have to move out of the palace for all kinds of reasons, even if only to get away from Jevaithi's obsession with her. More than anything, she *wanted* to be able to walk through the Harbour District without having to worry about Aranians chasing her because she'd applied to have her name removed from the Mothers' Register. But before she could be safe, she needed to face those people chasing her and stop them. Running was no longer an option.

"Then help me *do* something about it. Please, I consider you a friend. You have a strength of character that can make a lot of difference."

Zaina laughed. Strength? Her? She'd never stood up for anything except her own survival. "You think I should sign up?"

"Hell, yes. In fact, I think that's such a good idea, I'll sign up with you. Let's make a promise to each other: we will make a difference. We will make this city a safe place for law-abiding citizens of all countries."

He held out his hand for her to shake on their promise. Zaina hesitated. She had seen the damage from speaking up. Xalia had been adamant that she wasn't going to share a bed with any man. She was smart, she was rich, she was from an influential family, and none of that had been enough to save her.

"Let me think about it."

"All right, but don't think too long," Marek said. He withdrew his hand, disappointment on his face.

ZAINA THOUGHT a lot about it on the way back to the palace. She knew Marek was right, but being brave and heroic was not part of her life. She was busy enough trying to survive. She didn't want to draw any attention to herself. In fact, the less attention, the better.

But Marek was right, if she continued living like this, she would forever be running. If she did nothing, she would forever be mucking out stables and fixing simple engines in the palace. She would not be able to return to her workshop for a long time. Because if Nayek was still alive, he would want revenge. If he was dead, others would want revenge on his behalf. Or Denori would find out about her and would want her for a plaything simply because she'd been the lover of the woman who refused his army's commander. The princes despised women who didn't like men.

The persecuted and downtrodden in Arania didn't have the power to fight this by themselves. The Eagle Knights could help.

But it meant being seen. It meant showing her colours in public. Political opinions were something that Aranians were trained from birth *not* to display.

It was hard, very hard, to overcome that fear. She was too old, too damaged, too scared.

Zaina hadn't made up her mind when she came to the palace. She used the side entrance, but in order to get to it, she needed to walk past the front entrance and the garden with the stables.

She noticed a lot of people in the foyer. That was strange. As far as she knew, the Knight Council meetings were very basic, due to the absence of so many members; and anyway, she didn't think that a meeting was on today.

She went into the side entrance, changed into her work overalls and made her way towards the main foyer.

She could hear the voices long before she got to the foyer. They were angry.

A man was saying, "The Council has no right to meddle with our businesses. We demand an audience."

A more gentle male voice replied, probably one of the guards.

Several of the men shouted over the top of him.

Zaina slipped out the little side door that went from the hallway to the stables.

"What's going on?" she asked the stable hand, who was brushing one of the horses.

"They're mostly rich old men, getting upset that the council asks them to disclose their business interests."

Zaina thought of Marek and how he had been talking to Supreme Rider Barton.

"Don't they just want know which ones have business with Arania?"

"They *all* do. That's where the money is."

A chill went over Zaina's back. This was what Marek had talked about: the influence of the Aranian princes on people in business.

And he was right: it needed to stop, or Arania could pull the strings of almost everyone in the City of Glass.

The doors to the foyer opened and part of the group streamed into the front courtyard. Zaina and the stable hand watched them from the door. The man held a bucket of fish for the bears, Zaina held a broom.

All those haughty, opulently dressed people filed past. Most were quite old; most were men. They were soft, weak, and carried too much weight from doing too little. A middle-aged woman with a lot of jewellery and a painted face had trouble walking. She cast Zaina a disdainful look. Zaina was sure she would have trouble walking, too, if her backside was as fat as that woman's. She held the two sides of her collar close around her neck, and her hand had painted nails. Her expression was closed, horrified.

Those people were afraid.

Jevaithi, behind the window on the other side of the entrance, was afraid, too. Zaina could see that by the way her mouth was open and her eyes wide.

These people, Nayek and his friends, and Denori and *his* friends, and even Sferuk, were destroying her new home. The Aranians would fight to the death over the right to become their father's successor. They would claim ownership over whichever group of people they controlled and let those people carry out their whims.

The stable hand said, "Let's take the bears out when all these people are gone."

In that moment, Zaina made a decision. Yes, she could go on living the same life, go on hiding, shovel shit and fix engines and stay out of the public eye. Or she could help stop the fear.

"Here." She held the broom out to the stable hand who took it, surprise on his face.

"What are you going to do?"

"I'm going to fix something."

She took off her overalls, hung them over a hook on the wall and strode into the yard, in the direction of the main entrance.

A line of rich and noble people were still streaming out of the foyer and she went against the stream, drawing some wide-eyed looks as she charged into the entrance.

Rider Barton stood with a couple of guards who had cordoned off the hallway to Jevaithi's office and the stairs to the private quarters.

He was saying, ". . . no, but I don't think we can keep them out of the council meeting. It's their right to be in the gallery and attend the meeting. And they have valid points that we need to address."

One of the men with him said, "It will not be easy."

"No, it will not."

And then a second guard noticed Zaina and nodded. Rider Barton and his colleague turned to Zaina.

"Yes?" Rider Barton said.

Once more, Zaina didn't know what to say. She was good at *doing* things, but when she had to say something, the words would never come out in the right way. She'd sound stupid, or like a ten-year-old girl.

So she did the only thing she could think of doing: she knelt on the tiles before him.

There was a awful moment of silence, in which she feared he would tell her to get up and stop being ridiculous, but then he said, "A citizen never honours a Knight without a reason. Please do tell me what your reason is."

And Zaina said, with a voice hoarse through emotion, "Please, will you let me join the Knighthood?"

Zaina kept looking down. Her heart was thudding so hard that the blood roared in her ears. Two male hands came into her field of vision. They took her by the upper arms and drew her to her feet. It was Rider Barton, and he smiled at her.

"I've been waiting for this. I suggest you go to the second floor of the eyrie and get your uniform."

CHAPTER 21

WHEN THE ASTROLOGER announced that Lana was born in the sign of the Eagle, people in the hall gasped and stared at her, including Nashi, whose face was pale with horror.

"No, I didn't know that. Why didn't you tell me?"

Lana frowned at her. "Do you believe in this nonsense?"

"No, no, no, it's not nonsense. Everyone knows that it's an omen to be Eagle-born."

Lana was surprised that this star sign folklore had penetrated into Chevakia. Maybe a sign that Aranians had been crossing the border regularly for a long time?

"Well then, what does it mean?"

"I presume it means that the king wants you in his house."

The blood roared in Lana's ears. "Does that mean. . . ?"

"His harem. His Mothers."

Lana felt like the ground had opened underneath her. She'd heard and read about the mother's houses where the rich Aranian men kept women for the sole purpose of producing their children. Some of the Aranians she knew even spoke of the mother's houses with a degree of reverence, but as far as she was concerned, those women were slaves to their own bodies.

Lana thought of something, anything, to say that would stop this terrible thing happening, but everyone who was Aranian in the room bowed to her, and guards were already coming her way. They gestured for her to come forward.

Lana trembled from head to toe, afraid that she was going to faint or vomit. But she did neither of those things.

Both men also bowed to her and she walked between them out of the room. She didn't even get to say a few words to Nashi. What would she have said? Where to meet—she had no idea of the layout of this place and whether she would even be allowed out. How to escape —there probably was no escape.

With every step she took, her mind was screaming *No, no, no, no, no!* She was not going to have any man's children, not unless she chose to, and getting married was a long way from her mind. She didn't care if this was the king or not.

Her mind whirled. She had to tell her father and he would send the army to retrieve her, like Uncle Milleus had done. On the other hand, she didn't want to be responsible for another war. But she wasn't going to be in any man's harem.

They left the hall, turned right into the corridor. The king's astrologer walked behind them.

For a long time, Lana walked between the guards through a maze of corridors and big echoing halls. Sometimes they crossed a courtyard with palms and flowering bushes. She tried to remember the way, trying to get a feel for the layout of this warren of buildings and courtyards.

After a while, they came to a building a little separate from all the other structures in the crowded space of the citadel. It looked a little like a large house, and stood in its own yard, surrounded by date palms. It was three floors high with large open windows. It had an ornate arched entrance where two men stood guard. The astrologer spoke to them briefly. The two guards who had walked with her stepped aside and only the astrologer accompanied her into the building.

A broad, marble-floored corridor led from the entrance to a light-filled room at the very end. Against the walls on both sides stood miniature trees like the ones she had seen in the City of Glass. There were also large coloured vases and statues of women holding children, or pregnant women. Music and soft talk drifted from the rooms to either side.

"Come," the astrologer said. "This is the Mother's House."

"Did I tell you I don't want to be here? You have no right to keep me prisoner here."

"Lady, it is an extreme honour to be chosen for the King's house. There are many women who would like to take your place."

"Then let them. I'm not going to give any man what they want from me."

"You will be killed."

"Then kill me, and deal with the anger of my family."

He simply chuckled. "You do not understand the power of the king."

"I don't *care* about the king."

"You will soon. Do be quiet now."

He led her to the large and airy room at the end of the ground floor hallway, where women lounged on couches, looking on curiously as Lana came in. Many of them were pregnant, but the woman pushing middle age whom the astrologer addressed was not. She was not particularly pretty, and had a big nose and a face full of age spots. She carried a fair bit of weight and her hair—straight, thick and black —was flecked through with grey.

They spoke quickly, in soft voices, and Lana's Aranian wasn't good enough to pick up what they said, but the woman glanced at her a few times, a dubious expression on her face.

Then she waved the astrologer away, and he made a hasty departure, leaving Lana to stand by herself, feeling awkward in the middle of the room.

"Sit," the woman said.

She pushed herself rather awkwardly into a sitting position.

A young woman came to bring a tray with tea and cakes. Lana couldn't decide whether she felt ill or hungry.

"I'm Selwa," the woman said. "This is the Mothers' House of the king."

"This is a mistake. I shouldn't be here."

Selwa chuckled. "I assure you, we all felt like that when we first came here. It *is* an honour to be allowed to live here, and you will see this in due course. Now, your bloodlines. I heard the men found you—"

"Imprisoned me."

"They *found* you in northern Chevakia, close to the border. But you have a good deal of Perian blood, don't you?"

Lana didn't reply. She was so bad at these types of confrontations. She disliked lying, but everything she revealed about herself would be used against her, and heaven forbid if they found out who her father was.

"It is always a good idea to answer when I ask you a question."

"You can see what I am. I am a prisoner. The whole train was full of girls who *chose* to come here. Why don't you take one of them?"

"Honey, one thing you must understand, no one *chooses* to live in the Mother's House. Despite all these trappings—" She waved a hand with be-ringed fingers. "It is not easy to be a mother, to serve your man, to carry and birth his children in a dignified way. It *hurts*. It ruins your health. You can embarrass yourself and your man in many different ways. None of us *chose* to do this. But if the astrologer said that your birth sign is the Eagle—"

"I didn't tell him when I was born. Yes, he thinks I did, but how do you know that I told the truth? That whole business of casting stones is all rubbish to me, anyway. The stars are far away suns in the sky. They don't influence life on the Earth."

Now Selwa gave Lana a sharp look and an expression of uncertainty went over her face. "Are you an astrologer, too?"

"No. I'm a student of meteorology, but I also like astronomy, which is the factual study of the sky, without the interpretations and predictions."

Another uncertain look. "Does Kotori know this?"

"Kotori?"

"The King's astrologer."

"I don't know."

"He is a well-respected man. You would do well to show him the respect he deserves."

Lana didn't think that anyone who decided the fate of prisoners by throwing stones on a piece of cloth deserved anything, but she held her tongue.

Selwa fingered her upper lip, and then she set her tea down. "Right, since you have decided to embrace the bad side of the Eagle-born, let me show you around the house. Be warned that the king doesn't like difficult people."

She wormed herself off the reclining couch and waddled towards the door. The ground floor of the house, she told Lana, was taken up by the public section of the house, including the auditorium, the dining room, the reception room and the public meeting room, which was the best place to entertain your man, if he visited. The women in the house did not all serve the king, Lana heard. Some were on loan to the princes in exchange for favours.

"It's a favourable thing if you can warm the bed of both the king and a major prince. I am too old now, but you might be fortunate enough."

Lana could not think of anything worse than to be traded as a piece of meat.

Selwa warned, "The only thing we allow between us and the man in this house is talk and tea. Any other activities take place in the man's private quarters."

As fas as Lana was concerned, there would be no such activity.

Selwa led her up the stairs.

The top two floors contained a lot of bright and airy rooms—rooms for music, for resting, for talking. Even a library, which had a good number of shelves groaning with big and heavy tomes. Lana wanted to know what sort of books they were, but Selwa said that books weren't her thing. "The plays are much more interesting. They're usually on every week on Horse Day, and if you want you can take part. They get men in from outside to play the male roles."

There were also rooms for craft and art.

The bedrooms were all on the upper floor, big airy rooms with lots of beds and couches. Lana expected to be allocated a place to sleep, but she was told that she could sleep wherever she pleased. "You will make friends with one of the groups soon enough."

"Are you allowed to go out?"

"We can go anywhere in the citadel, but if you want to leave the citadel, you will have to get permission. I grant permission, so if you want to go out, you have to have proven yourself useful and trustworthy. I assure you, I don't grant this permission for women who have just joined and, yes, every one of them asks me this question. Even if I grant you permission, you must always be home at dinner time, because that is when the king lets us know which of us he wants to see."

Lana shuddered. Selwa was friendly enough, but with every word she said, the purpose of this place was further engrained into her understanding. It was crude, and it was terrifying. These women were prisoners for no reason other than to obey the king's whims.

They went back downstairs, where Selwa showed her the auditorium, a large room with curtains and seats in rows. A couple of drums stood to the side of the stage.

"Is this where you perform plays?"

The woman gave her a blank look. "No, this is where we have the birth ceremonies."

"You mean celebrations?"

"No the birth ceremony. When the Mother deposits the child she has carried."

Now Lana understood, and a deep chill took hold of her. "You do that on the stage?"

"That disturbs you?"

Well, yes. From what she had heard, birth was messy and could be risky and was not pretty to watch. Having been a midwife in the City of Glass, her mother had told her some horrific stories. Even thinking about it gave her the chills. Or thinking that people thought it was a form of entertainment.

One thing she knew: the first opportunity she got, she was getting out of here. "Where can I put my things? Which cupboard is mine?"

"Everything here belongs to everyone. We share everything. Including our man." She grinned.

Lana felt sick.

"Now come to the dressing room. We must choose some clothes for you."

"But I just got these."

"They would never do. Those are clothes for peasant girls going to work in the laundry and kitchens. You must look pretty. The king is likely to want to see you this evening."

A hand of panic clamped around Lana's heart. Was there anything she could do to get out of this? Be sick or claim that she had her bleeding? But the women would know that wasn't true. But at least she did have the seeds that Nashi had given her.

Selwa led her to a room that was full of wardrobes with thin gauze-like dresses.

She gave Lana a little singlet that just covered her breasts and a loincloth that covered little more than the hair between her legs. The gauze dress went over the top, letting air into places where it normally never came. Both items were orange, a colour Lana hated because it made her look pale.

"Give that dirty neck pouch to me. I'll have it burned."

Lana grabbed the pouch with the seeds that Nashi had given her. "No. I'll put it away if you want, but this belonged to my mother."

That seemed a good enough argument. The pouch did belong to her mother and, in Chevakia, she used it to keep a few coins for the train or to buy sweets. Lana took the pouch off and tucked it inside her singlet.

Selwa then combed out Lana's hair and put in a hair band and clips to keep it out of her face, yammering about how pretty she was and how nice her eyes were. She stepped back and looked Lana over. "You know, when he's getting older, the King has had some trouble getting excited about women, but you should bring that excitement right back to him. Do it well, and he will treat you like the Mother goddess herself. But do beware that almost all other women in the house will be jealous of you. Not all of them are nice. Wander about the house and introduce yourself to others. The more friends you make, the better your life will be. I'm going to take a rest until dinnertime. I suggest you do the same. The king likes to keep you up late."

Selwa went up the stairs, leaving Lana to stand by herself in the dressing room, feeling mortified.

How, how, *how* could she escape?

Not through the hallway, because the only entrance to the house was guarded.

The room overlooked the city. It had a small balcony, but the ground was a long way down with no means of getting there.

The *only* way out of this place was by using her brains and her mouth.

She might not have much time, but she should use that time wisely. And, because she wasn't much good at gossip or women's small talk but did understand knowledge, she went to the library.

This was a luxuriously appointed affair with lazy couches and young girls who went to get books off the shelf for the couple of mothers sitting there, many of them in various visible stages of pregnancy.

They all looked at Lana when she came in. Whispers went around the room.

Lana heard the name *City of Glass* a few times. Well, that was good if they thought she was from there, because it would never do to be seen as Chevakian.

She went around to each group and gave a small introduction, that she was from the south, that she was joining the house. Some women watched her with curiosity, but there were also outright expressions of jealousy. Selwa had warned her about this.

Lana wandered around the shelves, feeling those curious gazes on her. She realised that Mala was not a very Perian name, so she needed a story to explain it.

The library contained a good selection of classic plays and fairy tales, but also some surprises, like a thick tome on algebra, and Sizek's *The Star Signs And Their Meanings*, as well as a large-format book with maps of the coastline.

When she felt bad, even at home, books were her consolation. She pulled that book off the shelf and leafed through the delicate, hand-coloured pages.

Chevakian knowledge of the western coastline was poor. It was general knowledge that there were a couple of islands off the coast but she had expected people to live on those islands. Yet the maps showed little villages on the mainland coast in intricate detail, yet the islands were empty of any towns, roads or safe anchorage. It was very odd.

"What are you doing?"

Lana looked aside. The woman who stood next to her was one of the ones she had introduced herself to a bit earlier. She was Aranian, with sleek raven-dark hair and grey eyes. Her skin had a pale olive complexion, and there was rather a lot of it, since her belly was huge and protruding into space between her and Lana, and the gauze dress she wore did little to cover it.

Lana had to do her best not to stare at the belly button that had been turned inside out and pushed out of her stomach, like the tie on a balloon, by the sheer size of her womb. The skin looked tight as a drum.

"I'm looking around. Do you like reading?"

"No. But it's quiet in here."

True. Yet she was disappointed. She'd hoped to find like-minded women in here, and maybe start a little conspiracy to get out, but in all truth, the library was much too tidy to be used a lot for study.

"You're Mala, right?"

"Yes." She should really attempt to get used to that name.

"I'm Tynka. I'm from Chahek, south of Curack."

She let a silence lapse as if she expected Lana to react to that. When that didn't happen, she went on, "There is a rumour going around that you are going to be the one to turn around the King's flagging interest in women."

"Who said that?"

"Everyone. The king has been asking for a southern woman. I'm not southern enough."

Oh. Curack was a southern Aranian town.

"What do you know about pleasing a man?"

Er . . . nothing? Lana didn't even *want* to know anything about it. She'd had a few flings with fellow students, nothing lasting. "I'm just interested in books."

"There is a book about *that* particular thing, too. Wait, I'll show you. All of us have already seen it, but the librarian keeps hiding it. Because, you know, we're not supposed to talk about it's being fun."

She reached behind a row of books on the shelf and pulled out a thin, much-thumbed tome with the simple title, *Please Your Man*. It had no author name.

She handed it to Lana who didn't want to take it, but had no option. The flimsy cover of the book felt greasy with the touch of so many eager hands. The woman was watching over her shoulder, so she had to open the book.

There was little text inside, and most of the pages were taken up by men and women in acts of procreation. On the floor, on the bed, on chairs, on the edge of the table, in a meadow, in bath. There was even a section on how to go about it if the woman was pregnant.

Lana's cheeks burned as she leafed through, glancing out the corner of her eyes for a sign that it was all right to close the tome, which was both deeply disgusting and fascinating. People really did that sort of stuff?

"You don't know much, right?"

"I'm a meteorology student and study astronomy."

Tynka nodded at the book, scratching her distended belly. "About this, I mean."

"Well, I . . ."

"You don't. Study it. The king likes his women informed." She retreated, leaving Lana to stand with that silly book in her hands. Tynka could still see her, so she leafed through another couple of pages. The author really made an art form out of sexual interaction. Apart from positions, the book described oils and fragrances to enhance pleasure. It described places to touch a man or woman to increase excitement.

It was . . . fascinating, weird.

She read that men and women alike wanted to be teased and that the act should take the whole night, if possible, so that the desire for release can build. "It will be strongest the longer the woman can tease the man."

Well, that was . . . interesting. The only time she'd been involved, the whole thing was over in mere moments. She had not derived much pleasure from it at all.

Lana turned aside, shutting the book. Her cheeks burned and blood roared in her ears.

Tynka smiled at her. "It's good, isn't it?"

"Yes. Um. Is there an outroom here?"

"Silly. We have proper bathrooms. It's at the end of the hallway."

Lana scurried out of the library, and found the bathroom. The walls and floor were all covered in white tiles. There was a giant bath in the corner—empty—and a washbasin, dressing table, bidet and toilet in the other. She stared at herself in the mirror: the pale skin on her belly, the soft rounding of her breasts in the giant armholes of the singlet, the sweat on her forehead.

There was a shelf full of jars along one of the walls. She recognised some the names of ointments and oils from the book.

Her fate seemed sealed. She could fight it, but it would only result in harm to her, and it would help no one.

How many women in Chevakia could say that they had slept with the Aranian king? What was more, how much would he confide in her about his plans? Her uncle had defeated Arania, but they had come back, and were once again threatening her home country. Another war might not turn out so well for Chevakia, especially if Arania had sonorics weapons.

She remembered something that boorish fellow Scriptorium student Pavinius had once said: "The most powerful defeat comes from within."

He had been talking about acceptance for the discipline astronomy and how, in order to be accepted, students should show a single major breakthrough resulting from their work and that would cement the support of the Scriptorium for them.

Pavin was a student of warfare, and Lana had no doubt that this was the origin of his statement. It applied to everything in life.

Chevakia could go to war and defeat Arania a second time, but they'd stay angry and would invade again.

If, on the other hand, the Aranian king lost his desire to fight because he became more interested in trade or science, and could be enticed to *talk* his neighbours . . .

She thought of something her mother had said, *The way to a man's mind is through the bedroom.* She would say this in a joking manner, but just think of the influence a woman in good stead could have on a powerful man if he fell in love with her. The things she could whisper in his ear, the deeds she could quietly approve or disapprove, advice she could give.

This was what Selwa had hinted at.

She picked one of the jars from the shelf, opened the lid and sniffed. The clear gel inside smelled of fruit. A bottle next to it contained fragrant oil. She sprinkled a few drops on her hand and rubbed it over her upper chest.

Lastly, she pulled the pouch from out of her singlet, and shook out one of the seeds onto her hand. She put it in her mouth and bit the seed in half. A bitter taste exploded in he mouth. Urgh!

A jug of water with a glass stood next to a cup on the dressing table. She poured herself some water, and drank it, and then poured another cup. It only diluted the taste a little bit. Nashi had warned her about it.

Urgh, urgh, urgh.

The bell for dinner rang downstairs.

Lana tucked her pouch away, drank another mouthful of water, emptied the rest of the water in the sink and followed the stream of women downstairs. She knew she couldn't escape, and she knew the next best thing to do. Now she needed to wait for the opportunity to do it.

CHAPTER 22

*W*HEN JAVES LOOKED aside in the crowded street, where people walked past in groups, carrying all their possessions, the windwalker had already replaced the hood over his malformed head. With the growths hidden under the fabric, Karlen looked almost normal.

"Where can we go?" Javes asked. "We'd prefer to get out of town before the river cuts us off. We've got a long way still to go."

It had started raining again. The sky was darkening alarmingly and still a lot of people were making their way towards the bridge.

"Across the river? I know a place to stay on the far bank. It's not classy, but it's comfortable."

"We have no money, but we do have a tent."

"You don't need money."

"What about the animals? The camel and the goats are ours."

Karlen's pale gaze went to Tali who stood, hair dripping, a bit further down the street.

"The animals should be fine. There is a barn."

Javes hesitated. A comfortable place outside town sounded attractive. To be honest, just a *dry* place would do, preferably across the river, before it flooded the bridge. But how much could he trust this man?

He met Tali's eyes. She looked small, frightened, miserable. Drops of water ran down her forehead. Her lips had gone blue again.

Javes had to know what the deal was with these metal artefacts and why Karlen and the Aranians wanted them so badly.

He jerked his head and mouthed, "Let's go." Tali didn't reply, so he turned to Karlen. "We're coming. Lead the way."

A voice came from across the street. "Hey, what about my window?"

It was the owner of the antiques shop, looking dishevelled with his jacket askew and covered in dust.

Karlen dug into his pocket, and tossed the shop owner a handful of coins. The man only managed to catch one of them, and had to go scrambling for the rest. The ultimate way to embarrass someone you didn't respect: send him scrambling for money in a crowd.

Javes crossed the street and held the crossbow out to him. "Here is your treasure. I don't really have any money to buy it."

But the man refused to take it. "Keep it. I can't take that back now that he knows that I have it."

So. Another ancient artefact? "Are you sure?"

"Yes. Take it out of my sight. I've had far too much trouble over this thing already. Go. Please go."

"All right. Calm down. Take care."

"Make sure you have your wits with you dealing with that character. You're a good young man. He's a slippery. double-dealing bastard. Don't believe anything he says."

Javes retreated.

They started walking in the direction of the bridge. Javes and Karlen at the front and Tali with the animals at the back. Javes disarmed the crossbow, and wormed it into the bag he carried over his shoulder.

He glanced at Karlen. "So do you know the story about this weapon? It's not an ancient artefact, is it?"

"The ancient people had no need for weapons as primitive as that one. That man has many enemies. He makes weird twists and turns."

"What do you know about these ancient people?"

"They lived up north, in the desert. It probably wasn't a desert back then."

"Is that why they're no longer around?"

"What do you mean—they're no longer around?"

"Well, they aren't."

"Of course they are."

Javes frowned at him.

"We are their descendants."

What—

Well—

Javes guessed that Karlen *could* be right, but . . . "Why would no one know about that?"

"Myths? Magic? Death and destruction? Heresy? Beliefs?"

"So . . . you're saying that people have forgotten who they were and that they could make these strange artefacts?" Javes didn't know what to think about that.

"Forgotten, and snippets of truth have been expanded, in the absence of the people who wrote down and recorded the truth, until they were no longer true. Time is like the wash of the ocean: with its movement, it eats away at the rock, even if the rock seems permanent and immovable."

They arrived at the bridge, which was much longer than Javes had imagined based on the view from the hill on the other side of the town. This very long bridge reminded him of the railway bridge in Watya, which mostly went over a dry riverbed. This bridge went over a wide expanse of brown churning water.

This smaller river probably flowed into the Aramys River, which meant that the riverbed in Watya would be completely filled. It was hard to comprehend.

The sky had turned even darker, and squally winds were pulling at hair and clothing. The camel kept jerking up its head and the goats were pulling on the harness in all directions.

Tali had trouble keeping all the animals under control, and the crowds thinned, so Javes took the camel from her.

Karlen looked the animal up and down. "That's a nice camel."

"Did it used to be yours?"

"I don't trade camels."

"It was a windwalker camel before I came across it in the market-place in Ysherra."

Karlen squinted at it. "I don't know. Maybe an escapee. The wind-walkers are very precious about their camels."

"You're talking like you're not one of them. You're a windwalker, aren't you?"

"I'm not a windwalker. I'm something more cursed than them. They can live normally if they rub paint into their white skinned patches. For me, showing my face in towns is fraught with danger. I cannot count the times that I have been harassed over my looks, and it doesn't often end with just a few punches to the ribs."

Javes hardly dared glance at the hood that covered the hideous growths on his head. "Is your whole body like that?"

"It is. I can show you my back, if you want."

"No, thanks. I believe you." Javes shuddered.

They were now in the middle of the river, and the vast mass of water churned less than an arm's length under the bridge. Sometimes the bridge juddered with the force of the water battering the pylons.

Karlen increased his pace. "This is not going to hold out much longer. Either the bridge is going to get washed away or it's going to go under."

Javes agreed. He pulled on the camel's rope—it kept wanting to lick the railing—and followed. Tali didn't have to pull the goats along. They were all too keen to get off the bridge. Maybe goats were not as stupid as they looked.

At the far riverbank, a couple of armed guards had just arrived with a horse and cart. They were unloading trestles and lengths of wood. One took a large sign out of the back of the vehicle with the words *ROAD CLOSED* painted in white letters. He dragged it to the middle of the road as Javes and his companions passed, and then got back into the truck to collect the signs to put on the other side of the bridge.

Well, that was a stroke of luck.

"Where are we going?" Javes asked when they walked up the riverbank where the road was wide enough for the three of them—and the animals—to walk abreast.

"I told you I know a place. It's dry and warm."

"I hope it's in the right direction. We're going to Tiverius."

"Yah."

Then he said nothing for a long time. They followed the road up the crest of the hill and into the next valley. A few people were still making their way along the road, but most used oxen, and the companions were much faster on foot with the camel and the goats.

It was now so dark that the ground was hard to see. Rocks and the occasional tree made ghostly shadows against the deep grey sky. The stones on the road glistened with rain in the last of the light.

Karlen turned off from the main road onto a track that led up the hillside. He opened a gate to let Javes and Tali and the animals through. When Tali passed Javes, he could hear the chattering of her teeth.

Karlen flicked on a little device in his hand that made a pool of greenish light.

"What's that?" Javes asked.

"You better not come too close." He held the device hidden in the sleeve of his robe.

"Is that a sonorics light?"

Karlen didn't answer. Javes guessed that he was right.

"It doesn't harm you?"

A dry chuckle. "How can anyone still harm me? Something that kills me will put me out of my misery. The only harm that can hurt me has already been done: to be condemned to keep living this life where children scream and run when they set eyes on me. The adults may be more polite, but children are always right."

The incline became steeper. The ground was wet and slippery, with clumps of grass to trip over. Javes had to watch his footing. The camel was pulling on the rope again, although Javes could no longer see where it might want to go.

After a steep climb over a muddy path through a rocky paddock, Karlen's light revealed the rough stone walls of a farmhouse. The house's walls were covered in black growths, the windows were broken and the roof of a shed off the side had fallen in. This was the shelter? Comfortable and warm?

Karlen pushed open the door to the house and went inside. "Careful. There's a hole in the floor just here."

There was, too. A piece of the floorboards had rotted away.

"What about the animals?"

"Take them to the barn. You may even find some hay."

While Karlen went further into the house and lit a lamp, Javes stumbled with Tali and the animals into the shed. There was hay, but it smelled musty—not that the goats took issue with that—and also a proper water trough, as Javes found by accidentally tripping over it and putting his hands in the ice-cold water. Ugh. It was slimy on the bottom.

He tied the camel to a post and dragged a chunk of hay within its reach. Then he took off the packs and the saddle.

He picked up the bag that contained the essentials. "Come on, let's go inside."

"I don't like this man," Tali said in the darkness. "He looks creepy."

"He can't help that. You shouldn't judge people by how they look. That's why he has a miserable life."

"He acts creepy, too. Did you see how he broke the window?"

Javes hadn't. He wasn't sure that he wanted to know, because sonorics were probably involved. "Listen. I don't like him much either, but he knows things that we should know."

"I don't want to know anything. I just want to go to where you live and where all the people are rich."

"Well, it's not as simple as that." What would his mother say when he turned up with Tali anyway? She wouldn't want a scruffy, sullen kid too skinny to do any hard work in the house. "It's my job to find out what is going on. Come inside with me, because there will be two of us against one, and he doesn't look too strong or too fast to me. I need you to help me remember what he tells us. You can be my assistant."

That swayed her and she came, reluctantly.

Karlen had lit an oil stove.

Apart from the hole in the floorboards, the room was well-appointed, with cobbled-together chairs, a table, a simple bed with a straw mattress and a set of rough shelves that held boxes with metal items like the globe in Javes' pocket.

They sat at the table, and Karlen poured some tea. He had taken off his cloak. Tali had pushed her chair back against the wall and stared at his head. Side-lit by the lamp, the growths on his head and neck made him resemble an incredibly warty turkey.

He sipped from his tea before setting the mug down.

"I'll tell you my story and you can be one of the privileged few to know it. They call me Karlen the tree man, but Shen Mani is my name. I was born in the desert north of Ysherra. My mother consorted with an older man when she was a girl. When she became with child, that was a shame to her family, so she fled far into the desert, past windwalker land into the Badlands. I grew there and was born in a cave on foul soil, which is why I look like this."

"Does this mean that windwalkers are not born the way they are, with those white skin patches?"

"Oh, by now, they probably are, but they didn't always used to be. They would have been kids wandering too far north and their skin would break out in white patches or warts. But with time, those things became inborn for windwalker children."

He sipped from his tea again. Javes wondered why he had earned the right to hear this story.

"I was always much stranger than windwalkers, because my mother had been so far north. So when I grew up, no other child wanted to play with me, because I looked scary. I explored the desert instead."

"So that's where you found the artefacts. Did anyone find any before that time?"

"Not many. Most of the people who went into the desert never came back. Maybe some people had found them, but hadn't been interested. But not many people can go very far into the Badlands and come out alive. I brought my treasures back to the windwalker camp, because that was where I lived back then. No one was interested until a stranger came. He had light eyes like me and didn't flinch when he saw me."

"Aranian?"

"I guess so. I don't care. It was the first time anyone had ever given me money. He paid me to find things for him."

"Those metal things?"

"Yes, those and others. I knew where to find the stuff, and I was the only one who dared to go into so deep into the foul land."

"Why do people call it foul land?"

"You can't go there. The animals get nervous, and you're nothing without animals in the desert."

"How did you get there, then?"

"I walked the whole way, carrying all the water I needed. I got this man and his friends a lot of stuff, and they wanted more, so I went back and did it again."

"What are the Aranians doing with these things? People talk about collectors, but I bet there's more to it." He met Karlen's eyes.

Karlen took a deep breath and let it out with a sigh. "Why didn't you sell that thing I gave you?"

"Hey, that's unfair. I was asking the questions."

"I'll get to it later. Why didn't you sell it? I'm sure people would have offered you a handy sum for it."

"I didn't offer it for sale. I'd like to know what it is before I decide to sell something."

"Didn't you need money?"

"Yes, but my curiosity was greater than my need for money. I got the feeling that people thought this thing was worth a lot of money and I wanted to know why. Why did you give it to me?"

"It's a fairly long story, but the short version is that I didn't want to sell it."

"You wanted me to sell it?"

"I was hoping that you wouldn't sell it either."

"The Aranians were after this thing as well, weren't they? They were looking for you?"

"Not for me. Just for this thing, or others like it. The only value I have for them is that I can go into the Badlands."

"What is that thing?"

"That's where my long story comes in." He got up, poured some more tea and went to the shelf against the wall. He tucked a notebook under his arm. It was raining heavily outside, but despite the broken roof, none of the water came in, or at least none that Javes could see.

"I fixed a roof underneath the old one," Karlen said, when he noticed Javes checking the ceiling for leaks. "The house looks dilapidated, but it's quite sturdy with the repairs I've made."

"Apart from the hole in the floor."

"Apart from that, yes. But even the hole has a purpose. If an intruder comes at night, he will fall in and wake me up." He sipped from his tea. "So. During my first trip into the Badlands, I came across a strange contraption in a cave." He opened the notebook at a page which had a crude drawing across the spread of the pages of a square thing that looked like a stack of folded sheets with pipes running through each layer. He pointed. "This thing here. It was about as tall as I am, and was quite clearly out of action and had been so for many years. There was so much dust in this cave, the thing would probably have been buried had a colony of jackrabbits not been digging in the sand. It was far too big for me to take with me, so I made this drawing and set about trying to find out what the function of this thing could be. I wrote to a lot of people from all over the known world and sent them copies of this drawing. I didn't write to stuffy librarians, but I wrote to people who worked with engines, because steam engines had become popular and I thought this might be a similar design. It was not. None of the people knew what it was. Several people, though, told me that the machine reminded them of this thing that used to be underneath the City of Glass."

"You mean the machine that causes sonorics?"

"It's not there anymore, but yes, that one. Except this one didn't work anymore and hadn't worked for a long time."

He took another sip from his tea. Javes looked sideways. Tali had fallen asleep on the couch. Her cheeks were rosy red.

"I thought that was the end of that, so I continued to collect artefacts and continued to sell them. And then one day a man came to me during my travels. He asked me for a particular part called an igniter. I never took much notice of the things I found or sold and I told him I didn't know what he was talking about. But I brought him back more stuff, and he seemed happy for a while. But he came back. Through a roundabout way I had learned that his master had obtained a lot of old books from the City of Glass that told him about the function of this machine. It made magic so that people could use it. The trouble was that people couldn't quite reproduce this so-called igniter."

"I'm guessing the thing you gave me is one of those things."

Karlen nodded. "The biggest and most intact one I've ever found."

"And you didn't want it to fall into the hands of the Aranians."

Karlen blew out a breath. "Through another roundabout way, I had discovered that the Aranians had made their own machines, and that they were planning attacks with the magic rays. They only needed to bring a machine and could take their killing power everywhere. Except they lacked enough igniters."

"So you hid the one you had by giving it to me."

"They would never suspect you of having it, and they could ransack my dens for all they wanted. They could kill me, but they wouldn't find it."

"They can't make new ones?"

"Well . . . they can make small ones, but they've found it hard to make the larger ones and have been relying on putting several small igniters in a big machine, but they can misfire and create big problems."

"Like explosions?" Javes shuddered.

Karlen looked at his hands. "These experiments must cost thousands of lives in Arania. If they discover how to make the larger igniters, they will destroy the known world."

He looked back up at Javes. "Not much later, I discovered a second ancient machine in the desert, one that still worked. I knew this because I could see the strands of golden light radiate from the ground above the machine. I was dumb enough to go into the cave where it was hidden—that is why I look so much worse than I did as a child—and then I was dumb enough to tell my buyer about it. You have to understand that much of the truth about the machines I only learned later. I was much younger. I was starving. My Aranian buyer then begged me to dismantle the machine. He told me how to do it, but he also warned me not to pull the igniter out until I had shut it down, because the machine would keep working and no one would be able to get close to it. I asked him why the Aranians were so stupid to work with machines of the type that made entire swathes of land uninhabitable, and he just talked about how much he'd pay me. I thought about his offer for a long time. I may be strange and persecuted, but I am not a monster. So I went to the machine and I pulled the igniter out. That is the device I gave you. The Aranians know that this igniter exists, and they will do anything to obtain a complete machine they can take apart to see how it works."

"But can't they take it apart and find out anyway? It's not like there is a lot of border security in that area."

"The machine still works. They can't get near it."

"There are people that can."

"There are, yes, but will they know where the machine is? Only I know that."

"So they want the igniter and they want you to put it into the machine so that they can turn it off and move it elsewhere."

"That's my guess. They want to take it apart, see how it works and then build others like it. Somehow, they don't understand that a lot of people will die that way. Or they don't care."

The metal surface of the igniter almost burned against his skin. "And what do you want me to do with it? Do you want it back?"

"No. What were you going to do with it if you hadn't met me?"

"I had no plans. We are on our way to Tiverius, where my family lives. I was going to take it there and show it to the people at the Scriptorium. I'm a student there."

Karlen nodded. His mouth worked. He had little warts even in the corner of his lips. In one place an ugly scab marked his lip. Javes guessed Karlen had pulled a protuberance off his face, and he winced at the thought.

"Yes," Karlen said after a long silence. "Take it to Tiverius. I'll give you the map where I've marked the location of the machine. Let the learned men figure out how to destroy it and rid the world of this menace. I discovered it. I sold it. I shouldn't have done that, but at the time, I didn't know any better. Allowing for its destruction will be my final deed to the world."

Thank You

. . . for reading *Sea & Sky*. In the third and final volume of the Moonfire trilogy, *Moon & Earth*, Javes and Tali arrive in Tiverius, Isandor and Tamerane witness the secrets of the Aranian camps, and the Chevakian doga battles to keep the Aranians out of their territory while searching for a way to destroy the sonorics devices. And Lana makes a discovery that turns understanding of the world on its head.

ABOUT THE AUTHOR

Patty Jansen lives in Sydney, Australia, where she spends most of her time writing Science Fiction and Fantasy.

Her story *This Peaceful State of War* placed first in the second quarter of the Writers of the Future contest and was published in their 27th anthology. She has also sold fiction to genre magazines such as Analog Science Fiction and Fact, Redstone SF and Aurealis.

Patty has written over twenty novels in both Science Fiction and Fantasy, including the *Icefire Trilogy* and the *Ambassador* series.

pattyjansen.com

BOOKS BY PATTY JANSEN

MORE INFORMATION:

PATTYJANSEN.COM